MW00578712

THE ASSASSIN OF VENICE

ALSO AVAILABLE BY ALYSSA PALOMBO

Heavy Metal Symphony (as A. K. Palombo)
The Borgia Confessions
The Spellbook of Katrina van Tassel
The Most Beautiful Woman in Florence
The Violinist of Venice

The Assassin of Venice

A NOVEL

Alyssa Palombo

NEW YORK

This is a work of fiction. All of the names, characters, organizations, places and events portrayed in this novel are either products of the author's imagination or are used fictitiously. Any resemblance to real or actual events, locales, or persons, living or dead, is entirely coincidental.

Published in the United States by Crooked Lane Books, an imprint of The Quick Brown Fox & Company LLC.

Crooked Lane Books and its logo are trademarks of The Quick Brown Fox & Company LLC.

Library of Congress Catalog-in-Publication data available upon request.

ISBN (hardcover): 978-1-63910-787-2
ISBN (ebook): 978-1-63910-788-9

Cover design by Lynn Andreozzi

Printed in the United States.

www.crookedlanebooks.com

Crooked Lane Books
34 West 27th St., 10th Floor
New York, NY 10001

First Edition: June 2024

10 9 8 7 6 5 4 3 2 1

To my brother, Matt Palombo, who followed me through the back streets of Venice—and through that wild exhibit on crime and punishment in the Venetian state—as this book idea was coming into focus. Thanks for not letting me sit still when we travel together.

Part One

Domina Mortis

April–October 1538

Chapter 1

Sun beat down on the piazzetta as I scanned the crowd for the man I was going to murder. It was damnably hot, too hot for April—or maybe it was just all of the people packed together in too little space. But no one in Venice wished to miss the traditional ceremony of Sposalizio del Mare, the Marriage of the Sea. And the masters of this city that floated on the sea did not wish for any of its residents—and especially not its esteemed foreign visitors—to miss the ceremony that each year affirmed Venice's domination over the Adriatic and much of the East and Europe as well. Or so they fancied.

All of that mattered little to me. I had a job to do. And as much as the teeming crowd irritated me, with its heat and stench of unwashed bodies, it was actually crucial to the task set to me that day. In all the commotion, with so many people, no one would notice a man crumpling to the ground, and by the time they did, I would have melted away into the throng.

Up ahead, at the dock that led out into the lagoon, I caught sight of Ambrogio Malatesta turning to survey the crowd before boarding the Doge's great painted barge, the Bucintoro. Somehow, he caught sight of me among the masses and, consummate politician and spymaster that he was, gave no sign of recognition whatsoever. Yet I could read the look on his face even so: *"Do not fail me, Valentina."*

I fought the very strenuous urge to roll my eyes and instead jerked my head in a quick nod that I knew he would see and interpret correctly. By the Shadow God, one would think he would trust me a bit more.

But then that was the genius of men like Malatesta. They did not trust anyone and never would. It was a trait more people should cultivate, truly.

I turned my gaze from Malatesta and directed it back to the crowd. It was obvious that I was looking for someone, but no matter. Half of those out in the piazzetta that day were doing the same; I would not stand out. The eyes of the people around me would look over and past and through me, and later they would never remember me, even should they be asked.

Only once before had I seen my intended victim—or target, which was the word Malatesta preferred, as though the man still had some trace of delicacy left beneath his veneer of polished and barely leashed violence. But I had an exceptional memory for faces. Just another thing that made me so eminently well suited to my profession—well, to this second profession anyway. And I was equally well-suited to my first profession. Malatesta had seen to it that, the night before, the target had visited one of the girls in the house where I used to ply my original trade. Malatesta had joined me as I'd observed the target through the peephole in the wall in the voyeur's chamber. Wealthy men of Venice had all sorts of tastes, and the successful brothel catered to them all.

I'd arrived a bit late and received a hushed scolding from Malatesta when I finally sat before the peephole to see my victim for the first time. In the room next door, the main event was already well underway, and when I first looked within, all I could see was a man with reddish hair, nearly pink skin, and a rather hefty frame, pumping away between Marietta's thighs.

"Well?" Malatesta demanded, after I'd been looking for only a few seconds. "Will you remember him? Will you be able to find him tomorrow?"

"I've yet to see anything but his ass, and that is extremely forgettable," I remarked. "I hope for Marietta's sake his cock is more memorable."

Malatesta gave a huff of disapproval, which I disregarded. He could stand on his patrician sensibilities if that made him feel better than me—he would, and it did—but he was certainly not above consorting with courtesans, pimps, assassins, spies, and thieves, much as he liked to pretend he was. He wouldn't get anywhere in his business without the likes of me.

Eventually the target in question rolled onto his back. Marietta sat astride him, riding him, her moans loud and dramatic. I rolled my eyes. Her performances convinced no one except the men who patronized her, somehow. But I ignored her theatrics and squinted at the man's face. His eyes were closed, his face slack with pleasure as he grunted and groaned, but I began to commit his features to memory. A round face, plump like the rest of him. A bulbous sort of nose, thin lips, a smooth chin and brow, and the ginger-colored hair I'd noticed before. He wasn't handsome, but he wasn't ugly either. Marietta could do worse, though she often did better.

He had an unremarkable sort of face, really. But I marked it all the same.

I sat back from the peephole, the escalation of moans from the other side of the wall indicating that the show was reaching its climax, quite literally.

"And so?" Malatesta demanded. "Will you be able to find him in the Ascension Day crowd?"

"Just a moment more," I said. "I want to see him with his eyes open as well."

I listened, and indeed the activity within had come to an end. I waited a few beats, and when I looked in again, the man was sitting on the edge of the bed, smiling down at Marietta, who was sprawled out naked before his gaze. Then he turned his face away, looking about the room for the clothes he had discarded.

There. Now I had him.

He was tall, I noted, taller than me, and with his bulk would likely be stronger as well. No matter. A quick first strike to impair him before the killing blow was all that was needed.

"He pays for Marietta's company for the night and doesn't even stay," I commented casually. "A fool to not get his money's worth."

Malatesta snorted dismissively. "A fool, and worse, he's a spy. A traitor."

"You say that man is passing information to the Spanish?" I asked, inclining my head toward the wall that separated us from the next room.

"Yes. Without question. He is a merchant sailor from Spain originally who now resides in Venice between voyages. One of my informants stole his satchel in the Rialto a few days ago, and it had papers in it containing sensitive information. He might have copies and probably has additional documents, and we must assume he has committed at least some of the contents to memory. The Spanish crown must not get that information."

"Indeed they must not." Of all the mighty European powers, the Spanish wielded by far the most influence on the

Italian peninsula. It was no secret that they longed to add Venice as yet another jewel in their empire's crown.

I could not let that happen. I would not let it happen.

I pictured the man's face again: unassuming and indeed unremarkable. Hardly the sort one expected to be a spy helping plot the downfall of the Venetian state. But I well knew that appearances meant nothing—less than nothing, really, especially in Venice. A city of masks and shadows, deceptions and mirrors, and water that might hide any secrets within its depths.

This man wanted to betray my city, my adopted home. He wanted to bring blood and death and fire down on us all. Rage at the thought nearly choked me.

"And so you will be able to do it?" Malatesta asked me.

I arched one expertly plucked brow. "Why, is that anxiety I hear in your voice? Surely the great Ambrogio Malatesta, member of the Council of Ten and defender of the Most Serene Republic, cannot be nervous?"

"The man must be silenced, and it must be tomorrow," Malatesta retorted, his tone irritated, as it often was when he was forced to deal with me. In fairness, I rather enjoyed baiting him.

"Why must it be tomorrow? And why must it be in the crowd at the Sposalizio del Mare?" I asked, though I thought I already knew the answer. "Why did you not send him to me tonight? Then it would be done with already."

The look Malatesta fixed on me would—and had—chilled many people to the bone, caused them to quake in their shoes. I was used to him, though. "This must be done publicly," he said.

As I suspected. The redheaded Spaniard was to be made an example of, perhaps first and foremost to whoever in Venice was providing him with what Malatesta had called "sensitive information." If the Council of Ten had not disposed of them already. And it wouldn't be the first time nor the last that the Ten wished to show Venice—and the world—what became of traitors. Sometimes these traitors were dealt with quietly, albeit slowly and painfully, in the dungeons beneath the Doge's Prison. Yet sometimes it was felt that the public needed a reminder.

"Can you do the job or not, Valentina?"

I shoved aside all levity, my face becoming a blank, smooth mask—the mask I often wore to serve Malatesta and his colleagues on the Council of Ten. "I can do it. And I will do it, just as I always do."

A lesser man would have let out a sigh of relief, perhaps, but he only gave me a small nod. "Good. See that you do, and see that there are no mistakes."

"I don't make mistakes, Malatesta," I said.

With another curt nod, he rose and left the room, shutting the door behind him and leaving me alone.

I had sighed and closed my eyes, letting the silence still my mind for a few moments. I needed that quiet to focus on the task ahead. Then I too rose, in a rustling of skirts, and went downstairs to have my gondola brought up to the dock so that I might go home and get some sleep.

And then tomorrow arrived, and I was searching through the crowd for the man I'd last seen—only ever seen—naked in bed with Marietta.

Suddenly, there he was.

I spotted him to my left, standing over by the colonnades in front of the Doge's Palace, leaning against one of the massive columns. He appeared to be alone, but I knew it was best not to make assumptions.

I wove through the crowd toward him, moving at a leisurely pace, nothing in my movements to suggest that I was hurrying or indeed moving purposefully at all. Just a woman ambling along the piazzetta, perhaps trying to get a better view of the Bucintoro as it rowed out into the lagoon.

I came up behind him, this man whose name I had never been told. But it didn't matter what his name was or who his family was or any of the rest of it. All that mattered was that the Council of Ten wanted him dead, that Venice *needed* him dead, and so dead he would be.

I felt eyes on me and turned my head slightly to the left, only to see a man lurking behind one of the columns behind me, nearer to the basilica. I recognized him—another of Malatesta's hired hands. He saw me notice him and gave a subtle nod that no one would have seen had they not been looking. He was there to watch my back should this job start to go badly, and also—perhaps more likely—to make sure that I did the deed.

I drew my dagger from its sheath, hidden within a secret pocket in my dark red gown that I had sewn in myself. I had always had a gift for stitchery, even if I had put it to a use that my mother would be appalled to learn of, were she still alive. It was a long blade, slender but strong and deadly sharp. Easily concealed and easily wielded.

I came up behind the victim, the blade laid along my wrist so that no casual observer would see it. Then, with a flick of my fingers, I flipped it about so that the handle rested securely in my palm and the blade protruded from the front of my fist. Swiftly I came around the column, and saw the man's ginger head turn a bit, as though he'd heard my footsteps. Mentally I cursed myself for not being stealthier, but there was nothing for it now. I placed one hand on his left shoulder and quickly plunged the blade into his right side. He crumpled, and my free hand immediately reached up and covered his mouth, at the same time pulling his head back toward me. In a flash I brought the blade up to his throat and sliced it open.

"The Council of Ten send their greetings," I hissed in his ear. Then I released him, and he crumpled silently to the ground, his lifeblood flowing from him over the cobblestones.

I was already melting into the crowd again before his body had fully gone still, sliding the now-bloody dagger back into its sheath and hiding my stained hands in my gown's pockets. I did not think I'd gotten too much blood on me, but the gown's color would mask it even if I had.

I did not escape back across Piazza San Marco and into the warren of streets and canals that was Venice, as any amateur assassin or hired killer would think to do. Rather, I went further into the thick of the crowd, closer to the lagoon, my eyes trained on the Bucintoro, just as the eyes of those around me were. It wasn't long before I heard a commotion behind me, as the man's bloody body was discovered. I glanced over my shoulder at the noise, as if with passing curiosity, but continued making my way to the edge of the piazzetta, an ordinary Venetian woman out for the holiday celebration. I waited and watched the moment when the Doge rose and threw a gold ring into the water, symbolizing Venice wedding the sea, and assuring another year of prosperity and dominance over the water.

It felt as if only I saw all the waves of blood that truly kept La Serenissima afloat.

CHAPTER 2

Immediately following the events of Ascension Day, word traveled around the city about the man found murdered during the celebration. Some claimed it was a robbery; others, that the man had been carrying on an affair with a married woman, whose husband had caught wind of it and killed his rival in a jealous rage upon seeing him in the crowd. All of the usual scandalous, salacious stories that were passed around when a murder or other noteworthy crime occurred with no obvious reason.

Soon enough, though, the tenor of these rumors changed, and a new set of whispers began to emerge beneath the others, hushed at first, then growing louder.

"Spy."

"Plot."

"Spanish."

"The Ten."

"Assassination."

And as those particular whispers began to permeate every level of the city, from the bankers at Rialto, to the beggars in the streets, to the whores on the Bridge of Tits, slowly but firmly the Council of Ten's grip on the Republic strengthened.

Oftentimes one could go about one's business forgetting about them altogether. And that was good, for the Ten very strongly preferred that no questions be asked about their doings. But then, every once in a while, they needed to remind their fellow Venetians of what befell those who crossed them or who sought to betray the Republic. It was ever the same in the wake of such a reminder: fear snaked its way through the streets, the paranoia as thick in the air as the stench and humidity that rose off the canals in summer. And then everyone would go about their business a bit more carefully, mind whom they spoke to and what about, and avoid foreigners as though they carried pestilence. And so the Ten kept Venice and Venetians in line—but also kept Venice and Venetians safe.

To discourage corruption and prevent any one man or small group of men from becoming too powerful, those elected to the Ten served a term of one year and, once the year was up, could not serve another in their lifetime. The Tre Capi, or three heads of the Ten, were elected to serve a month at a time and could not leave the Ducal Palace during their tenure. I had worked with various members of the Ten over the years; Ambrogio Malatesta was only the latest in a long line, if perhaps the most ambitious thus far.

I certainly never forgot about the existence of the Ten, not even for a minute. How could I? After all, what they paid me helped keep me in the style to which I was accustomed. And while I, like any Venetian, had a healthy fear of the Council of Ten, my fear had a bit of a different tenor, for I was useful to them. Very useful.

I did not wish to find out what might happen should there come a day when I was no longer so useful.

But that day, I flattered myself into thinking, was far in the future, should it come at all.

⋆ ⋆ ⋆

A few days after carrying out my most recent assignment, I had just awoken to the sun streaming through the gap in my velvet curtains. I was stretching my naked body languorously beneath the covers when the door to my bedchamber flew open. I looked up to see Bastiano Bragadin standing in the doorway, looking pleased with himself—which was his habitual expression.

"The last man to enter my bedchamber uninvited lost his balls," I remarked from the bed.

"I don't doubt it in the least," Bastiano said, stepping into the room. "But here I thought that I had a standing invitation."

"That is exceedingly presumptuous of you, Bastiano. Who let you in?"

"Your maid, of course. What is her name? Lauretta?"

"I might have known," I said, heaving a dramatic sigh and sitting up, letting the coverlet fall so that my breasts were almost, but not quite, exposed. "Lauretta would allow you entry anywhere, you scoundrel. Including into her own bed."

Bastiano shut the door behind him and removed his cloak. "Why would I want to sport with the maid when I can have the lady of the house?"

"Again you presume. The gall is shocking, truly. Is this what they teach you young Venetian patricians?"

"Presumption and entitlement? We take it in with our mothers' milk."

"And they say courtesans are ruining the morals of Venice."

Bastiano grinned, and heat pooled between my legs at the sight. His smile usually had that effect on me. I'd have sooner cut out my own tongue than admit it to him, though. "Very well, let me try again, then: Why would I sport with the maid when I would seek to seduce the most beautiful woman in Venice?"

"Better," I said. If not exaggerated. There were plenty of women in Venice, many of them fellow courtesans, more beautiful than I. But that was for the best. If I were as breathtakingly beautiful as some, I would stand out in a crowd, would be more memorable. That in turn would hinder my work for the Council of Ten. I had a face that I could make forgettable when needed and also make strikingly beautiful when I chose. Such was the magic of jewels and cosmetics and fine clothes.

But so long as Bastiano Bragadin thought I was the most beautiful woman in Venice, then I was perfectly satisfied.

And he was, in my estimation, one of the most handsome men in Venice—something else I would never admit to him. He was tall, well-built, and muscular, with hazel eyes that gleamed with mischief and a head of thick chestnut curls.

Bastiano tossed his cloak over the back of a chair. "Then I can stay? And keep my balls?"

"I'll allow it this time," I said. "I see you've returned to Venice."

"You know I do so love to make an entrance."

Bastiano was the third son of Gasparo Bragadin, the patriarch of one of the oldest and most distinguished patrician families in Venice. As such, he wasn't expected to marry and produce heirs. Indeed, were he to do so, it would leave less of the family fortune to go around. He had a seat on the Great Council, as all patrician men did, but though he attended meetings when in Venice, he desired to cut no great political swath through the Republic, as his eldest brother did. Instead, he traveled across the Mediterranean to see to the Bragadin family's mercantile interests, which were considerable. Such activity made him the perfect spy for the Ten, as well as a conveniently placed assassin should someone abroad be found—or thought—to be working to undermine the Venetian Republic.

And when Bastiano was home in Venice, he spent much of his time with me.

He moved to the chair against the wall and sat down, his eyes never leaving me. "I heard about the man killed on Ascension Day," he said. "Right outside the Doge's door, they say. Was that yours?"

I shrugged, trying to appear nonchalant even as my body tensed at the reminder. "I don't believe I know what you're talking about."

"Who was he spying for? The Spanish is the rumor I've heard most often, but some are saying the French or even the English."

I snorted. "When has the English king ever concerned himself with the affairs of Venice?"

"So the Spanish, then?"

"If you weren't informed, Bastiano, then you do not need to know."

"Ah, but I so like being well informed," he said. "It was well done, Valentina. There is not a soul who can claim to have seen the act committed."

"Or no one willing to claim they saw it."

"What difference? It means the same thing, in the end."

"True enough," I conceded.

"Who gave you the job?" Bastiano asked. "Malatesta, I assume?"

"I have not even said it was I who did it. Even if I did—"

"This modesty is most unbecoming of you, Valentina Riccardi."

"Even if I did," I repeated, "what is there to be gained from me telling you who gave the order?"

Bastiano threw up his hands, his grin back in place. "Very well. Have it your way."

I stretched my hands up over my head, affecting a casual gesture, but I marked well the way Bastiano's expression turned hungry as the coverlet slipped down, exposing my bare breasts and the smooth skin of my abdomen. "You've an unfortunate habit of poking about where you're not wanted," I informed him. "It will lead to nothing good for you."

"And here I thought that was one of the benefits of our relationship," Bastiano said, his eyes trailing over my body. "Since we both have the same, *ahem*, employers, we might discuss the finer points and perils of our positions."

"Is that what you came here for this morning, Bastiano? Discussion?"

In a flash, he was beside the bed. "It was, but I could be persuaded away from my current line of questioning."

"And what might such persuasion look like?"

He pulled his doublet off over his head and unlaced his breeches, his eyes never leaving me, until he was completely naked, his manhood erect and straining toward me.

I shook my head. "The presumption, yet again. What ever shall I do with you?"

"I can think of several things I'd like you to do with me," he said, and joined me beneath the coverlet.

"Oh, can you?" I said, forcing out the words as my breathing grew heavy with anticipation.

While I was as fond of bed play as the next courtesan, Bastiano had been gone for some weeks, and I found I did not wish to wait any longer. I pressed him down into the mattress, swung one leg over his hips, and lowered myself onto his cock, sheathing his full length within me. He let out a groan of pleasure, and I began to move atop him. "Is this one of the things you were thinking of?" I asked, my breath coming in pants.

"Yes," he said, the word coming out in a half groan. His hands reached up for my breasts, my back arching as his fingers toyed with my nipples. "Yes, God, yes, Valentina."

I had thought to tease him a bit, to continue our repartee, to make him wait for his release. But the sensation of him inside me, our bodies moving slickly together, his hands on my breasts, soon overtook me. I kept moving, faster and faster, his hips bucking beneath me to thrust deeper into me, until my own cries of pleasure joined his, ringing unashamedly through the room.

Afterward, he cradled me against him in the bed, his body warming mine and our breath mingling until there was no telling where he ended and I began.

Chapter 3

A little after midday, Bastiano finally departed. He had declared his desire to never leave my bed, but that, alas, he had pressing matters requiring his attention. I did not ask what those matters might be—partly so as not to give him the satisfaction, but partly out of caution. If he did not share his doings with me, then it may be that I was better off not knowing.

It was true, what he'd said: the two of us both working for the Council of Ten meant that we could share certain stresses and fears that we could not share with anyone else. But even so, we had both learned well enough not to pry. We knew firsthand what happened in Venice to those who knew things they ought not know.

Well, I had learned it anyway. Bastiano, as I'd told him only hours before, still had a tendency to stick his nose where it didn't belong and wasn't wanted. Hopefully, he only displayed that tendency to me. No doubt that was the case, and that was why he was still alive.

My principal maid, Marta, was just finishing pinning up my hair for the day when Lauretta, my other maid, peeked her head into the room. "Begging your pardon, signora, but you have a visitor."

My body tensed ever so slightly. "Who is it?" I asked. None of my regulars were scheduled to visit me that day, and having just come from bed with Bastiano, I had no intention of seeing any client. Fidelity is a quality that many would not expect a courtesan to possess, but possess it I did, in my own way.

And if it was Ambrogio Malatesta, I did not particularly wish to see him either. But I would have to receive him regardless of my personal feelings.

Thus was I steeling myself for Lauretta's answer when she replied, "It is Amalia Amante, signora."

I allowed a smile to touch my lips. Amalia Amante, fellow courtesan, next-door neighbor, and the best friend I would ever have, was the one person I *did* want to see. "Very good," I said, waiting for Marta to slide the last pin into place before standing up. "Show her up, Lauretta, and into my sitting room. Then bring us some wine and whatever delicacies might be found in the kitchen."

Lauretta nodded. "Of course, signora." She disappeared around the doorframe to do my bidding.

"Signora, we have not discussed your gown and jewelry for tonight," Marta said as I turned away to go into the sitting room.

I let my smile slide across my face again. "I am staying in tonight, Marta. I've no engagements."

"Were you not set to receive Giovanni Acri?"

"I wrote to him to cancel," I said. "I told him I've my monthly courses and am feeling poorly." It didn't do to be *too* terribly available to one's clients; a bit of withdrawal built mystery and kept them interested and hungry. And since men had a horror of thinking about women's monthly courses, it was the perfect excuse. Men simply assumed a woman's body was always available to them unless they were told otherwise—and sometimes not even then.

By the time I swept into the sitting room that adjoined my dressing room, Amalia was seated on a cushioned daybed, her eyes sparkling with joy and mischief, as they often were.

Amalia Amante was one of those women who put to lie Bastiano's claim that I was the most beautiful woman in Venice. She was all voluptuous curves where my own body was more slender than was fashionable; she was of an average height, whereas I was a few inches taller than was usual for a woman. Her hair was a rich brown that needed no heated metal rods to curl it, her eyes a warm amber, and her skin a deep olive tone that positively drew the light to it. The daughter and only child of a Venetian cittadino father and a Turkish mother, Amalia had been born in the Venetian quarter of Constantinople and had moved to the city of Venice proper after both her parents had died of plague when she was a young woman. The convent had not appealed to her—it did not appeal to many women, in truth—and so she had used her inheritance from her well-off father to set herself up as a cortigiana onesta. Her beauty, her gift for music and poetry, and her fluency in several languages, not to mention her desire to live an independent life, made her ideally suited for the courtesan's profession.

But few people knew that behind her striking beauty was a brilliant head for numbers and a sharp insight that missed nothing. That, far more than her beauty and talents, was what kept her not only alive but thriving.

She was a marvel, and I did so adore her. She put most of the men running the Venetian Republic to shame. What a tragedy that they would never know it.

"Dearest Valentina," she said, rising to embrace me. She brushed a perfumed kiss on my cheek. "It has been too long."

I raised an eyebrow at her as we both sat down. "We saw each other less than a week ago."

"You see? Far too long," she said. She gave me a sparkling smile. "I meant to come earlier today, but I thought I saw Bastiano Bragadin come in this morning, so figured I'd best leave you two alone." She winked.

"You should have come over anyway. It would have given me an excuse to throw him out."

"Oh, I'd never want to deprive you."

"It would be good for him to doubt my affections a bit, I think," I mused.

"Doubt your affections? Amica mia, you have borne him a child. Him, and no other man. I would venture that he is in fact quite secure in your affections."

"Even so," I said. My body flushed with maternal warmth at the thought of my daughter, Ginevra. I had never borne another man a child, nor would I. Courtesans knew well the ways to prevent conception, and if and when those failed, we also knew the ways to rid ourselves of an unwanted pregnancy. I'd had to take the herbs to void my womb twice in my life before—an unpleasant process, full of blood and sickness, but a necessary one for me and so many other women. But as a general rule I took less care with Bastiano, and when I had found myself with child by him a few years back, I had been nothing but happy. A fresh chance to give a child the safe world I had not had. "His pride could do with being brought down a notch or two," I added, smiling.

"Could it indeed," Amalia murmured. I could tell by her knowing look that she didn't believe me, as she never did when I said such things. I might be flippant about my feelings for Bastiano to everyone else, but she—and he, damn him—knew the truth.

Yet I could not help that flippancy, it seemed. I remembered all too well what had come of the last—and only, before Bastiano—man I had truly loved.

"And what of you?" I asked. "Any recent visits from your . . . favorite?"

Amalia had long had a lover with whom she had a relationship much like mine with Bastiano. He wasn't a paying client, though I thought he'd started out as one, and I knew she loved him very much.

She laughed. "Just last night, in fact," she said. "He was very pleased about something, though he wouldn't tell me what. Something political that had happened in his favor, were I to guess." She rolled her eyes, then giggled. "But I benefitted from his good mood, I can tell you that much."

"Ah, so he *is* a politician," I crowed. "A very powerful one, no doubt, as I've always suspected. Let's see, there's few of those young and handsome enough to tempt the exquisite Amalia Amante. Could it be that newer senator, that—"

Amalia was shaking her head before I'd even finished speaking. "You know I cannot tell you, Valentina," she said gently. "I wish I could, but he wants our relationship kept a secret. Says it is important for his good name and his family."

"You know I would never tell anyone, Amalia, if you asked me not to."

"I know. Of course I know that," she said. "But I just . . . I cannot betray his confidence." She stared at me beseechingly. "You understand, don't you?"

I sighed. "I do, I suppose," I grumbled. But someday, by the Blessed Virgin, I would know the man's name. If only so I might know who had the power to make Amalia Amante blush and swoon like the convent girl she had never wanted to be.

Just then Lauretta appeared, bearing a tray with wine, cheese, some cold meats, and pastries from the baker a few streets over. She poured the wine for us before leaving and shutting the door behind her. Our talk then, as it often did, turned to gossip about the people we knew in Venetian society, which between the two of us was just about everyone. Given the scope of our acquaintances and the amount of news we heard, it wasn't really a surprise when our talk turned to a darker matter.

"I assume you've heard the bloodiest piece of gossip," Amalia said, daintily picking up a pastry between her fingers.

My heartbeat accelerated slightly at the change of topic. I was quite practiced at deception and at keeping my secrets close, away from the prying eyes of others. But Amalia knew me like no other and was most likely to spot such deception. I could never allow her to know of the sinister work I did on behalf of the Council of Ten. Even if it was for the good of the Republic, I could not bear for her to hate and fear me, as she surely would if she knew the truth. I did what had to be done, to protect Amalia as well as others.

"This is Venice, cara," I said languidly, leaning back against the cushions and eyeing her with practiced disinterest over the rim of my wineglass, a sparkling, multifaceted clear glass, some of the finest they made on Murano. "You shall have to specify which bloody rumor you mean."

She huffed a sigh. "Assuming you've left your house since Ascension Day, you *certainly* know which one I mean."

"I have, and I do," I allowed. "Senator Querini could talk of nothing else last night." It had been amusing, in a perverse sort of way, to listen to him speculate about the murder, repeating gossip he had heard and assuring me that his work in the

Senate would certainly lead him to learn of the culprit in due course. The widowed senator, while from an old Venetian family and therefore blessed with a prestigious name, was something of a bumbling fool, always longing to appear more important that he was. He was the sort of man who didn't believe that a woman—even an educated cortigiana onesta—could truly grasp the intricacies of power and politics. Yet I could only laugh, for despite all his posturing, I knew far more about the affairs of the Venetian state than he did.

Amalia wrinkled her nose in distaste, momentarily diverted. "Querini? You still have him as a client?"

"Regretfully, yes."

"Poor dear."

"I simply lie back and think of all the gold he adds to my coffers. He pays a rate higher than most."

Mirth entered Amalia's eyes. "Because he is foolish enough not to know better?"

"Exactly."

"Bless him," Amalia said fondly. "We all need one like him, I suppose, don't we?"

"Men like him certainly have their uses."

"Indeed they do. But look here, now we have gotten off the true matter at hand. The murder. Have you ever heard of such a thing? Right in broad daylight, in the middle of the Ascension Day celebrations?"

"Of course I have, and you have as well," I said. I didn't particularly want to discuss this any more than I had to. "It happens every time the Council of Ten wishes to remind us of who truly rules Venice. Therefore, not infrequently."

Amalia pursed her lips, studying me. "You think it was the Ten?"

"Who else?" There was only so far I could play the fool with Amalia before she would become suspicious. And in any case, I knew perfectly well that she would have come to this conclusion—the correct one—on her own.

"Who else indeed," she mused. "But does this not seem . . . blatant, even for them? In the middle of the crowd on one of the Republic's most important holidays? What could the poor bastard have done—invited the Spanish armada to sail right into the lagoon?"

That was more or less exactly what he had done, or at least had been planning to do. Even now the thought filled me with rage anew. "Perhaps," I said, with a noncommittal shrug.

"There are scores of rumors in the streets, of course," Amalia went on. "Jealous husbands, cheated merchants or business partners . . . anything you can imagine."

"I've heard all that as well, and more," I said.

"But I think you're right," Amalia said, meeting my eyes and holding them a moment longer than necessary. "I think it was the Ten. I don't suppose we'll ever know precisely why."

And that, of course, was why I did what I did. So that the residents of the beautiful city of Venice, the jewel of the Adriatic, would never know how close ruination regularly came to their doorstep. So that the Venetians would never have to go through what I had suffered as a young woman. "No," I said. "I don't think we ever will."

Chapter 4

The next night I went to a party with a client who was a wealthy and influential member of the Great Council, Iacomo Bergamasca. It was a pleasant enough evening, even if many of the guests in attendance were still gossiping about the murder on Ascension Day. I did what I had to do for Venice and had made my peace with that long ago, but that did not mean I enjoyed reliving my actions over and over again.

Luckily most of my assignments were much less public.

The following night I had another free evening, and so I sent a messenger boy to Bastiano's palazzo to invite him to join me for the night. The messenger returned, saying he had left the message with one of the Bragadin servants, as Bastiano had not been in. I shrugged it off, telling myself I wasn't disappointed and that I would enjoy the very rare night to myself.

I had Girolama, my cook, fix me a simple meal, then had Marta undress me for the evening before I dismissed the servants.

My home consisted of a grandly appointed piano nobile for entertaining, a smaller adjoining parlor, a dining room, and a bedchamber that took up the whole second floor of my palazzo, along with my office. The kitchen was on the ground floor, opposite the water entrance. On the third floor were my private rooms, a guest room, and servants' quarters for Lauretta and Marta. Bettina and Girolama, the cook, had their own homes nearby, and came and went as their duties dictated, while Luca, my loyal gondolier, had a small room on the mezzanine above the water entrance. I did not like to conduct my business—any business—in the same rooms where I slept and lived my life. The only people ever permitted access to the third floor, aside from my servants, were Bastiano and Amalia.

Wearing nothing but my shift and a silk robe, I settled into my private sitting room on the third floor with a book of poetry that I had yet to read and had been a gift from one of my clients. A courtesan must be current on arts and literature so as to better converse with her patrons and their peers. But even more than that, I simply enjoyed reading and did not often find myself with much time for it.

So engrossed was I in the volume that night fell, the last of my candle burned down, and I was forced to get up and light another. I had quite lost track of time when suddenly the door to my sitting room burst open.

I shrieked and was halfway to the small table, in the drawer of which was concealed a dagger, before I realized who it was. "Bastiano," I gasped, heart pounding. "God's thumbs, don't *do* that. I might have stabbed you. Who let you in?"

"Once again, your maid," Bastiano said, and instantly I became aware of the slump of his shoulders, the dullness of his eyes, the flatness of his voice. He was not his usual buoyant, arrogant self. "On her way out, it seemed."

Lauretta was no doubt off to debauch herself, for which I could only applaud her. But her antics were of no concern to me just then. I picked up my book from where I'd dropped it in surprise, and set it down on the daybed I'd been curled on, studying my lover all the while. "Bastiano. What is wrong?"

He shook his head, seeming unable to speak for a moment. I could not remember the last time I had witnessed that particular phenomenon. "I . . ." he started. "I had to come here. Didn't know where else to go."

"You got my message, then? The one my messenger left at your palazzo?"

He shook his head again. "Messenger? No. I haven't been home. How could I, like this?"

He withdrew his hands from the folds of his cloak, where they had been tucked ever since he'd come in. I could see now that they were covered with blood, as was the front of his doublet beneath his cloak.

I gasped, and he hurriedly reassured me. "It's not mine," he said. "It's . . ." He shook his head again.

"The Ten?" I asked, certain he could hear the relief in my voice. Now that I knew the blood wasn't Bastiano's, we could deal with anything else.

He nodded. "Who else? They gave me the assignment almost as soon as I returned to the city a few days ago. And then, tonight, just now, after . . . I didn't . . . I didn't know where else to go . . . I had to come here . . ."

It was quite the stroke of luck that I hadn't had a client here tonight. How would I have explained my blood-covered lover storming in? But I didn't need to, and what mattered now was tending to Bastiano. "Come here," I said, steering him into the room that held my bathing tub and chamber pot. "Sit." I pushed on his shoulders lightly, and he sat on a small upholstered stool beside the tub, usually used by Marta when she was helping me bathe. "Don't move."

Since I had dismissed the servants, I would need to do this myself. I realized as I hurried down to the kitchen that that was a boon as well. No explanations would be necessary.

I built up the kitchen fire and set a pot of water to warm. It would take me ages to heat and haul enough water for a full bath; by the time I did that, the servants would likely have returned for work in the morning and begun asking questions. But I could get Bastiano cleaned up before then.

While I waited for the water to heat, I went back upstairs and took the small pitcher and bowl from my bedroom and brought it into the bathing chamber. Bastiano was sitting right where I'd left him, the backs of his hands pressed against his knees, staring at nothing.

"Here," I said, setting the bowl on a washstand and pouring the water in it. I produced a small bar of fine soap, imported from France for an exorbitant price. "Wash your hands, at least. Soon there'll be enough water to clean whatever other parts of you we need to clean."

Bastiano obeyed wordlessly, dipping his hands in the water and using the soap to scrub away every last trace of blood. I watched him for a moment as the water in the bowl began to turn pink.

I returned to the kitchen, where the water was now warm enough for washing. I hauled the pot upstairs, got some of the clean clothes Bastiano kept there, and returned to him. His hands were clean, and he had removed his cloak, which, being black, would hide any traces of blood until it was washed. His doublet with its linen sleeves, however, was another matter.

"Off with that," I said, gesturing to the garment. "We'll have to burn it."

He obeyed, still without speaking, and I could see that some blood had soaked through onto his chest, but not much.

And there was not a scratch on him, thank the Shadow God—my own personal deity, whom, I liked to imagine, watched over the doings of those such as Bastiano and me.

I dipped a cloth into the warm water and began to wipe the blood from his skin. He made a sound in the back of his throat as I did so, a contented sound, almost like a cat's purr. I allowed myself to smile as I kept working.

After a moment of silence, I finally spoke. "You seem troubled by this assassination," I said softly, keeping my eyes on my task. "Do you wish to talk about it?"

He shook his head and laughed mirthlessly. "Should I not be troubled by killing a young man in the prime of his life?"

Still I did not meet his eyes. I wished for him to speak freely, to say what was on his mind without fear of my judgment or censure. I would be a liar if I said that the actions I took on behalf of Venice never bothered me, but Bastiano struggled with it more than I. He always had. But then, he had never lived through what I had lived through, never seen what the consequences could be if we did *not* do as the Ten bade us. His life, for the most part, had been much easier than mine. What my life should have been before it all collapsed in a maelstrom of blood and fire. But who knew better than I the need to speak of these unspeakable things from time to time? "I suppose you should be troubled," I said, dipping the cloth back into the water. "That means your soul is still intact."

"Soul," he spat. "What of a soul have I left?"

"You are not a remorseless killer, Bastiano."

"The man I killed tonight is just as dead, remorse or no," he said. "My remorse does not change the fact that his body is being eaten by fish in a canal somewhere at this very moment."

I was silent for a moment before speaking again. "Why this man?"

Bastiano exhaled sharply. "An Ottoman spy, so I was told," he said. "He got some shipbuilders drunk and learned more than he should have about the Arsenale. He posed as a merchant sailor but was a member of the sultan's own household. Or so I was told."

"Then you did the right thing," I said simply. "He was a threat to Venice."

Bastiano met my eyes, held them. There was a depth of agony in them I could never remember having seen there before. "He screamed for his mother," he said softly. "Just before I slit his throat."

I dropped the wet cloth and, from where I knelt beside the stool, threw my arms around Bastiano. He took a deep, shuddering breath, burying his face in my loose hair. We stayed like that for a long time.

Because both things were true. The man had been a threat to Venice and had needed to die. But he was also a young man with a mother and a family who would wail out their grief when they learned of his death. And people like Bastiano and I had to grapple, somehow, with those twin yet disparate truths. Had to carry them both without them crushing us, even if the weight, I secretly suspected, was bound to crush us eventually, some day.

And when Bastiano could no longer carry it all, I was here to help him and always would be.

Interlude

Rome, March 1527

"Maria! Maria Angelina!"

I turned toward the voice whispering—loudly—my name in the deepening twilight. A grin spread slowly across my face as I spotted Massimo peering around the door of the stables, smiling at me.

I hadn't known he was coming to see me that evening, but I was not surprised. He snuck out to come to me as often as he could, riding from his parents' fine house in Rome proper to our lovely villa just on the outskirts, on the edge of a vineyard with rolling hills to one side and the seven hills of Rome to the other, church domes and steeples rising against the sky.

I glanced around to ensure no one was observing us, then walked quickly across the stable yard and into the stables themselves. Massimo pulled the door shut behind me, and I fell into his arms.

Immediately his lips were on mine, and I returned his kisses hungrily, sliding my hands under his jacket and untying the strings of his doublet.

His hands covered mine, stopping me. "Your parents?" he asked in a whisper, his breath hot against my cheek.

"Out. Some banquet or another."

"Your maidservant?"

I shrugged. "In the house somewhere. She'll not come looking for me."

"Are you sure? Last time . . ."

"Last time you left the door open, you silly thing. It's closed this time, is it not?"

That was all Massimo needed to convince him. "Indeed it is," he said, and without further ado, drew me into one of the empty stables.

We undressed each other quickly, bringing our bodies together in an inexperienced fumbling that was all the more thrilling for it being so new. We had first made love not even a month ago, and I was overjoyed at how it seemed to grow more pleasurable each time, how Massimo and I kept discovering new ways to delight each other.

We had kept our trysts from my parents and his, of course; it was not worth the lectures and wringing of the hands that would occur if we were found out. But even if they did discover us, what could they truly do? Massimo and I were betrothed, which was almost the same as a marriage, both legally and in the eyes of God. It was an arrangement made between our two wealthy merchant fathers, in the interest of uniting family businesses and fortunes. My father owned extensive vineyards outside Rome and exported his fine wine all over Europe. Massimo's father dealt in luxury goods from abroad, and it made sense for them to go into business together, so my family's wine might reach an even larger market, and

Massimo's family might share in the profits. And what better way to seal such a profitable business alliance than with a marriage?

The difference between our arrangement and those of other young couples—both in the Eternal City and, I imagined, elsewhere—was that Massimo and I had fallen in love. I fancied that I'd loved him from the very first time his father had brought him to visit, when our families had dined together and Massimo had stared unabashedly at me across the table while I had cast him flirtatious looks from under my eyelashes. He was as handsome as a painting of a saint, with golden hair that curled lightly as it fell over his forehead, and eyes the bright blue of a hot summer's day. He was taller than me and well-muscled from swordplay, riding, and wrestling with his brothers. I loved to touch him, to run my hands over every part of him, reveling in the beauty of his form and the fact that he was mine.

Afterward, as mio carissimo Massimo and I lay sweaty, with limbs entangled and bits of hay sticking to us both, he turned to me, propping his head up on one arm as he regarded me.

"Why such a serious look, caro?" I asked him. My smile faded slightly. "Did I . . . did I not please you?"

"No," he answered immediately with a gratifying swiftness. He grinned. "You could never not please me, Maria."

I let out a breath of relief. "Oh. Good."

His face turned serious again. "I . . ." He cleared his throat. "I love you, Maria Angelina."

My breath froze, just for a moment, before joy flooded through my entire body. It was much like the ecstasy of lovemaking, but emotional rather than physical. "I love you too, Massimo," I said, not hesitating for even an instant. "So much."

We had never said those words to each other before, though I had known them to be true, had felt them in every glance and touch and kiss between us. Yet hearing Massimo say it aloud . . . how could I not be overjoyed?

He leaned over to kiss me, his body covering mine again, already hungry for me once more. As I was for him.

I knew I was the luckiest girl in Rome, probably the luckiest girl in the world. I was going to marry the boy I loved. We were going to share a bed together every night of our lives. We could make love whenever we wanted, and no one could stop us. He could kiss me in the street, right in front of everyone, and while the old women might cluck in disapproval, it would be with a smile on their faces. I would keep his house, and he would bring me lovely gifts, and someday I would bear his children. He loved me. And I loved him.

How many other girls could possibly be so lucky?

Chapter 5

Once Bastiano was cleaned up, I got him into bed, where he fell asleep almost immediately. I spent an hour at least getting rid of the bloody water, scouring the pot, and burning Bastiano's clothing. Then, finally, I collapsed into bed beside him, exhausted. He turned to me in his sleep, drawing me against him, and I reveled in his warmth, his closeness.

The next morning, Bastiano dressed and gave me a deep, sensuous kiss before taking his leave. "My, my," I said when we drew apart. "Careful, or I shall pull you back into this bed."

My heart lifted to see his old cocky grin flash across his face once again. "I would like nothing better," he said. "But alas, I must get home. My parents are likely to be worried that I never returned last night, and I have some very dull mercantile business to attend to today."

"Very well." As he turned to go, I reached out and grasped his hand, squeezing it once. "I will see you soon, Bastiano," I said softly. "And don't . . ." I cleared my throat. "Don't worry."

He squeezed my hand in return, his eyes catching mine in an embrace, understanding everything I was saying with those two simple words. "No," he said. "I won't."

And with that he was gone, standing straighter than he had last night, bearing the weight a bit more easily.

Once I'd risen, broken my fast, and dressed, I had business of my own to attend to. I settled myself in my office, to go through my correspondence for the day, putting the night before from my mind as best I could.

I had received a letter from Sonia Abate, the country woman with whom Ginevra was staying. I had not had the luxury of suckling my child myself at her birth two years before, and the life I led was not one in which I could involve a child, in any case. So I paid a married couple in the countryside of the Veneto to take care of Ginevra along with their own brood. The woman had suckled Ginevra along with her own daughter, born around the same time. And this way Ginevra would spend her babyhood away from the stenches, plagues, and danger of Venice.

And the danger of her own mother, really. It was a less palatable truth, but it was a truth, nonetheless. I was a dangerous woman, and I did dangerous work. So did Bastiano, Ginevra's father, and his work for the Ten aside, he was often abroad and in no position to raise a child. I would not have her put in the way of that danger—not if I could help it. Not to mention that a courtesan's household was not the best place for a young girl—a young girl with noble blood, no less—to grow up. I would not do as other courtesans in the city did, grooming their daughters for their trade, selling their daughters' virginity to the highest bidder as soon as the young girls had their first blood. Should Ginevra someday become a courtesan, it would be because she had chosen that path after coming of age, and not for any other reason. And it was not a bad choice to make if a woman wished to live freely, to be beholden to no one man for her existence and livelihood. But I meant to work hard enough to have enough security—that is, money—to give my daughter a choice. As a Bragadin by blood, she could make a good marriage as well, if she so chose.

Someday I would bring her back to Venice to be with me. I could not let her spend her whole life as a stranger. I could not bear it. But not yet, not while she was still so small, so fragile. And so, for the time being, I had to content myself with letters from Sonia Abate.

She wrote that Ginevra was well, healthy, and had a good appetite. She was growing fast and talked up a storm. *She speaks more than my husband does!* Sonia had written. I smiled at that. It would seem that Ginevra had inherited her father's penchant to speak simply to hear himself.

All good news, and I vowed again that that summer I would make the journey to the country to see Ginevra and spend time with her. Much of Venetian society left the city in the hot summer months anyway, the better to get away from the heat and stink of the city, as well as from the pestilence that was so much more prevalent in the hot weather. After Ginevra's birth, I had bought a modest country villa not far from the village where Sonia and her husband, Vito, lived. And whenever I could, which was sadly not terribly often, I stole away there to see her. Bastiano came with me, sometimes. I saw no clients in my country villa, entertained no important personages. No one other than Bastiano, Amalia, and my servants even knew I owned the villa. And I intended to keep it that way. The country villa was where I could imagine, if only for a brief time, that I might have a family again, even if it could never be. It was an escape from the realities of my life in Venice, but only ever a temporary one.

I set the letter aside to show Bastiano when next he came to visit, for he read each of Sonia's letters without fail and would be delighted to hear our daughter was well. Bastiano also sent money for Ginevra's upkeep and had helped me arrange for her care by the Abate family. He would have liked to keep our daughter nearer as well, but understood all the reasons why we could not.

Someday, perhaps, he could acknowledge her as his own. When that day might come and what it might look like, I could not say, but so long as Ginevra always knew who her father was, that was all that truly mattered to me.

I remained at my desk and spent the rest of the morning going through my correspondence. Every so often I'd pause to glance up around me, to take in the fine desk and the chair in which I sat, the gilt-framed Murano glass mirror on the opposite wall, the silk curtains that framed a view of a small canal outside, the beautiful glassware and expensive spirits on the mahogany sideboard that was positioned in between the windows. I appreciated the fine things in life and would never apologize for it. It seemed there wasn't a day that went by that I didn't look around my lovely home and the beautiful things in it with satisfaction—and almost a bit of disbelief as well. Disbelief that I truly had all of this in my keeping, at my command; that I could truly be living like this after everything I'd been through in my younger years, and all I'd lost. I would never take it for granted.

Other than Sonia's letters, there were stacks of invitations and requests to visit me to sort through, most of them from current clients and also some from men hoping to make my acquaintance. I discarded the latter. It took more than a letter out of the blue, no matter how prettily worded, to gain my attention. I instead went through the ones from current clients. My sole ecclesiastical client wished to come the following night, and I quickly wrote a reply in the affirmative. I had not received Father Valier in some time and smiled in pleasure at the thought of a visit with him. Francesco Valier was about thirty-five years of age, handsome, and quite vigorous and thorough in the bedchamber, more than one should rightly expect of a man of the cloth. Perhaps it was that thrill of the forbidden that also helped in my own attraction to him, but nights spent with Francesco were never a chore, as they were with those like old Senator Querini. Francesco was one of many whose patrician family had wished to gain power and influence within the Church, and so sent their second son to take holy vows, regardless of how well-suited he was for his profession. And Francesco, though possessed of the sharp intelligence and strategic mind needed to rise far within the Church, was not at all suited to certain other aspects of his position, such as celibacy.

Luckily for me.

I wrote replies either accepting or declining the remaining invitations, then stood from my desk and stretched. It was early yet, and there was plenty of time before I would need to start readying myself for the evening. I was accompanying Niccolo Contarini, eldest son of a venerable family and who much preferred my company to that of his dull wife, to a salon that evening. Aside from Francesco, Niccolo was perhaps my favorite client; I always enjoyed myself with him. In bed we knew exactly what the other's body craved. Out of bed, we were friends.

I rang the bell to summon Marta. "Just a plain dress, and pin my hair up simply," I told her when she appeared. "I will accompany Bettina to the market today."

"Of course, Madonna," Marta said, turning to the wardrobe to do my bidding.

If I was dining in, either by myself or entertaining a client, Bettina would have been at the market at dawn, looking for the best catch or cut of meat that could be had that day. As I was going out that evening, she likely had not been. We could go and stock up on a few things together.

There were many courtesans in the city who would not be seen out on the streets doing any sort of mundane task. This helped them maintain an air of mystery, the illusion that they were not like other women, but were closer to goddesses. This served neither my work for the Council of Ten nor my own personal inclination. I lived in what I was certain was the most beautiful city on earth. What good was that if I did not go out and enjoy it? I had certainly not become a courtesan to lock myself away in yet another cage, not even one of my own making.

Besides, my clients and lovers came from the strata of society wherein I would be unlikely to run into them among the crowded and smelly fish stalls of the Rialto market. I could have my freedom and still maintain that air of mystery.

In short order, Bettina and I were setting out from my palazzo, which was not so old or grand as many of those owned by most of the patrician class, but a fine one, nonetheless. We headed toward Rialto and the market.

"There'll not be much left at this hour, Madonna," Bettina warned.

I waved this aside. "I know. I am more interested in the walk, in any case."

"It is a fine day," my stalwart housekeeper agreed, and we fell into a companionable silence as we navigated the narrow calli, crossing bridges and weaving among the throngs of Venetians taking in the lovely spring day. I breathed in the salty air of the canals, the damp and earthy smell of the bricks and stone of the buildings. We passed both fine palazzi and smaller houses where multiple families lived. We followed the maze of streets until we came out at the base of the Rialto bridge, the wooden structure arcing over the Grand Canal, that main waterway of Venice, the artery in the throat of La Serenissima from which all life flowed.

I took a deep breath of the breeze off the lagoon again, sighing contentedly at the sight of the sun on the water, on the stone faces of the beautiful palazzi lining the Grand Canal, the magnificence of this city that floated in the sea.

I knew what went into keeping it afloat. I knew of the horrors and the blood and the death required to stop it all from sinking into the waves. Yet such beauty, such prosperity, was worth it all. I had seen what the alternative was, and I would do whatever it took to stop the flames of war from engulfing La Serenissima.

And after all, I had chosen this city, and she in turn had chosen me, or so I'd always thought. And I had not been much of a choice, not when I first arrived. And still Venice had given me a second chance. Why would I not be willing to let so much blood stain my hands on her behalf?

Bettina and I climbed the steps of the bridge to cross to the other side, where the market was located. I could not help but linger at the top of the bridge, admiring the glorious view down the Grand Canal. Bettina waited impatiently, shaking her head. "It looks the same as the last time we walked this way," she said, when I finally moved away from the railing and down the other side of the bridge. "And it will look just the same tomorrow."

"I stop to take it in *because* it looks the same," I said. "Because each day it is somehow just as beautiful as the last. That seems to me the true miracle."

She clucked at me. "You're getting sentimental in your old age, Madonna."

"Old age? I'm young enough to be your daughter!"

"But old enough to be as sentimental as a poet."

"You are old, and you're the least sentimental person I know," I pointed out.

"And it's served me well," Bettina said.

"I will strive to be more like you, then, Bettina," I said. But inwardly I scoffed. *Sentimental? Me?* If I was, certainly I wouldn't be able to bring myself to slit a man's throat or put poison in his wine.

But I stole one last glance at the Grand Canal shimmering in the sunlight and let the sight fill me up like a fine meal. I remembered the weight of Ginevra in my arms when I'd been with her last summer, and the unique scent of her hair, her skin, the knowledge that she was mine and I had made her. I thought of lying beside Bastiano in bed, not making love, not even speaking, just staying close to each other.

Perhaps I was sentimental about some things. The things that mattered.

I wandered behind Bettina among the stalls, pointing out some vegetables and sausages and leaving her to haggle with the vendors.

As we moved through the market, I began to feel the uneasy, prickling sensation of eyes on me. I glanced over my shoulder several times, only to feel as though someone was hovering at the edge of my vision. Bettina, missing nothing, frowned at me after I'd quickly turned a couple times, but I merely smiled to attempt to put her at ease.

Then, finally, I saw him, lurking near a fish stall: one of Malatesta's hired hands, the same one who had been keeping an eye on me on Ascension Day. If he noticed that I'd seen him, he did not react; he merely continued perusing the stall before moving along to one next to it, closer to me.

Could this be mere coincidence? Malatesta's hired thugs must eat as well, so perhaps there was a perfectly innocent reason he was at the market.

But . . . no. I knew what being watched felt like, and someone had most certainly been watching me. Why, though? To what end? If he was meant to be discreetly monitoring me, he hadn't done a very good job; I'd spotted him quickly enough. He knew I knew his face, if not his name.

Or perhaps I was meant to see him. Perhaps I was meant to know I was being watched. That idea was somehow most chilling of all.

I shivered, causing Bettina to frown at me again. "What is it, Madonna?" she asked.

"Nothing," I said. "I . . ." But when I looked around for him again, the man was gone. "Nothing," I said again. "Let's get home, shall we?"

When we arrived home, Bettina and I, carrying our purchases, entered through the servants' door, the one that opened onto the street behind the palazzo, and immediately Lauretta was upon us. "Oh, Madonna, forgive me," she said, anxiously wringing her hands. "One of your regulars is here—that one . . . is he a senator? Oh, by the Blessed Mother, I've forgotten his name . . ."

"Ambrogio Malatesta?" I asked, my stomach sinking.

"Yes, that's the one. He's in your parlor, Madonna," Lauretta said. "He demanded to be shown in, even after I said you were out."

"Of course he did," I muttered, yet a shiver went down my back all the same. Had Malatesta sent his man to find me when I was not at home? Or did he make a habit of having me watched? Louder, I said, "Thank you, Lauretta," and stalked upstairs.

I put the man at the market out of my thoughts as best I could. I needed to be sharp now. There was only one reason Malatesta would come to my house unannounced: he had another job for me to do.

Chapter 6

Without preamble or bothering to announce myself, I flung open the doors to the second-floor parlor in which Malatesta was seated, although *enthroned* was perhaps a better word. He occupied the richly upholstered chair as if he owned it, the room and everything in it, and the palazzo and its occupants as well. I did not much like to think of the ways in which that was true.

If he was startled by my sudden arrival, he didn't show it in the least, damn him. His cold, dark eyes simply met mine calmly as I entered. Ambrogio Malatesta was in his later years, to be certain; his late fifties at least. Yet even I had to admit that he was an attractive man; he had likely turned many a lady's head in his younger days and perhaps still did. He was tall and well built, if on the thin side. He kept his thick iron-gray hair combed away from his face, which still remained sculpted with perfectly balanced features, like a statue of some old Roman emperor or hero. He was dressed that day, as always, in the black robes of Venetian patrician men, and his were never less than impeccably clean and pressed.

Malatesta had just begun his term on the Council of Ten a few months prior, in January of that year. I had worked with others on the Ten prior to Malatesta, most often passing information that I gleaned from my clients, and eventually began eliminating those who sought to bring harm to the Venetian Republic. I had met Malatesta several years ago, when he was an ambitious member of the Great Council, and eventually a senator, who discovered that he had a great use for my particular talents. Of late, I tended to work exclusively with—and for—him. And this year, finally, he had achieved his long-held desire of being elected to the Council of Ten.

"Signor Malatesta," I said briefly, in response to his impassive gaze in my direction. I settled myself in a chair opposite him. "To what do I owe this unannounced visit?"

His eyes locked on mine. "What else? I have a target I need you to eliminate."

"I'd figured as much. More traitors to the Venetian state?"

"Of course. Their numbers, alas, are never ceasing."

"Indeed." Relaxing somewhat into my usual poised, deadly, seductive persona, I lightly ran my fingers over the velvet upholstery of my chair and purred, "One would think that a nation as great as Venice would inspire a bit more patriotism and loyalty, or at the very least, fear."

He scowled. "This is no laughing matter, Valentina."

"Treason never is, and incidentally, I was not laughing."

His scowl remained in place. He knew that there was mockery in my words somewhere but didn't have the patience to tease it out or spar with me further. "This is deadly serious."

"Quite literally," I observed. "Who is my next victim, then?"

It was a wonder that scowl did not stay permanently etched on the man's face. "The *target* is one of your regular clients, which should make matters quite easy."

My hands stilled in their idle stroking of the upholstery. "Who?" *By the Shadow God, let it not be Niccolo or Francesco,* I prayed. I had killed clients of mine before, of course: one of the things that made me so valuable to the Venetian government and the Ten was that I had access to many wealthy and powerful men while they were completely vulnerable. I'd always had the uneasy understanding that I might be asked to kill any of the men who paid for my body; that in my bed, death and intimacy were woven together like strands of silk cord. I had long dreaded the day when I might be asked to assassinate one of my own favorites. With one exception, the clients I'd killed had all been men Malatesta had sent to me under the guise of facilitating an introduction to one of Venice's most popular and sought-after courtesans.

So to hear that my next victim was a regular client . . .

"Dioniso Secco."

I gasped—I could not help it. Part of it was relief, and part was genuine shock.

Secco was a very wealthy patrician with mercantile interests all over the Italian peninsula and eastward. He held great power and influence on the Great Council and aspired to the Senate, as many patrician men did. Most thought he would make it there eventually.

But that, I saw now, was not to be.

I would be sad to lose Secco. Not because I enjoyed bedding him; he was the sort of man who took his own pleasure and cared nothing for his partner's. Nor even because I particularly liked him. But he was known to often pay more than my usual fee to ensure I was not otherwise engaged when he wished to see me, and he often gave me extravagant and interesting gifts from the far-flung places where he did business.

"Is there a problem?" Malatesta asked acidly when I did not immediately reply.

"Dioniso Secco," I repeated, leaning back in my chair, my flip tone covering my unease. "I would not have guessed it. You and the Ten are very bad for my business, Malatesta, I must say. Secco pays well. Very well."

"Your business is what the Ten says it is," he snapped.

"If you have me kill all the rich men in the Republic, there will be none left for me to fuck to keep me in fine dresses," I said, noting his wince with satisfaction. Malatesta always hated when I used profanity, which was, of course, why I used it in his presence. "And then where will I be?"

"Naked, and no doubt doing better business than ever."

"Ah, Malatesta, you flirt. Spend much time thinking about me naked, then?"

Saints damn me—and surely they would—but was that a spark of desire I'd seen in his eyes? As quickly as it had come, however, it was gone. "How much does Secco pay you in a year?" he asked impatiently.

I tilted my head to one side, calculating. "Hmm, let me see . . ."

"Whatever it is, I'll double it."

I bit back another gasp and instead arched an eyebrow at him. "Does the Ten have that kind of money at their disposal?"

"For this we do. Secco must go."

"By the Virgin. What has the man done? Plotted to assassinate the Doge?"

"Worse. He owns a share in one of the glassworks on Murano, and we've intercepted some of his correspondence with a highly placed nobleman in France. He is making arrangements to send one of the glassblowers to France to teach the French artisans Venetian glassmaking."

I had not expected this either. "Is he," I said, pondering. This was indeed tantamount to the gravest political betrayal. Venice had a monopoly on fine glass, and it made the Republic, and its rich and powerful men, a considerable fortune. That the secret of making the glass would get out to other nations was the greatest fear of many in Venice, and so the Ten kept a special eye on Murano, on the glassblowers and their families, and on anyone who did business with them. The glassblowers themselves were not permitted to leave the city without the express permission of the Great Council, for fear of a betrayal exactly like the one Malatesta was describing.

If the Ten said Secco was a traitor and that he needed to die, then so he did. Yet something about this did not quite add up to me. Why would a man with plenty of money and influence already, and with grand political hopes, take a gamble this large? He would have to know that the Ten would eventually uncover such a plot. Why risk everything he yet stood to gain in his life? "One would think Secco had plenty of money already," I commented.

"Apparently the substantial weight of the gold already in his coffers is not enough, and he must betray his country for more. Per the letters, in addition to an outrageous fee for simply sending the glassblower to France, he has also negotiated a percentage of the profit made by everyone who learns from his man."

"Hmm," I said thoughtfully. "Truly I would never have thought it of Secco." And yet who knew better than I how inconspicuous spies and traitors could be? Had I not thought the Spanish spy I'd killed was similarly innocuous?

Malatesta ignored this. "So you see why he needs to die."

"I suppose," I said.

More death. More blood. More stains on my soul. And for what, this time? For money? So the men of the Venetian Republic could stay as rich as they'd always been? A man who threatened to bring the Spanish armada down on us had to be eliminated, certainly. But simply to protect the monopoly on glass?

Yet Venice was not like anywhere else on the Italian peninsula. I knew that well. Statecraft and economics were entwined such that they became one and the same. And from the economic security of the Republic flowed its naval might and, therefore, its safety. Not to mention that, just from what I knew, this would not be the first time the Ten had killed to protect the secrets of the glass.

"When is Secco scheduled to see you next?" Malatesta asked.

I had just had a letter from Secco that day and had replied to let him know that I was free to see him on the evening he had requested. "Four nights hence."

Malatesta nodded. "Very good. See that it is done, then, however you feel is best. I will have men standing by to remove the body."

There it was: the cold, efficient brutality that characterized so much of what Malatesta did. "Good. But Secco is quite powerful, you know. He wields much influence on the Great Council. What if his death should be linked to me?"

"The only people who matter know what he has done and know he deserves to die."

"And what of those who don't know? What if his powerful friends should ask questions?"

"You are under my protection."

It was somewhat reassuring to hear him say it, at least, even if Malatesta's protection was often like an itchy, stifling blanket I wished I could cast off. "Surely even you have enemies, Malatesta. Perhaps especially you."

He rose from his chair, clearly done with the conversation. "To cross me is to cross the Ten," he said. "All of Venice knows that. And if they don't yet, they will soon." He moved toward the door and then stopped to look at me down the length of his nose. "You're not losing your touch, are you, Valentina?"

I lifted my chin. "Hardly," I said. "You want Secco dead? Then he'll die."

"It isn't what I want, but what the Ten needs. What Venice needs. And so I know you will act accordingly." With one more short nod, he turned and left the room, and I could hear the sound of his expensive leather boots going down the marble staircase.

I shook my head at his fading footsteps. It was a dangerous man who mistook his own will for the best interests of a nation. Even more dangerous when he had the power, the means, to enforce that will.

And what was I but one of the tools he used to do just that?

Chapter 7

I had, of course, other business to attend to that night. Once Malatesta left, it was time for me to ready myself for my evening out with Niccolo Contarini.

It was always a process, preparing for an evening with a client, especially an evening out. I usually bathed, a lengthy affair in and of itself, with the maids having to haul heated water upstairs from the kitchen. If I washed my long, thick dark hair, then I must wait for it to dry. I wouldn't have time for that today, though, so instead I pinned my hair up to bathe and, when I stepped out, wrapped myself in a silk robe and sat at my dressing table for Marta to do my hair and cosmetics.

She and I had already chosen my gown for that evening: a lovely sky-blue silk, very low-cut and trimmed in creamy Burano lace. Niccolo loved me in blue, or so he claimed. I knew he loved me best in nothing at all.

Marta braided and pinned back a few strands of my hair, like a crown, and wove a yellow ribbon through it. Courtesans were required—though the word *required* was often applied, or at least enforced, loosely—to wear something yellow when in public. This was to distinguish us from patrician ladies, who often dressed as richly, or indeed sometimes less so, as we did.

She then curled the rest of the strands with a metal rod heated in the fire and left them loose down my back, the dark, glossy hair shining in the firelight. She applied cosmetics lightly, and as a final touch I donned an elaborate necklace, worked in gold and set with diamonds, as well as matching diamond earrings. The set had been a gift from Niccolo himself.

"Remind me where the party is this evening, Madonna?" Marta asked as I slid the earrings into place.

"The home of a friend of Niccolo's—Ottaviano Lotti is his name," I said. "He is from Rome, exiled for displeasing the pope with some of his writings, or so they say. I've yet to meet the man."

"One of those rabble-rousing intellectual types, then?" Marta asked with a smile.

"They are Niccolo's favorites. It'll be a rather mixed crowd, I expect—some patricians, some artists, some poets, the like."

"Lots of men talking over one another, sounds like."

I laughed at this astute observation. That was, more or less, how such gatherings often went, and I had certainly been to my share. "Of course. At least until they call for one of us courtesans to entertain them for a short time. Then they'll be back to wanting to hear themselves talk."

Just then, Lauretta poked her head into the room. "The Contarini gondola is moored downstairs, Madonna," she announced.

"Very good. I'll be down shortly." I rose from my seat at the dressing table, tugging the bodice of my gown down a bit, enough to almost, but not quite, expose my nipples. Many of the common prostitutes on the streets wore bodices cut low enough to reveal their breasts entirely, both as a way to display their wares, so to speak, but also to avoid harassment by the authorities. There was a robust underground sex trade in which men sold their bodies to other men, which was illegal in the Republic of Venice as well as elsewhere in Christendom—though, of course, such illegality did little to hinder it. Many of these male prostitutes dressed as women, and so female prostitutes were sometimes asked to show their breasts to prove that they were female and thus working legally. As such, some chose to save themselves both time and trouble and simply wear lower-cut bodices. The authorities tended to be a bit more delicate in their policing of cortigiane oneste such as myself, and so more than once I had been asked to pull up my skirt and reveal a leg to an inspector's gaze, on the assumption that a man's leg could not be mistaken for a woman's.

I took the time to straighten my dressing table, putting the box of hairpins and pots of cosmetics away. Marta watched me with a half smile. She was more than capable of doing all this after I left, but I liked to keep Niccolo waiting, at least a bit.

I allowed perhaps ten minutes to elapse before I finally moved to leave. "Have Lauretta put some wine in the downstairs bedroom for our return," I said to Marta. "We shouldn't need anything else, as we'll eat at the party, so you are all dismissed for the evening."

She nodded. "Very good, Madonna. Have a good night."

"And you."

I went downstairs to the water entrance, my fine silk skirt sweeping over the marble. When I stepped outside, I found Niccolo waiting solicitously for me on the dock. "Ah, and so the exquisite Valentina Riccardi decides to grace me with her presence at last," he teased, a smile on his handsome face.

"I was debating whether I wanted to come at all," I said, walking past him and toward the gondola. I accepted the hand his gondolier offered to help me into the craft. I ducked my head to enter the felze, the canopy that created a private space within the gondola and helped keep the heat in on cold nights.

"You would never abandon me, surely," Niccolo said, coming through the felze behind me.

I settled myself against the velvet cushions and threw him a glance out of the corner of my eye. "If I got a better offer, I might."

"Who pays more than me? I'll double it."

His words, an echo of Malatesta's earlier that day, gave me an unpleasant jolt that I had to quickly master. "Ah, but a lady never divulges the secrets of the bedroom." My lips curved into a smile. "Or of her ledger."

"Humph," Niccolo said, seating himself right beside me. "Yet I know I am the most fun, am I not?" He slid a hand beneath my skirts, his fingers expertly probing between my legs.

"For shame, Nico," I said, biting back a sigh of pleasure as he stroked and teased. "You are a gentleman, are you not? Surely you have the patience to wait until later . . ."

Yet soon even my prestigious skills at clever banter were bested by the pleasure rising in me. I leaned back against the cushions and no longer tried to hold back my sighs.

When I opened my eyes and emerged from my haze of pleasure, Niccolo was smiling down at me with satisfaction. He bent over me and kissed me thoroughly. "I find my patience is sorely tested this evening," he said, "especially when you're looking at me like that." He kissed me again, deeper this time. "Perhaps we should turn this gondola around," he said, his breath warm on my skin.

"And disappoint your friend? Surely not," I said, though my own breathing was heavy.

Niccolo sighed and drew back, putting a respectable distance between us. "I suppose you're right," he said, the reluctance plain in his voice as he eyed the swell of my breasts at my neckline.

I straightened my skirts and patted my coiffure to make sure it was still in place. "What news since I saw you last?" I asked.

Niccolo had recently taken up the place on the Great Council guaranteed him by his patrician birth, and so he helped keep me duly informed. As the gondola sliced silently through the canals on its way to the home of Ottaviano Lotti, Niccolo regaled me with everything from new trade deals to the recent arrival of legates from the Holy Father, to a scandal involving a man from a minor patrician family whose name was unfamiliar to me.

"He aspired to make his way up to senator, but that'll never happen now," Niccolo concluded.

"Doesn't everyone aspire to become a senator?" I asked.

"Not the lazy ones."

"Fair point," I conceded. "But I fail to see how being caught bedding another man disqualifies him from the Senate. You know as well as I do that there are current senators with that very same preference."

"Indeed there are, but the difference here is that those senators have enough money and influence to persuade people to look the other way. This man does not—he has a distinguished name, but not the wealth that once accompanied it."

"Poor man," I said, and meant it. Such hypocrisy, with all sexual pleasures outside of the marriage bed officially frowned on by the Church. And yet even so, some were considered acceptable and others were not. I was certainly not one to raise an eyebrow at anyone's choice of consenting partner.

"Indeed. A shame, that. He's intelligent and capable. He'd be useful in the Senate, no mistake."

"Then why don't you champion him?" I challenged. "If he is such an able politician? To have a Contarini take up his cause would surely convince everyone to overlook the scandal."

"And risk alienating my own political allies? I think not."

And so Venetian politics—and the world—turned.

By then, we had arrived at the rented palazzo of Niccolo's friend Lotti. Niccolo's gondolier tied up at the dock to let us out, and we went in through the water entrance and up the stairs to the piano nobile, the floor of Venetian palazzi where life was lived.

The gathering was already in full swing when we entered, my hand securely on Niccolo's arm as we were shown to the ballroom where the guests had gathered. Upon our entrance, a tall, solidly built man with dark hair and olive skin detached himself from the rest of the company and came to great us. "Niccolo Contarini! An honor to have you among us, signore," he said, shaking Niccolo's hand enthusiastically. The man's Roman accent triggered a sudden burst of memory, and suddenly I was a teenage girl again, making eyes at the handsome merchant's son seated across my father's table in our fine villa on the outskirts of the Eternal City. But in the space of a blink, I had mastered myself again and was turning my usual charming smile on the man who was surely our host.

"Thank you for extending your hospitality, Ottaviano," Niccolo said warmly. He indicated me. "Have you yet had the pleasure of making the acquaintance of the enchanting Valentina Riccardi?"

"I have not," Lotti said, eyeing me up and down as though I were a piece of fine statuary, a look that for me was something of an occupational hazard. Lotti took my hand in his and kissed it. "I must confess to a great sorrow," he said.

"Sorrow, in such fine surroundings and company as this?" I said, my voice warm. I took great care that my accent, almost flawlessly Venetian after my years in the lagoon city, did not slip. No need to let a Roman vowel seep through and invite any unwanted questions from a man who would surely recognize it. "What might that be, Signor Lotti?"

He pressed both hands to his heart. "That I have spent my time in Venice thus far *not* in the company of such beauty," he said. "I hope you might help me rectify this immediately."

I laughed. "That is why I am here."

He took my hand again and bowed over it. "The beautiful Valentina will do me great honor by using my Christian name," he said.

"A small enough favor, Ottaviano."

He pressed his hands to his heart again, this time in delight. "Che bellezza," he said rapturously. "Please, come in, the both of you, and make yourselves comfortable. What will you have? Wine? Spirits? There are some small delicacies on the table just there—please help yourselves."

Ottaviano Lotti would no doubt have trailed us—me—all over the room, but just then another guest appeared at his elbow and claimed his attention. With a last regretful look in my direction, he turned to speak to the man who had approached him.

"I think you've just found your next client," Niccolo commented as we each accepted a glass of red wine from a servant and stepped into the ballroom, which was richly appointed. The floor was of marble polished to a shine, and the walls were a soft cream color, trimmed with gilt, lighter than the heavy reds and blues one usually saw. Columns around the periphery held up a loggia ringing the room, with an upper level that guests could ascend to in order to look down on the crowd below and gossip. Tables holding refreshments were adorned with flowers and were arranged at the sides of the room, and an assortment of chairs, cushions, and daybeds had been arranged about the room for guests to sit or recline on as they saw fit.

As we entered, another courtesan was playing a lute and singing a charming love song that had captivated most of those in attendance. And rightfully so, for she had a lovely voice, as well as the blonde hair, pale complexion, and wide blue eyes that were all the rage in Venice. Her name was Felicita Cavazza, and she was quite popular for her beauty, talent, and wit. Our paths had crossed fairly frequently, and we enjoyed each other's company enough that I considered us friends, if only casually so. I nodded in her direction when our eyes met, and she returned the nod, smiling briefly even as she never missed a note in her song.

I returned my attention to Niccolo. His tone, when he'd spoken, had been even, but when I glanced up at his face I saw his mouth was contorted into a moue of displeasure. "So long as his money is good, then he is welcome to my attentions," I purred.

Niccolo didn't speak.

"Would that bother you?" I asked. Certainly Niccolo knew, as all my clients did, that they were not the only one. I could not afford to take just one lover, no matter how handsomely he paid. Not if I was to save enough money to support myself once my looks faded, and also to provide for my daughter and allow her to lead the life of her choosing.

Still, men were men, and they got jealous. Though, as yet, none of my clients had gotten so jealous that they had slashed my face or committed some such vile act, as sadly happened to courtesans from time to time. Not many of my clients came to me for just a quick fuck; they could go to the whores on the Bridge of Tits for that, and pay a lot less for the privilege. Courtesans, after all, provided much more than just sex; that was the point. We were also cultured, elegant, well dressed, well spoken, and well educated. We could join in discussions of politics and literature and art and music, just as men could, unlike the patrician daughters of Venice, for whom education was all but forbidden. Far be it for a woman to be better educated than her husband. The result was that these highly educated patrician men who ran the Republic were married to women who could barely read or write, let alone converse on important topics, and so they must turn elsewhere for intellectual companionship. They may as well get sex in the bargain. As well, there were all of the younger sons of the noble houses like Bastiano, who, in the interest of keeping family fortunes intact, were often not permitted to marry and have legitimate children of their own. Such younger sons kept the courtesan's trade afloat just as much as the elder sons dissatisfied with their wives.

And so, as I well knew, in the course of the companionship that came with being a courtesan—intellectual and physical and all the rest—occasionally emotional attachments developed as well. Not in all cases, but in some.

For Niccolo, for the sake of our mutual attachment, I would do something I would do for perhaps no other client: I would turn away Ottaviano Lotti if Niccolo wished it.

It was also good business. Niccolo was a generous patron, both with his money and his gifts. If it would prick at his pride to see me entertaining a friend of his, then I would refuse that friend. A courtesan had to be strategic about what invitations she accepted and which she declined. The bedroom was as political as any hall of government. Many learned that lesson too late.

Niccolo glanced down at me with a half smile. "And if I said it would bother me?"

I shrugged and took a sip of my wine, as though this conversation did not matter to me in the least. "Then if Ottaviano Lotti comes to call on me, I shall send him next door. Amalia Amante will appreciate the business."

"Ottaviano has been looking for a mistress among the famed Venetian courtesans since he arrived here, so I've heard," Niccolo said, his eyes following our host around the room. "Apparently he has yet to find any that suit his fancy. I am given to understand that he much prefers brunettes, so I'm sure Amalia's charms will be precisely to his taste."

I smiled. "Amalia bends every man's taste toward her, I think."

Niccolo laughed aloud at this. "No doubt she does." He bent down and pressed a quick kiss to my lips, one I was too surprised to return. He rarely made such gestures in public. "And yet she pales in comparison to you."

I tried to think of a response to this, one in my usual flippant style, and found myself coming up short.

Just then, Felicita's song came to an end, and after the gathered company had applauded, she took her bow and returned to her patron's side. He was a man I did not recognize—one of our host's friends from Rome, perhaps. Ottaviano Lotti appeared in the center of the room. "Who shall regale us next?" he asked. His eyes lit as they came to rest on me. "Ah, the exceptionally lovely Valentina Riccardi! Have you a song for us, perhaps?"

I smiled and moved from Niccolo's side to where Ottaviano stood. "Alas, I have no musical gifts to speak of," I said, addressing both our host and those in attendance. "But poetry I can offer, if that would please your guests, amico mio," I said, turning a flirtatious look on Lotti.

"Poetry! Beautiful verse from the mouth of a beautiful woman!" Lotti said. "Please, bella Valentina."

"Petrarch, perhaps!" a male voice in the crowd called out.

I kept my smile in place, though inwardly I was grimacing. Did no one know of any poets save Petrarch and Dante? But it was a courtesan's duty to please, above all. Lord knows I had enough of those dead men's verses memorized by then. "One of Petrarch's love poems, then," I announced, and allowed my voice to both deepen slightly and grow louder as I prepared to cast my spell over the room. "*'When I utter sighs, in calling out to you/with the name that Love wrote on my heart . . .'*"

I did not declaim so much as perform the poem, bestowing fleeting glances on some of the men gathered while gazing into the eyes of others as I spoke entire lines, thus making each man believe I was speaking only to him. By the time I reached the end of the sonnet, I had them all enraptured. The applause that followed was as hearty as that following my colleague's song. I inclined my head and dipped a slight curtsey, allowing myself to appear demure for just an instant so that they might think they had imagined my boldness of moments before.

"Another!" Lotti called, still clapping.

I inclined my head to him again. "Since our gracious host insists," I said, "this poem is one written by a woman, a fellow courtesan and citizen of Venice." I arched an eyebrow at the gasps and murmurs of excitement, then began to recite a poem that Amalia had written. As I delivered the last line, I threw a wink in Lotti's direction. Perhaps he might inquire as to the poet's name, and then I could introduce him to Amalia. She would adore him.

The guests applauded again, then Lotti clapped twice, loudly. "Dinner is served, my friends," he said. "Please! Come through to the dining room."

I returned to Niccolo's side, and, bless him, he had a fresh glass of wine waiting for me. "Such lovely verses, and beautifully recited," he said, his arm tightening possessively around my waist. "Although I can think of a different use for that lovely mouth of yours."

"Someone is impatient indeed tonight," I murmured, watching the guests filter into the dining room next door. "I thought you liked poetry."

"Never more than when you speak it," he said.

"Perhaps I will regale you with poetry all the night long, then."

"I think you'll find yourself quite out of breath with me in your bed."

"Impatient *and* altogether too certain of yourself."

"I shall most certainly rise to the challenge."

I was saved the need to reply to such a terrible pun, however, when Niccolo spoke again, his attention now on someone else nearby. "Ah. Buona notte, signore. Valentina, I trust I need not introduce you to Bastiano Bragadin?"

Speaking of jealousy.

My head shot up to see Bastiano standing before us, his expression tight in a way likely only I would notice. He must have just come in, for I would have noticed him right away had he already been there when we entered. I never failed to sense his presence.

"Indeed you do not," I replied. It was an open secret among those of both Bastiano's and my social circles that we were lovers and that we had a child together. Open secrets, after all, could still be overlooked by the most powerful. And by Bastiano's parents. "And how are you this evening, Bastiano? I did not expect to see you here."

"Nor I you," he replied shortly, nearly glaring at my hand on Niccolo's arm.

I sighed inwardly. *Please, Bastiano, do not cause a scene,* I prayed, hoping someone inclined to answer the prayers of courtesans was listening.

Niccolo, on the other hand, was positively beaming at this turn of events. "Are you here alone, Bragadin?" Niccolo asked conversationally.

"I am, as you see," Bastiano said, holding his arms out to his sides as if to emphasize his solo state.

"A pity. But then I suppose only one man can have the most beautiful woman in Venice on his arm on a given night. Tonight it seems I am that lucky man."

"Niccolo, really," I said, my voice low.

"I only speak the truth," he insisted, his eyes never leaving Bastiano's. "I am a lucky man."

Bastiano lifted his chin, his habitual arrogance and charm flooding back to his face, his bearing. "Tonight you are," he conceded. "But on most nights you'll find that I am luckier." He nodded to me. "Valentina. I shall see you soon." With that, he turned and followed the rest of the party into the dining room.

Once he was gone, I slapped Niccolo's arm. "Was that entirely necessary?" I demanded.

"I thought so, yes."

"Saints spare me from men and their pissing contests," I muttered. "You are all like children—you know that, do you not?"

Niccolo shrugged. "I suppose we are, in that we do not like to share if we can help it."

"Shall we forget this foolishness and have a pleasant evening?" I said, arching an eyebrow at him as I took another sip from my wineglass.

"Oh, I plan for it to be very pleasant indeed," Niccolo said, eyeing me hungrily.

As we stepped into the dining room, I happened to glance over my shoulder and noticed Felicita Cavazza whispering into the ear of Anzolo Balbi, a man I knew only in passing. He was a young member of the Great Council and was said to be very ambitious. Whatever she was telling him he was listening to intently, nodding, a serious expression on his handsome face. I recognized the clandestine passing of information when I saw it, though they could both stand to learn a bit more discretion. As if feeling my gaze on her, Felicita glanced up, her eyes meeting mine. So she was not entirely without awareness of her surroundings, then.

The prudent thing—the Venetian thing—to do would have been to avert my gaze immediately, pretending I hadn't seen anything. Yet, before I could think better of it, I nodded to her once, a slight, subtle motion of my head, nothing more.

She froze just slightly at the moment of recognition, no doubt panicking that she'd been caught in her spying and scheming. Yet almost immediately, it seemed as though she read the understanding in my gaze, and she visibly relaxed a fraction. She returned my nod, equally as subtly, all without breaking stride in her report to Balbi. He, for his part, noticed nothing whatsoever of the exchange.

I turned to face forward again, an unsettled feeling writhing low in my stomach. It should have made me feel better to know that I was not alone in the work I did, at least in some of it. And in truth, never had I dreamed that I was the only courtesan in Venice used as a source of information about the city's most powerful men. We were too perfectly placed, too easily able to gain the kind of knowledge that could make or break political fortunes or literal fortunes. Of course I wasn't the only one.

And yet, somehow, seeing the truth of it before my very eyes made me both sad and angry at the same time.

★ ★ ★

It was not until the early hours of the morning that Niccolo and I returned to my palazzo, where a jug of wine and two glasses were waiting for us in the bedroom where I entertained clients, just as I'd requested before I'd left. Niccolo, however, had had enough to drink at Lotti's. Or he wished to claim me as his own after our encounter with Bastiano or had simply felt his desire building all evening—perhaps all three—for he eschewed my offer of wine and rather quickly stripped me of my clothes. He made love to me hard, rough, in a way he knew I liked, but I was also certain I wasn't imagining the possessiveness in his touch.

Men. Honestly.

After we'd both come to our pleasure—and I usually did with Niccolo, I had to give him that—we fell asleep next to each other. In the morning, all was back to normal between us. Niccolo stayed to break his fast, as he often did, before kissing me deeply as he prepared to take his leave.

"When shall I see you again?" he asked. "There is a musical performance at the Gradenigo palazzo three nights hence. Would you join me?"

I would have liked nothing better, but I remembered, with a sinking sensation in my stomach, that three nights hence was the date of my deadly assignation with Dioniso Secco. I could under no circumstances cancel or reschedule with him, or Malatesta would hear of it and think that I'd lost my nerve or that I was playing some game with him and with the Ten. Neither would do me any good. "I cannot," I answered with true regret in my voice. "I am otherwise engaged that evening."

He bent to nuzzle my neck. "Cancel," he whispered in my ear. "I shall triple whatever he is paying you."

I laughed mirthlessly. "Even you cannot afford that, Nico."

"Oh no?" He drew back. "Who is he?"

"A lady never—"

"Oh, don't be coy with me, Valentina," he said. "Who? I would know his name, that's all."

I could not tell him, not when Secco's body would likely be found floating in a canal the next morning. I had no fear of anyone else putting two and two together, should Secco mention his plans for the evening to someone. It would just be assumed he had fallen afoul of some thief or worse when leaving my house. No one would suspect me.

Niccolo, though . . . he might wonder, at least.

"Who is it?" he repeated. "Who is the man who can pay more than the future patriarch of the Contarini family? My vanity demands you tell me."

"I have powerful clients that I cannot risk offending, Niccolo," I bit out at last. It was more than I should have said, but it was true, if not in the way that Niccolo would interpret it. "I am not your wife. I cannot be simply at your beck and call because you will it."

Niccolo drew back from where I sat at the dining room table. For a moment I wondered if he was offended. He had never been so by my frank speech in the past—and indeed, it had helped form the friendship between us. But I thought that perhaps this time I may have gone too far.

Instead, he said, softly, "I am sorry, Valentina. You are right." He stepped close and bent to kiss me once more. "I am privileged to spend with you whatever time you can grant me, and know that I consider myself so." He donned his black patrician's cloak. "I will write to you," he said, "and hope I can see you again soon. Buon giorno, mia bellezza."

"Buon giorno, Nico," I said. "I hope to see you again soon as well."

He swept me a bow, and with that, departed.

I groaned and put my head in my hands.

I was still sitting at the head of the table that way when Bettina came in to clear away the breakfast dishes. She had obviously been listening in on the conversation, for she said, "He's in love with you, that one is."

I heaved a sigh. "I know."

"What are you going to do about it?"

"Niente. Nothing I can do about it," I said, finally raising my head. "He is simply going to have to live with the disappointment."

Chapter 8

Since, of course, I could have no peace in my life, that afternoon I was in my office going through correspondence and bills when I heard a rush of footsteps outside the door, which was then opened abruptly. Lauretta poked her head in. "Forgive me, Madonna, but Signor Bragadin is here, and he insists—"

"Yes, yes, there's no need for all that." Bastiano's voice came from behind her, and he pushed the door open the rest of the way and strode into the room.

"Mi dispiace, Madonna, he—"

I sighed and rubbed my temples. "It's all right, Lauretta. You are dismissed."

She did not need to be told twice, and made a hasty retreat out of the room, shutting the door behind her.

"Why are you here, Bastiano?" I asked, not in the mood for pleasantries.

"Do I need an invitation to come see you, my love?" he asked, the last two words spoken with a note of scorn. "Do I need to write ahead of time and arrange a rendezvous, like your paying customers?"

"Jealousy is beneath you, Bastiano," I said, my tone bored, even though I wanted nothing more than to let my anger show.

"Was I supposed to be pleased to see you on Niccolo Contarini's arm, then, and watch you stand by as he mocked me?"

"You know he is one of my clients," I said. "You knew from the beginning, when I began entertaining him."

"But I'd never seen you with him."

"And so?" I asked, rising from the chair behind my desk. "What of it?"

"I'd never *seen* you with him," he said again, nearly spitting the words. "You like him. You care for him."

"We are friends, Niccolo and I. We get along well."

"You like him," Bastiano repeated. "You care for him."

"And if I do?" I demanded, finally exploding. I spread my arms wide, the same gesture he had made last night when emphasizing that he had come to the gathering alone. "This is my profession, Bastiano. You know this; you have always known this. You know what it means, what I do. You have known the truth of my life all along." I laughed. "You know more of my life than anyone else living. So why do you now begrudge me? Why the jealousy? And do not pretend to me that you have not had other women since you and I took up with each other."

"And if I told you I had not?"

"You—what?" I stared hard at him. "Surely not."

Yet I did not have time to press him further, for he went on, back to our previous subject. "But Niccolo is more than just a client to you, isn't he?"

"And so?" I said. "Do you prefer that I am miserable with every man who pays for my company, Bastiano? Is that what you want? Would it be better if I loathed every man who touched me, if I simply had to endure them all to make a living? Would you rather I suffered in that way, simply so you need not be jealous?"

That silenced him, a feat not many could claim to have accomplished.

"Well?" I demanded. "Have you nothing to say?"

He took another moment before responding. "I do not want you to be miserable," he said softly. "I do not want you to suffer. Of course I don't. How could you think that?"

"What else am I to think when you barge in here and reprimand me for actually liking one of the men who pays for my company?"

"Do you love him?"

That brought me up short. So that was what this was about. I should have known. "Niccolo?" I asked, stalling for time.

"Yes. Niccolo Contarini. Who else have we been talking about this whole time?"

"No. I do not love him."

"But he loves you."

It was a statement, not a question. "Yes," I conceded, "I think he does. But it changes nothing for me, Bastiano. Nor for him, not really."

Bastiano laughed shortly. "It's obvious enough to anyone who sees the two of you together. And why wouldn't he love you? Why wouldn't any man love you? Why don't they all?"

"Not all men are capable of loving a woman," I said quietly. "Or of loving anyone but themselves."

"I suppose that is true enough," he said. "But I am. I am capable of loving one woman, at least."

"Bastiano," I whispered. "Don't. Please."

"You know it's true. Why may I not say it?"

I shook my head. "It . . . it just makes everything harder."

For that, he had no answer.

He knew as well as I did that our circumstances were not likely to change. I was a courtesan, and he was the third son of a venerable Venetian patrician family. His elder brother was married and would inherit the family fortune in its totality, then pass it on to his own son in time. Bastiano would not be permitted to marry, and even if he were, he would never be allowed to marry a courtesan, a woman who had known countless men, who had sold her body for coin. The allowance he was given would be cut off if he dared to marry me, and then how would he support me and our daughter?

And of course there was what had happened to the last man I had loved, to whom I had confessed that love. And so while Bastiano knew the truth of my feelings for him, I could not bring myself to speak the words. It was a foolish superstition, and I knew it, yet each time I'd ever even thought about saying the words, they'd stuck in my throat as if I'd swallowed a splinter of glass.

Surely it was for the best, this slight distance between us. It allowed me to pretend that I could survive losing him, should it come to that.

What did it matter, in the end? There was no way out of it all for the two of us—the three of us, counting Ginevra. I had been over and over it in my head. The calculations always came out the same. We were always short.

He sighed and dropped into one of the chairs I kept facing my desk. "I am sorry, Valentina."

"I understand."

We were silent for a moment, then he spoke again. "May . . . may I stay tonight?"

I winced slightly and sat down again myself. "Not tonight. I am—"

He sighed. "Otherwise engaged?"

I nodded. "I'm sorry," I said, and meant it.

"Can't you . . ."

"No," I said. "It is Francesco Valier. I have not received him in some time."

Bastiano laughed mirthlessly. "Oh, the priest. Another of your favorites."

Damn him, but he knew me too well. "Do we need to have the same argument all over again, Bastiano?"

"You're right. I am being childish. I'm sorry."

"And you know as well as I do that I may have need of the priest someday."

Famous for her courtesans though Venice was, and as much as the Republic appreciated the taxes we paid into its coffers, from time to time the city would turn on us: in times of plague or war, or of some other privation that led people to think God had turned his face from the Republic, or simply in a sudden fever of religious fervor. In the past courtesans and whores in the brothels and the prostitutes on the Bridge of Tits alike had been arrested for all manner of crimes, real and imagined, witchcraft being one of the most popular charges. Should such a day come again—and there was no reason to believe it would not, eventually—having a churchman, especially one from a respected patrician family, as a lover who might be inclined to protect me would come in most handy.

And, I added silently to myself, *someday I might have need of God's forgiveness, the sort that only a priest could provide.* If ever I could bring myself to ask for it.

Bastiano sighed. "I know. I do know it." He thought a moment. "Tomorrow night I am commanded to dine with my family. The night after, then?"

That damned night. Why did everyone suddenly wish to see me three nights hence? "I cannot, Bastiano."

"Who now?" he demanded.

"I can't—"

"Yes, you can, Valentina. It's me. Please."

I hesitated at his tone: not angry nor exasperated, but simply weary, weary of fighting with me. But surely it was best not to tell him the truth of what I was obliged to do on that night.

"It . . . it is better if you do not know," I said at last.

Instantly Bastiano leaned forward in his chair. "Malatesta," he said. "What is he having you do this time?"

"Stop, Bastiano. You know I cannot say."

"Who is the target? He's having you kill one of your regulars, isn't he?"

"It wouldn't be the first time," I said.

"It isn't fair to ask of you."

I laughed mirthlessly. "This, from you? Why, a moment ago I'd swear you were ready to kill all my regular clients yourself."

"I am in earnest, Valentina. This is too much to ask of you."

"Tell that to Malatesta and the rest of the Ten," I said. "This is why I am so valuable to them, as you well know. I won't be suspected, and it is no trouble at all for me to get men alone."

Bastiano rose from his chair and stalked to the window, looking out at the canal below. "Has he no scruples at all, the bastard? Have none of them any scruples?"

"If they did, they would not be sitting on the Council of Ten."

When he did not speak again, I sighed wearily. "Enough, Bastiano. I must do what they ask me to do, just as you must do the same when they call. How I may feel is irrelevant."

He turned from the window to face me. "But it isn't irrelevant."

"It is. It must be."

He came toward me and turned my chair to face him so that he could kneel at my feet. He took my hands in his own. "How you feel isn't irrelevant to me," he said, looking up solemnly into my eyes. "Tell me. Who is it?"

"I can't," I whispered. "For your own safety, I can't—"

He waved this aside. "I enjoy being alive, so rest assured I will not say a word. So tell me. Who is it?"

I glanced at the closed door, as if I would somehow know by looking at it whether anyone was listening on the other side. I dropped my voice to below a whisper, just in case. "Dioniso Secco."

Bastiano watched my expression carefully as I spoke. "Not one of your favorites, then."

"No. He pays well, though." I sighed. "But I . . ."

Bastiano stood, drawing me to my feet as well, and embraced me, holding me tightly. "I know," he murmured in my ear. "I know."

INTERLUDE

Rome, May 1527

Shouts. Screams. The smell of smoke.

I jolted awake, straw in my hair as I sat up. Beside me, Massimo, always a deep sleeper, stirred. "Maria?" he asked drowsily. "What . . ."

"Wake up," I hissed. "Something is wrong."

"Cosa?"

"Don't you hear that?"

Massimo opened his eyes, and it only took an instant for it all to register: the cacophony of voices outside the stable, shouting in anger and screaming in terror; the sounds of hoofbeats and horses whinnying; the ring of steel on steel.

Almost immediately, Massimo scrambled to his feet, fumbling for his clothes. "Stay here," he said as he dressed hastily. "Whatever you do, don't leave the stables until I return for you."

"What is it?" I asked, a tremor of fear in my voice that I tried desperately to hide. "What is happening?"

"I'm not sure, but I think . . . soldiers," he said distractedly, opening the door of the stall we'd been ensconced in and scooping up his belt from where he'd dropped it just outside, fastening it about his waist. From it hung his sword and a small dagger as well.

"What soldiers?" I demanded.

"The soldiers of the Holy Roman Emperor," Massimo replied, looking toward the door of the stables. "They were said to be coming this way, but I never thought they'd really dare . . ."

"What? Who?" I got to my feet and pulled my shift over my head, making to step out of the stall.

Massimo blocked the doorway, placing his hands on my shoulders. "Stay here," he said again. "Bar the door after I've gone, and whatever you do, whatever you might hear, don't come back outside. Don't let anyone in save for me or your family."

"But what are you going to do? I still don't understand what's going on. How am I supposed to wait—"

Massimo silenced me with his lips on mine, kissing me hard, and it was a kiss that tasted more of desperation than affection. "Just stay here, Maria Angelina," he said, and for the first time I heard the panic in his voice. "I will come back for you. I promise."

I often wondered, after, if he knew that kiss would be our last one.

Before I could protest again, he turned and fled from the stables, opening the door to the inferno outside. For just a moment, the screams and shouts grew louder, and I could see the flickering light of a fire spill into the stables. Then Massimo closed the door behind him and was gone.

I did as he said and went to bar the door behind him. I listened as the sounds of mayhem grew more and more terrifying until I could listen no more. With a sob, I fled back into the stall in which Massimo and I had so recently made love, curled into a ball in the hay, and pressed my hands over my ears.

I stayed there until morning. No one came for me.

★ ★ ★

I was greeted by the gray light of a bleak dawn when I finally emerged from the stables. It had been quiet for a few hours, though I could hear the same sounds of violence off in the distance. Surely it was safe to come out. I did not allow myself to wonder why Massimo had not returned for me as he'd promised.

Yet soon I did not need to wonder at all.

Halfway between the stables and the house, Massimo lay on his back, his beautiful blue eyes staring sightlessly up at the slate-colored sky. His hands were clenched to his abdomen, as though he had tried and failed to keep his innards from spilling from the gaping cut in his belly.

A scream rose in my throat, but at the last second I bit it back. What if those who had done this still lingered nearby? What if they heard me and returned if I should scream?

I wanted to drop to my knees beside Massimo, to sob and wail and rage at the sky. But I didn't—not then. The sobs and screams would come later, and they would come in force. In that moment, I had the curious certainty that if I fell to the ground beside Massimo just then, I would never get up again. And so I averted my eyes from him because I could not bear to look any longer. Because, some small voice told me, if I was going to survive, I had to keep moving.

Tears streaming silently down my face, I moved slowly toward the front door of my family's house, stepping around piles of rubble and ashes and what I told myself were bundles of clothes. I knew they were not, but I could not let myself see them for what they really were.

Inside, the house had been ransacked. What wasn't broken and strewn about the floors had been stolen. Muddy boot prints crossed the downstairs, and there was blood smeared along the floor and the walls.

And the bodies.

Our cook, Paolo, in the kitchen, along with Agata, one of the maids. My nursemaid, Giovanna, near the back staircase. My father, in the rear room that overlooked the green hills covered with grapevines and the winding road into Rome. My mother, upstairs in her bedroom.

I do not remember much else. Just the mess. And the blood. And the bodies. And the blackness that consumed me just when I could bear no more; the blackness that I fell into eagerly in the hope that I would never need to emerge from it again.

Chapter 9

Because of his position, Father Valier only ever visited me at my home, with the occasional exception during Carnevale. During that time, all went about masked, and there was no way to know a churchman from a senator, or a courtesan from a fishwife. Therefore our evenings together were almost always spent in my palazzo, where I'd have Girolama prepare us a fine meal before Francesco and I retired to the bedchamber. Bettina had been at the market that morning, likely before Niccolo and I had even stirred from bed, looking for the best fresh seafood that was to be had. True Venetian that he was, fish and shellfish were always what Francesco preferred.

Francesco arrived and was shown up to the second-floor parlor, where I swept in a few moments later. "Good evening, Father," I purred, looking up at him from beneath my dark lashes. "Dinner is being prepared in the kitchen as we speak—fish fresh from the lagoon this morning. Would you care for an aperitivo before then?"

Without waiting for an answer, I was already moving toward the carafe of chilled white Veneto wine waiting on the table. But just as I reached it, Francesco put a hand on my arm, stopping me. "I would just as soon that dinner wait a while," he said, voice low, and I looked up, startled, into his warm eyes, set in a face like a dark-haired Adonis. Just then those eyes were heavy with the weight of desire.

I smiled coyly to cover my surprise. Francesco was usually a much more patient man, and I had always found it to be worth the wait. The thought that I had inspired this more urgent lust in him was heady indeed. "Whatever you prefer," I said, releasing the carafe and stepping back. "Shall we, then?"

I led him into the bedchamber, though he knew the way well enough by then. He closed the door behind him as he entered, already beginning to remove his clothing—the breeches and doublet he usually wore when he visited me, rather than his priest's robes.

"If you'll excuse me," I murmured, "I shall have my maid help me undress."

I went into the small adjoining dressing room and rang the bell for Marta. She appeared moments later, startled. "Before dinner?" she asked in a low voice, quickly unlacing my gown.

"Apparently so," I murmured. "I wonder what's gotten into the good father."

"What's about to get into you, more like," Marta muttered, and we both giggled at the crude joke. In short order, Marta had me out of my gown and underthings and helped me into my silk robe so that I might make my reentrance into the bedchamber.

I did so to find Francesco dressed only in a long shirt, waiting. His eyes eagerly latched onto me as soon as I entered the room. "Valentina," he said, sighing more than speaking my name.

"Yes, Francesco mio?" I said, closing the door behind me.

"Come here."

I obeyed, and he immediately reached out and drew me to him, crushing his mouth to mine. He kissed me urgently, roughly, like a man starving. "Ah, it's been so long," he murmured against my jaw, his teeth biting at my lower lip. I could feel his erection pressing against me through the thin cloth that separated us.

"Then let us not wait any longer," I said, drawing him to the bed. He spun me around, my back against his chest, and kissed and nipped at my neck, causing me to sigh with pleasure. He slid the robe from my body and gently guided me to the bed with his hands around my hips, so that I was on my hands and knees. I heard the soft swish of cloth as he pulled his shirt off over his head, felt him draw close to me. My body pulsed with desire. I felt his hardness just briefly at the entrance to my body before he entered me from behind, his hands on my hips, pulling me toward him as he thrust into me.

I let out a moan of pleasure—entirely unfeigned, as it usually was with Francesco—and pushed my hips back against him as he thrust, taking his entire length inside me, my movements urging him to bury himself ever deeper. He began to thrust harder, his breath coming in short groans of pleasure. "Valentina . . . yes," he gasped. "Good Christ, yes! *Yes!*"

My breath came quicker as I felt my own pleasure near. "Yes. Yes, Francesco. Harder. Harder—"

My words cut off sharply as ecstasy washed over me, so sharp it was almost painful, and I let out an animalistic cry, shuddering with the force of it, my body rocking back and forth against Francesco's. Dimly I heard his own moan, felt one last hard thrust into me as he reached his own pleasure, his fingers digging into my hips.

I remained on my hands and knees, trembling and weak in the aftermath of my climax, and after we'd both caught our breath, Francesco withdrew. I felt his seed trickling out between my legs, and reached for a cloth I kept beside the bed to discreetly clean myself. Meanwhile, he laid back against the pillows, still breathing heavily.

Once I was done, I lay beside him, the satin sheets cooling the sweat from my body. He drew me close against him, skin to skin. "You are an absolute treasure, my Valentina," he said, one hand idly toying with my nipple.

"And I suppose I need not tell you that I enjoy your company just as much, Francesco," I murmured. My body still hummed with the pleasure he had drawn from it.

He kissed my neck again. "Might we still have that meal your talented cook has prepared? I find myself quite in need of sustenance after our exertions."

"Ah, so now you are hungry."

"I was hungry when I got here," he said, his hand gently squeezing my breast. "Just not for food."

I laughed aloud at that. "I see that. Very well, then. I'll let Girolama know we are ready to dine."

A few moments later we were in the dining room, still in a state of only partial dress—me in my silk robe and him in just his shirt and breeches. I sat at the head of the table as the lady of the house—no man, no client, however important, would displace me from the seat of honor in my own home. Francesco sat immediately to my right. As we began to eat, I asked the question that had been niggling at the edges of my mind since Francesco had arrived.

"So," I began, "what is troubling you, Francesco?"

He merely raised an eyebrow at me as he took another spoonful of soup, waiting for me to elaborate.

"As you said, it has been quite some time since you have been to see me," I said. "And when you arrived it was obvious that you were quite . . . tense." I gave him a sly smile as I took a sip of wine.

He smiled wryly. "Indeed. I do apologize for such a long absence; it is not what I would have chosen. But I confess I am pleased to see that I was missed."

I heaved a fake sigh. "I was forced to find other amusements, of course."

That wry smile again. "No doubt," he said, raising his wineglass to his sensuous lips. He took a sip and then set the glass down again. "But since you ask, what else could keep me away but church politics?"

"What else indeed," I murmured.

He sighed, and I could see a trace of frustration return to him. "There is a distinct possibility that I could be made vicar general," he said. "Very soon. For this reason, the patriarch of Venice has been keeping a rather close eye on me." He sighed. "He wishes to be sure I am behaving in a manner as befits a man of God."

I laughed. "And is that what you were just doing, then?" I asked, gesturing in the direction of the bedchamber. "Behaving as befits a man of God?"

He laughed. "One might say I was merely delighting fully in the human body. God's finest creation, no?"

"Worshipping indeed," I said, winking at him.

His face turned serious again. "But alas, I fear the patriarch would not see it that way. And so I have been forced to be more discreet than usual. I must, if I am to advance."

I sipped my wine again as I considered this. The only churchman in Venice who would outrank the vicar general was the patriarch himself. Above the title of patriarch was cardinal, something that Francesco's sharp mind, political savvy, and family name put him in excellent standing to receive when next the Holy See needed to grant a boon to Venice.

And above cardinal, of course, was only the pope.

"And so," Francesco went on as my servants cleared away the soup dishes in preparation for the main course, "it has of late seemed prudent to deny myself your company and your rather considerable charms."

"I can understand that well enough," I said, "though I hope that when you become Vicar General Valier, I might still have the pleasure of your company."

He smiled at that. "You shall from time to time," he said, "even if we needs must be more discreet than before."

"Indeed," I said, "although it seems not quite fair that the patriarch would seek to punish you for something nearly every churchman in Venice has been known to do, himself included."

Francesco, who had just taken another sip of wine, nearly choked at my words. I eyed him evenly over the rim of my own glass as he coughed and sputtered. "What?" he finally gasped, once he'd somewhat gotten a hold of himself. "The patriarch? You . . . you mean to tell me that he has a mistress?"

"He does indeed," I said. "You didn't know? Why, I thought all of Venice knew."

"I did not," he said, his voice still sounding somewhat strangled. "Who is she? A courtesan, I assume? Someone you know?"

I shook my head. "Surprisingly, no, on both counts. I am not even certain of her name, but I know he keeps a mistress in a house over in Castello."

"Castello?" Francesco burst out incredulously. "With all the shipbuilders and fisherman and thugs?"

I shrugged. "Whoever would think to look there?"

"Who indeed," he said. "And she is not a courtesan, you say?"

"It seems not. As I said, I do not know who she is or where she comes from, but what I have heard is that she has never been a courtesan and is not set up as one now. She is mistress solely to the patriarch."

"Extraordinary." After a moment, Francesco began to laugh aloud. "Oh, you are a treasure indeed, Valentina. I did not know this, did not even have an inkling. This information will prove useful indeed, very useful . . ."

I hid my smile behind my wineglass. "My talents, Father Valier, are many."

"Indeed they are." He raised his glass to me in a toast. "To you, Valentina Riccardi. A woman of not only beauty and skill in the art of love, but a woman possessed of a fine and calculating mind."

I raised my glass as well and drank the toast to myself. There was more than one way to please a man.

Chapter 10

All too soon, the evening of my rendezvous with Dioniso Secco arrived.

I had decided that poison would be the easiest and least messy means by which the deed could be done. The Ten, via Malatesta, kept me well supplied with arsenic and hemlock so that no suspicion would be raised by me acquiring any of it myself. When I did use poison, arsenic was by far my favorite: it was tasteless, odorless, and colorless, which made it perfect for slipping into a glass of wine. Belladonna, which I also kept on hand, was easy enough to come by without even a trace of suspicion; many ladies in Venice, from courtesans and prostitutes to noble ladies, liked to put a drop or two in their eyes to cause their pupils to dilate in what was considered an attractive way. Knowing of its efficacy as a poison, however, I wanted no part of it in my beauty regime, and I warned every woman I knew away from it.

I also kept a dagger and a length of woven silk cord hidden in the bedchamber should I ever have need of them. Whether a courtesan engaged in my second profession or not, our work could at times be dangerous. Men were dangerous. Every courtesan and every whore knew more than one story of a client who had gotten angry, who had become violent, and the woman had paid for it. So even when I was not planning on assassinating anyone, I always had weapons and ways to restrain someone close at hand, just in case.

Men may be dangerous, but I was more dangerous. I made sure of that.

So that evening, long before Secco arrived, I measured out a heavy dose of arsenic powder into a large ring I wore, one with a hidden compartment in it. The purple gem on top was actually set as a small door, with a hinge that was invisible unless one knew to look for it. At the press of a tiny, equally invisible button, the little "door" swung open to reveal a compartment within. Perfect for storing poison that could easily be dispensed into a goblet of wine.

I had done it before and could do it again. *Would* do it again.

When Secco arrived that evening, I was, as always, dressed, hair up, and cosmetics applied. He awaited me in the dining room, where we would have a meal together before adjourning to the small parlor. Once there, I would confess a craving for a bit more wine before we went into the bedchamber. Then, so long as I had measured the correct dose, the poison would take effect very quickly, before we ever made it to bed.

By the Shadow God, let me have measured the dose right, I thought as I paced my dressing room anxiously, awaiting his arrival. I did not want to have to bed this man who was marked for death. I wanted the deed done as quickly as possible. I wanted it over with.

I took several deep breaths to steel myself. *He is a traitor to the Venetian Republic, Valentina,* I reminded myself. The doubts that had drifted uneasily through my head when Malatesta had first told me of the need to eliminate Secco began to rear their heads again, and I ruthlessly tamped them down. I could never go through with the task at hand if I acknowledged them. *He deserves this. Even the Ten cannot afford to have a powerful man assassinated for anything less than the most grievous treason. Which betraying the secret of the glass is.*

When he arrived, I went into the dining room almost immediately. "Dioniso," I said, with a wide smile, and crossed the room to him. His smile was just as wide upon seeing me, and he took my face in both hands and kissed me. "Valentina," he said fondly. "Ever you are a sight for weary eyes."

"I hope that I may alleviate some of that weariness this evening," I said, showing him to his seat, to the left of my own. "Girolama is preparing a fine cut of beef for us even as we speak."

"Ah." He smacked his lips in anticipation. "Not cooked too long, I hope?"

"No, no, just as rare as you like it."

"Excellent." He reached for the glass into which I'd just poured him some wine. "And a fine vino rosso to accompany it, I trust?"

Oh, if only I might slip the poison into his glass then and have done with it, but no, I'd need to wait. I could not have him breathing his last at the dining table, where the servants might see and panic and raise an alarm. Once we were ensconced in the bedchamber or the parlor adjoining it, we would not be disturbed. "Indeed," I said. "What else? I have just acquired a barrel of this; it is from Tuscany. You must let me know how you like it."

He drank deeply from the glass and held the wine in his mouth a moment, considering, before swallowing. "Excellent," he said, "excellent. You must provide me with the name of the vintner before I leave. I'd like to order some myself."

"Indeed. I'll write it down for you in the morning," I said easily.

I barely heard him throughout the meal as he talked about this acquaintance and that business deal and this colleague on the Great Council. Surely I could hardly be expected to focus on anything else with such a grim task before me. Yet even as I tried not to dwell on it, I could not help but feel a sort of angry bafflement. How did anyone live in Venice in this day and age and think they stood a chance of getting away with treason and betrayal? How did anyone think they were clever enough, powerful enough, cunning enough to outwit the Council of Ten? This was the same body of the Venetian state that was rumored to have been responsible for the death by poison of the Ottoman Sultan Mehmed II in 1481. If a man as powerful—and presumably well guarded—as the sultan was vulnerable to the plotting and machinations of the Ten, how on earth did a man like Dioniso Secco think his treachery would remain undetected and himself unpunished?

And when a man had a homeland as beautiful, as prosperous, as safe and secure as Venice, why would he ever dream of betraying it? Of threatening all those wonderful things? Of putting at risk everyone who lived there, everyone going about their lives and doing their work and raising their children and putting food on the table and amusing themselves?

Had men such as this never seen war before, never experienced the horrors and atrocities that conflict brought with it? They must not if they sought to court more of the same for Venice.

But I had. I had, and I would do whatever it took to keep such violence from La Serenissima. I had killed to stop it, and would again.

"Valentina?" Secco's voice broke into my thoughts, and I found myself blinking at him across the table. "I say, you seem a bit distracted this evening."

Inwardly I cursed myself and pushed my past back into its dark box, hoping the locks on it would hold this time, at least for the rest of the night. "I'm so sorry, Dioniso," I said sweetly. "Just . . . a bit anxious for the meal to be over." I winked at him.

He chuckled. "Ah, as am I. But anticipation only heightens the pleasure, no?"

I thought this particular anticipation was likely to kill *me*. "Indeed it does," I purred.

Eventually, *finally*, the meal was over—I barely tasted Girolama's beef, which was a shame, for I could tell that it was excellent—and we adjourned into the parlor. I shut the door behind us with a steady hand. Now that the moment was upon me, the deadly calm I had worked so hard to cultivate came over me, and I embraced it like a familiar, dark, warm cloak, tucking my anger and pain beneath it.

"More wine, Dioniso?" I asked sweetly. "I have a bianco dolce from our very own Veneto that is perfect for the after-dinner hour."

He hesitated for a moment, and the slightest trace of anxiety slithered through the pit of my stomach. What if he declined? What then? There were always the daggers in the bedchamber, and yet another dagger in this very room, if it came to that. But oh, poison was so much easier.

But true to his namesake, the Greek god of wine, Dioniso assented gamely. "Why not," he said, nodding for me to pour. "But not too much, mind. I imbibed a bit more of that excellent vintage at dinner than I meant to, and I should hate to be unable to perform—they say too much wine can do that to a man. Not that it's ever happened to me, mind," he hastened to assure me. "But a friend of mine, poor fellow . . ."

He rambled on, telling me some story about this friend who had drunk too much and found himself unmanned in the company of a very beautiful woman—a famous courtesan, no less. It was a story I already knew, for while the man's name escaped me, the courtesan had been Amalia, and she had been nearly helpless with laughter as she related the story to me. As Secco continued speaking, I put my back to him ever so briefly to pour the wine from the carafe. With one quick, fluid motion, I opened the hinged door on my ring and dumped its contents into one of the glasses. Careful to mind which was which, I turned back to him and handed him his deadly cup. "There you are, Dioniso," I said. "How unfortunate for your friend, indeed. But I should hardly think one more glass would at all trouble a man of your virility and stamina."

He puffed up his chest at my words. "Of course not," he said. He swirled the wine in his glass, at which I had to hide a smile: doing so would help the poison dissolve all the more swiftly. "From the Veneto, you say?"

"Yes, indeed. You must let me know how you like this one as well. If it pleases you, I shall be sure to have more on hand when next you visit."

He smiled at me. "Ah, but you are so thoughtful, Valentina. Ever your house is a veritable oasis of pleasure."

"I am honored that a man of such worldly and refined tastes should think so."

Still smiling, he raised the goblet to his lips and drank.

I looked casually away, drinking from my own glass.

"Ah," he said, after he'd swallowed. "Very fine as well. A pleasant sweetness after a large meal." He sipped again.

I smiled. "Precisely. I am glad you enjoy it."

"Indeed I do." He took a chair and continued to drink, and I seated myself on the chair next to him.

"A friend of mine is hosting a party next week, and I hoped that you would accompany me," he said. "Thursday next."

"Certainly," I replied.

"Very good. I shall indeed look forward to it." He took another sip of wine, then began to cough. He coughed again and again, his hand fumbling at the collar of his doublet as if to loosen it or pull it away from his throat. "Excuse me," he said, recovering slightly. "Some bit of dust, perhaps . . ." He took another swig of wine, as if to clear his throat. "I . . ."

But then he could no longer speak. His tongue was swelling, I knew, and his stomach would be contorting itself painfully. Indeed, just then he dropped onto his knees on the parquet floor and vomited.

I watched him, glad that I had asked Lauretta to remove the carpet from this room today, ostensibly to be beaten free of dust.

Heaving and gagging, Secco looked up at me from where he crouched on his knees. "Poison," he slurred. "Why?"

No point in either of us dancing around the issue, then. I set my glass on the side table and stood up. "Sending a glassblower to France," I said impatiently. "Did you truly think the Council of Ten would not find out, Secco? Did you think they would allow the Republic's great monopoly to fall?"

Confusion crossed his face. "I didn't . . . I never . . ." He groaned and vomited again.

"They have your letters, Secco. It was only a matter of time." I observed him for a moment as he writhed on the ground in agony. "I am sorry it came to this, for what it's worth."

"No," he cried, "no! Lies! I never . . . I swear . . ."

"No point in protesting to me," I said. "Even if I could save you now, it isn't up to me, I'm afraid."

Understanding dawned on his face then, as sharp and clear as a shard of glass, and it cut me just as deeply as it did him.

"Malatesta," he gasped, causing me to go still. "He wanted . . . I wouldn't do . . . he thought I would agree to . . ."

"You are a traitor," I said, though the words did not have the confidence behind them that I would have liked. How could he have known Ambrogio Malatesta gave the order? The Ten made their decisions as a group; why would one man among them even be suspect? I pushed this aside, but it took a mightier shove this time. "You are a traitor," I repeated, "and you will die for it. You should have known you wouldn't escape the Ten."

He gagged and choked again, his eyes becoming more and more bloodshot. "Bitch," he spat. "Whore. Murderess."

"Come, come, now, are those to be how you waste your last words? Telling me what I already know?"

He was lying on his side now, his head in a pool of his own vomit. With all that was left of his strength, he lifted his head up one more time. "Burn in hell, Valentina," he spat. "You and that lying whoreson Malatesta."

With that he collapsed, letting go one last rattling breath, and then went still.

I stood motionless for a moment, observing him, making sure that this was not some sort of trick to get me to move closer so that he could attack. With the amount of arsenic I'd given him, it was highly unlikely he'd have the strength to try any such thing, but it was best to make sure. I watched him for a few minutes, and when I saw no movement that would indicate he was still breathing, I cautiously approached. Careful not to step in his vomit, I reached out and pressed a hand to his chest.

No heartbeat. He was dead indeed.

There was no time to think, no time to parse through what Secco had just said, just implied, in his final moments. I stepped back and moved into action.

I went into the adjoining bedchamber and pressed the lever behind the headboard that opened a secret door in the wall. The door led to a hidden staircase, one that opened out into the extremely narrow alleyway at the side of the palazzo. I had hired a building crew to make these renovations when I'd first bought the palazzo, for circumstances such as these. While my servants knew about the secret door and staircase, they believed—for so I'd told them—that it was for clients who wished or needed to leave discreetly. Indeed, it had been used for that purpose more than once. It's true, darker purpose was known only to me and a few others who did the Ten's dirty work.

I sped down the stairs and cautiously opened the door to the outside, poking my head out. There was no one immediately visible. I stepped outside and moved a few steps to my right, peering around the corner of the building, into the wider street that ran behind the palazzo. Still no one to be seen.

Goddamn it, Malatesta! I swore to myself. He had promised to send men to deal with the body afterward, as he always did. How was I to dispose of Secco by myself? I could not carry him; I'd be lucky if I could drag a man of his size into the bedchamber, down the staircase, and into the alley. And then what would I do with him? It would hardly do for him to be found floating in the canal right outside my door, and that was if I could get him outside at all without being overheard or seen.

"Damn you, Malatesta," I muttered, out loud this time. Yet just then, I heard a whistle to my left, from the narrow slice of canal just visible there. A gondola pulled up to the half-submerged, algae-slicked steps that waited at the end of the alley. A pair of men wearing hooded capes stepped out and came to stand before me.

"We're here on the business of the Ten," one of the men said. I recognized his face beneath his hood, even in the dim light. He had an angry scar across his face that was hard to forget. Malatesta had sent him for such tasks before.

"Upstairs," I said to him and the other man, whom I did not recognize, and led them back up the staircase, through the bedchamber, and into the parlor where Secco lay. One of them grunted assent, and they threw a long winding sheet over his body, then rolled him up in it rather unceremoniously. That done, one lifted him by the legs, the other by his shoulders, and they made to take him back out the way they'd come.

"I don't suppose you're going to clean up my floor, are you?" I called after them.

I got no response.

I followed them back down the staircase and watched as they loaded Secco's body into the gondola and pushed off, out into the canal, without a further word to me. It was just as well. There was nothing more to say.

I went back inside, making sure the door to the alley was closed securely behind me, then went back up to the parlor, where I rang the bell for Lauretta.

She knocked twice before entering, as my staff always did when I was with a client. "What did you need, Madonna—oh, sweet Jesus," she gasped, once she saw—and smelled—the vomit on the floor. "What happened? Where is Signor Secco? Is he well?"

"He became quite unwell, as you see," I said, "and so has left. He went out the back staircase." None of that was technically untrue.

"Let me get some soap and water and clean this up, then," Lauretta said, sounding extremely reluctant.

I smiled thinly. "It was for that exact purpose that I summoned you, Lauretta. Thank you. I am for my bed. Send Marta up to help me undress, won't you?"

Lauretta nodded and hurried to do my bidding.

I left the room and went up the stairs to the third floor, my sanctuary, where no blood or death or the will of others could touch me. Marta arrived shortly thereafter, helping me out of my clothes and into one of the soft shifts that I slept in. She left, and I blew out the candles in the room and lay down to sleep.

Except that sleep was the furthest thing from me just then. As soon as the room was dark and quiet and I was alone, I could no longer hide from my own thoughts.

I had had my doubts about this assignment from the moment Malatesta had told me the intended victim's name. It hadn't added up then, and it certainly didn't add up now. A part of me insisted that it still didn't matter whether it added up or not; Secco was dead and his body certainly already dumped in some back canal. Nothing would change that.

Yet the rest of me knew that it did matter, that it mattered more than anything. Because if what Malatesta had told me wasn't true, if he had lied to secure my assistance, then I had just killed an innocent man.

Killing was, I'd found, unfortunately, like many things in life: the more one did it, the easier it got. And yet it had never been without guilt for me. How could it be? Even when I knew the men I killed were traitors and would bring death and destruction down on Venice if I did not stop them . . . still it sat uneasily upon me. But I had decided long ago that I would take that sin on my own soul to protect the innocent, unwitting people of the city. Someone had to.

But this—this had seemed different. From the beginning, my instincts had doubted what Malatesta was telling me. What Secco was accused of didn't make sense. And what's more, even as he lay dying, Secco had denied—with his very last breath—that he had done anything wrong. Even when confronted with his treachery, with the fact that the Ten had proof, he had denied it. Not confessed, as they often did, nor pleaded for his life, as they did still more often. But he had denied it all. Usually they thought that if they admitted their wicked deeds, they might more easily be granted forgiveness. But it was the Church that was the giver of mercy and absolution, in the end. Not the Ten. Never the Ten. And therefore not me either.

What was it he had said? *"Malatesta . . . he wanted . . . I wouldn't do . . . he thought I would agree to . . ."*

Agree to what?

He had said nothing about the glass, or France, and had seemed genuinely surprised when it was mentioned. If a man was selling one of the Republic's most important secrets, he surely could not be that surprised that it led to his death. And if what Malatesta had told me was true, why would his name have ever come into it? How could Secco possibly know that Malatesta had been the member of the Ten to give me the order?

He couldn't. He couldn't have known. Which meant that there was something else at play here, of which I knew nothing. Malatesta had used me for some end of his own that I knew nothing about. Perhaps that end was still in the service of the Council of Ten, and ultimately of Venice.

Or perhaps it was not.

There *was* the very real question of whether I could have refused what Malatesta asked of me, and avoided imprisonment, torture, or even execution. I knew too much about the Ten and their doings; if I were not going to cooperate, there was no question I would be deemed quite dangerous.

But whatever the reason, whatever the whys and hows and whatever I could or could not have done, I had very likely killed an innocent man.

My body trembled and shook beneath the covers; this realization was too much to physically bear, and so my very muscles and bones were rebelling against it. Try as I might, I could not stop shaking.

I was still lying awake when I heard the door of my bedchamber open softly. In a flash I was sitting up, the dagger I kept between the mattress and headboard in my hand. "Who goes there?" I demanded.

The interloper held up a candle so that I could see his face. "It is me," he said softly so as not to wake the rest of the household. "Bastiano."

I slumped with relief, allowing the dagger in my hand to clatter to the floor. "Bastiano," I repeated, as if to confirm it.

He moved closer to the bed. "Will I ever surprise you in your bedchamber without you threatening to stab me or cut off some vital body part, do you suppose?"

"Not when you persist on barging in uninvited," I grumbled, hoping I'd hidden the tremble in my voice.

He set the candle on the bedside table and sat on the bed beside me. "Is it done?" he asked quietly.

"Do you think I would be abed if it were not?"

He nodded, then stood to remove his doublet and breeches.

I sighed. "Not tonight, Bastiano. Please. I can't. I . . ."

"Such a filthy mind on this woman. I did not come here for that."

Dressed only in his long shirt, he slid beneath the velvet coverlet with me, pressing his body against mine, and gathered me in his arms. With him holding me tightly, my trembling ceased, and I took what felt like my first deep breath in hours.

Interlude

Somewhere in Tuscany, June 1527

A dagger clattered down onto the ground beside my face, causing me to wake with a start. I sat up quickly, still half asleep, scrambling backward across the threadbare blankets I had spread over the dirt to try to get some sleep.

When I squinted upward in the dim light of dawn, I eventually recognized the figure looming over me to be Fernando Cortes, the rather grizzled Spanish soldier with whom I was traveling. He had taken pity on me when he'd ridden by and found me trudging along the side of the road bound northward, away from Rome, in my dirty breeches and shirt and vest that I'd taken from my father's room. Cortes had gruffly told me in his accented Italian that I could come along with him and serve as his page until he got where he was going. Dangerous times to be alone on the road, especially for a boy like me, he'd said.

He'd hardly needed to tell me how dangerous the times were.

"Get up," he said, his tone as gruff as ever, "and take the dagger."

I reached out cautiously and wrapped my dirty fingers around the handle of the dagger. It was a plain weapon, but well made of good steel. Even I could tell that much.

Slowly I rose to my feet, keeping my eyes on Cortes. "What do you want me to do with it?" I asked, only barely remembering to pitch my voice an octave lower than its normal register.

"I'm going to teach you how to use it."

"Me?" I protested, baffled, years of being taught to behave as a lady choosing that moment to assert themselves. "Why?"

He met my gaze, his eyes canny and calculating. "I don't know where you're going, but I know well enough what you're running from," he said. "And a young woman alone needs to know how to defend herself."

I froze, my fingers only tightening on the dagger at the last minute so that it didn't fall to the ground again. "You . . . you know I'm a girl?"

"Of course. You haven't disguised yourself as well as you think you have."

I said nothing.

He sighed impatiently. "And you're gently bred too, if I don't miss my guess. It's in the way you move, the way you speak."

When I finally spoke again, I didn't bother attempting to disguise my voice. "You knew all along.

"I did. When I saw you on the side of the road there, I figured I'd better take you under my protection before someone with evil intentions happened upon you."

I lifted my chin haughtily, like the well-born lady I was. Had been, before the world had burned down around me. "I do not need your protection."

"In fact you do." He nodded toward the dagger I still held loosely in my hand. "But if I teach you to use that, you'll not need any man's protection again."

I closed my eyes for a moment. I remembered Massimo belting his sword about his waist, placing his hands on my shoulders, and making me promise to stay put, to hide, to let him go into danger on his own and do nothing to help, nothing to try to protect him. Making me promise that I would allow him to protect me. And I had listened, like the soft, shrinking lady I'd been raised to be, had let the man I loved rush headlong into the fray, to keep me safe. And Massimo had died for it.

And I had died too. Or at least, Maria Angelina, that soft gentlewoman who would let others die for her, was dead. And good riddance.

What good, then, was the protection of others? If Maria Angelina was dead, then this new woman that I had become might do things differently. Might make different choices. Might move through the world differently.

Maybe then I could be safe.

It took me naught but that moment to make my decision. I hefted the dagger in my hand, wrapping my fingers tightly around the handle. "All right," I said. "Show me."

Chapter 11

I startled awake, pulled from sleep by some dark dream that I could, thankfully, no longer remember. I tensed slightly as I noticed the weight draped across my hips, but quickly enough I realized it was Bastiano, who had wrapped an arm around my waist in his sleep, drawing my back securely against his chest.

I settled against his comforting warmth and closed my eyes, trying to go back to sleep, but it was a futile effort.

Luckily, I did not have much time to review the events of the previous evening nor examine my guilt and doubts again, for beside me Bastiano was stirring. I twisted to look over at him, and he opened one eye sleepily, his mussed brown curls falling across his face. "Morning," he murmured.

"Buon giorno to you," I said. "Sleep well?"

"With such a beautiful woman beside me? Of course." His smile faded as he lifted his head from the pillow a bit and considered me, as if just remembering why he had come the night before, what had driven him from his own home and to my bed to sleep beside me. "But what of you? Did you sleep well?"

The words *"Not particularly"* were on the tip of my tongue. But what good would come of admitting that? Maybe he'd worry. Maybe he'd think I wasn't as strong as he'd always believed me to be. I knew that was faulty reasoning in both cases, but I couldn't seem to help it. "Well enough," I settled on at last. I sat up in bed, the coverlet sliding off me as I stretched.

I felt rather than saw Bastiano studying me carefully. "And you are well today?" he asked conversationally. "After—"

"Of course I am," I said, cutting him off. "I am as well as ever."

I wanted nothing more than to share my doubts with Bastiano; wanted to take him through the line of reasoning I had been unable to escape the night before, after the poison had been administered and it was too late. I wanted to share the burden of what I might have done; wanted to share the terrible knowledge I now suspected I had.

But reluctantly, very reluctantly, I decided against it. For his own safety, I needed to keep what I knew, or what I suspected, to myself. If I was right, and Malatesta did have some nefarious purpose separate from the rest of the Ten, no good could come of Bastiano knowing such a thing. I knew him. He would not be able to leave it alone, especially not if he thought I had been used for some ill purpose. He would begin to look into it, begin to ask questions of his various contacts, and soon enough word would get back to Malatesta himself.

I could not lose another man I loved. And so I would keep this terrible burden to myself, to protect him.

But by the Shadow God, it did get wearying, protecting so many others all the time.

As though he could somehow sense the inner turmoil I was in, Bastiano looked for a moment as though he meant to question me further, but then—wisely—decided better of it. "Shall I go, then?" he asked, one arm propping up his head.

I smiled and bent down to kiss him, feeling how quickly his body responded to mine. I knew one surefire way to push aside the fears and doubts and ugliness, if only for a little while. "You shall not," I said, reaching up and removing my shift over my head. "Not before I've had my way with you."

As we made love, I let the feel of Bastiano's skin on mine, of him inside me, of the love mingled with pleasure in his touch, chase away everything that had happened the night before. And thus I'd be able to go on.

⋆ ⋆ ⋆

"Will you be at Flora's tonight?" I asked Bastiano as he dressed later on, preparing to take his leave. Flora was a courtesan known for her extravagant parties, and as she was the mistress of Lorenzo Corner, a great friend of Bastiano's, I thought it likely he would be in attendance.

I saw the tension in his body for just a moment before he forced himself to relax. Only someone who knew him, knew his body as well as I did, would have seen it, but it was there. "No," he said briefly. "Why, will you be?"

"Yes, Alvise Gasparo is taking me," I said, naming one of my regulars whom I liked well enough. "Why aren't you going? Surely Lorenzo invited you?"

"I am otherwise engaged, I fear."

Instantly I rose from the bed and grabbed my silk robe, wrapping it about me. "By the Ten?" I demanded. "What now?"

"Whatever do you mean?" Bastiano asked, turning to face me, trying and failing to keep his tone light. "I was already set to go to another party before I got Lorenzo's invitation, that's all."

I ignored this. "Who on the Ten gave you the assignment?" I asked, trying to keep the urgency from my voice.

"I am not doing anything on behalf of the Ten," Bastiano said, at last meeting my eyes, and in them I found naught but sincerity.

"Then why will you not tell me what you are doing?"

"There is nothing to tell. Another party, as I said. And perhaps I simply don't wish to see you on the arm of Gasparo—had you thought of that?"

I waved this aside. Gasparo, though a wealthy and well-connected member of the Great Council, was not the sort of man to make Bastiano jealous. "You are a terrible liar, Bastiano Bragadin."

"And perhaps this is something you are better off not knowing. Have you thought of *that*?" Bastiano flared. "I am doing what I can to keep you safe, Valentina."

This gave me pause. I believed that whatever he was up to was not at the behest of the Ten; yet what on earth else could he be doing that he did not wish to tell me about?

What did it mean that we were both embroiled in things that it was not safe to tell each other about?

"What are you about, Bastiano?" I whispered.

He paused in dressing himself and looked over at me, and I knew he had heard the anxiety in my voice. He sighed. "I am looking into something on behalf of my father," he said. "A . . . political matter. It is delicate, and better if you do not know."

"Hmm." As I stood there puzzling it all over, debating whether to press him on the matter, Bastiano finished dressing and came over to me, startling me slightly from my thoughts when he placed his hands on my shoulders. "All will be perfectly fine," he said, bending to kiss me on the lips. "Enjoy the party and give Lorenzo my best. I'll see you again soon?"

"When?" I found myself asking.

He paused, studying me. "Whenever you want me," he said softly, kissing me again.

I grabbed his collar to keep him close to me and kissed him again. "The night after next," I said. "I've no engagements that night and will keep it that way."

"I will eagerly await it," he said, and we kissed once more before he reluctantly drew away. "Ciao, Valentina. I will see you in a couple days." With that, he left to let himself out.

Chapter 12

Flora's party that night was the usual crush, a mix of patricians, courtesans, intellectuals, merchants, and a few foreign guests. The ballroom was marvelously appointed: gilt trim, expensive tapestries on the walls, and a spectacular Murano glass chandelier hanging overhead, fitted with so many candles that it was bright as daylight. Doors at one side were thrown open to the cool night air, giving onto a balcony and providing the guests a magnificent view of the canal beyond.

Alvise Gasparo paraded me about on his arm, pleased at the admiring attention I drew from a great many of the men in attendance. I was dressed in a favorite gown, a purple brocade that complimented both my dark hair and eyes and the olive tone of my skin. My jewelry was a dark jet, and a yellow feather had been inserted jauntily into my elaborately pinned-up hair. I attracted even more admiring glances than usual, or so I fancied.

I was surprised, on entering, to see Ambrogio Malatesta huddled with a group of patrician men. He glanced up as I entered with Gasparo and, on catching my eye, gave me a brief nod. Heart pounding, I returned the gesture, then quickly looked away. I was surprised to see him there; he was not known to be much of a social creature, and I had not thought parties like this to be his style. Yet any fool knew that political capital in Venice—and, I'd venture a guess, in most places—was not gained solely in the halls of government.

I could likely rest assured that he would not seek me out that evening, though. Necessary fiction that he was one of my lovers aside, he would not wish to draw too much attention to any interaction between us, thankfully. I did not wish to face him again so soon, not when I had so many doubts, so many unanswered questions.

So many suspicions.

Much to my delight, Amalia Amante was also present, on the arm of a middle-aged patrician who was one of her regular clients and dressed in a gown I suspected was new, of a sea-green color. She threw me a wink across the room as our respective escorts walked us about the party, and I gave her a saucy wink in return, already eager for the moment when we might draw into a corner for a bit of gossip together. If anything could serve to distract me from Ambrogio Malatesta's presence, it was my dear friend.

Finally, having greeted everyone he knew—and all the important people he wished to know—Gasparo was drawn into a robust discussion of politics. He did not notice when I wandered away from him and approached my friend. "Amalia, cara, so good to see you," I said, kissing her on the cheek.

"My dearest Valentina," she said. "But you do not have any wine! We must remedy that immediately. Pier'Antonio," she said, addressing her escort, whose arm she still loosely held but who had turned away from her to engage another man in conversation, "I must speak to the lovely Valentina Riccardi for a moment. Do not miss me too much."

"Very well," he said, giving her a lustful grin. "But do not leave me alone too long." He turned back to the group of men he'd been conversing with. "The most exotic beauty in all of Venice!" he declared, admiring Amalia as we walked away together.

The smile froze on Amalia's face as she turned her back on him. "Honestly," she muttered under her breath. "As though I am some trinket from the East he can place on his shelf."

I groaned. "I am sorry, Amalia."

That description, "exotic," was often applied to Amalia because of the shade of her skin, her dark hair, and her unusual amber eyes. She took more offense at it than any of the epitaphs flung at women of our profession—we were both used enough to those, after all. "I was born a Venetian citizen," she had complained to me more than once. "There are Venetians who go their whole lives without ever setting foot in the mother city, who learn any number of languages before our own. And yet somehow *I* am the one who is exotic simply because of the color of my skin."

That night Amalia simply rolled her eyes and shook her head, perhaps shaking off her client's words at the same time. We moved to the table laden with wine and food, and she snatched up a goblet and handed it to me. I drank it gratefully. "Don't tell me Gasparo has kept you parched all night," she said disapprovingly, taking a sip from her own goblet.

"Alas, it is so," I said regretfully. "There were many people he wanted us to greet."

"Of course," she said.

"Where have you been of late?" I asked, looping an arm through hers and drawing her to a less densely populated area of the room. "I've scarcely seen you."

She sighed dramatically. "I've been very busy with a new client," she said, a hint of a smile on her lips and in her voice.

"He is a Roman, living in Venice for the foreseeable future. Actually, I received a letter from no less a person than Niccolo Contarini, recommending him to me, and so I agreed to receive him."

I laughed aloud. "Is the new lover in question Ottaviano Lotti, by any chance?"

"Why, yes! Do you know him?"

"I have made his acquaintance," I said. I gave her an abridged version of my attendance at Lotti's party and Niccolo's jealous snit, including our encounter with Bastiano, and my comment that, should Lotti come to call on me, I would send him to Amalia instead. "I did mean to facilitate an introduction between you and Lotti, but it slipped my mind." *And no wonder,* I added silently, *given what occupied me between then and now.* But I pushed these thoughts firmly aside. "I see that Niccolo decided to save both me and poor Lotti a step," I said, laughing.

Amalia was also laughing at the folly of men, as she often did. "So I see," she said. "And poor Bastiano! That Niccolo is really a devil, isn't he?"

I rolled my eyes. "He can be a bit much," I conceded. "But it is worth it to me to keep him happy."

Amalia nodded, understanding. "Of course. Though I regret to inform you that Niccolo did not do you any favors in keeping Lotti from your door."

My eyebrows raised. "Oh no?"

"Mmm." She made a little noise of pleasure, half laugh, half sigh, that I didn't think I'd ever heard from her before. "He is most attentive in the bedchamber." She giggled. "*Most* attentive. And he is most free with his purse strings."

"Generous in bed and out of it," I observed. "The ideal client."

"Indeed. Oh, there is Pier'Antonio waving to me." She sighed with only a touch of irritation. "No doubt I'm needed to bat my eyelashes at someone and make a business deal of his go more smoothly."

"You'd best do more than bat your eyelashes, then, with what he pays you," I said. I reached out and tugged her bodice down a bit, so that a hint of her nipples could be seen above the neckline. "There. Now go."

She laughed and leaned in to kiss my cheek. "He will be grateful, I'm sure. I'll see you again before the night is over."

"Indeed," I said. I watched her flit back to her client's side, beaming up at him and at the man he was speaking to, a man I was sure I'd seen out and about before, but whose name I did not know. Pier'Antonio smiled widely at Amalia as she said something. "Ah, there you are," he said to her—or, more accurately, to her breasts.

I stifled a laugh and turned away, slipping back through the crowd to find Gasparo.

* * *

Later in the evening, while the after-dinner drinks were being served and the crowd had started to thin a bit, Malatesta found me.

"Ah, Valentina," he said as I approached the table that held the remaining refreshments, having promised to get Gasparo another glass of wine.

I looked up to see Malatesta approaching. I gave him a deep, deferential nod, only because we were in public. "Signore," I said, "I trust you are well."

"I am, thank you," he said. He regarded me closely. "Nothing puts me in finer spirits than a bit of successfully conducted business."

My heart began to beat a bit faster, if for no other reason than his gall in speaking of such things here. I lifted my chin. "The same is true of me," I said.

"And you have reason to be in such fine spirits this evening, then?"

By the Shadow God, had the men he'd sent to dispose of Secco's body not given him a full report? Or perhaps he simply took a perverse pleasure in speaking of murder more or less openly. "I do," I said, my tone even. "My work is always concluded satisfactorily." I gave him a flirtatious smile for the benefit of any onlookers, who would interpret my words in a much different way should they be overheard.

He smiled, which on his face was a stiff expression, as though it was not one often used. I realized, thinking back over all my encounters with the man over the years, I could not rightly remember ever seeing a smile on his face before. Not a genuinely joyful one in any case.

"I am delighted to hear it," he said, moving closer to me. "And I have no doubt that what you say is true."

"Nor should you." I turned my gaze from him, back to the table of refreshments, hoping he would realize that I considered the conversation to be over. When he lingered, however, I glanced back up at him.

He stepped closer to me. "Perhaps, Valentina," he said, his voice low, "you might someday soon show me just how . . . satisfactory your work truly is." He brought a hand up to stroke my cheek, his fingers cool.

For a moment, I was frozen in shock. Not at a man making overtures to me, certainly—if it only happened once at a party I was attending, it was an unusual night.

But this was Malatesta, of all men. If there was any man in Venice who I had thought immune to my charms, it was he, he who never let me forget the difference in our stations; he, who acted as though he was lowering himself to have any sort of dealings with me at all.

But men's lust, as I knew well, had no such refinement or fastidiousness.

And so, deep in the pit of my stomach, which felt like it was descending into my silk-and-diamond shoes, I was not wholly surprised. I remembered the last time I had seen him, when he had given me the assignment to kill Secco. I had made some offhand comment . . . what was it? Something to the effect of *Spend much time thinking about me naked, do you?* And I remembered marking the desire that had flashed through his eyes as I'd said it, that brief spark that belied the disgusted expression he'd retreated behind like a Carnevale mask.

I truly should have expected something like this.

I could, of course, have played it all off as a joke and saved his pride. I could have retreated behind false modesty or insisted I could not entertain such an offer when I was here accompanying another man. But that would solve nothing, ultimately. And so I decided to be direct.

I drew back from him and met his eyes. "Oh, Ambrogio," I said, my voice flat, "I rather think we know each other too well for that, don't you?"

He looked surprised, as though he truly had not been expecting this response. "Surely—"

"You have seen enough of my ugliness, and I enough of yours," I said. I reached past him and plucked the glass of wine I'd promised Alvise Gasparo from the cloth-covered table. "Let's keep that ugliness out of the bedroom, hmm?"

With that, I turned and glided away.

But not before I saw confusion flicker across his face, followed closely by rage.

★ ★ ★

The next day, I set off to see about having some new clothes made for Ginevra. I was heading down to the water entrance of my palazzo when Luca, my gondolier, met me on the stairs coming up. "Madonna Valentina," he said, voice low, "please wait here a moment."

"Why? Whatever is the matter, Luca?" I asked.

Luca had ever been a man of few words, but now he stuttered and stumbled over them to a degree that was unusual. "There is . . . I mean to say . . . trust me, Madonna, you don't wish to see . . ."

Dread curdled my stomach. "See what?"

"In the water just outside, there is . . . I came to find you first, to tell you not to come out, and now I must alert the authorities . . ."

Quickly I pushed past him, ignoring him calling after me. I strode out the water entrance and down the dock and saw clearly enough what had Luca in such a state.

There, bobbing face down in the canal at the end of my dock, like so much rubbish, was a man's body.

Luca came up behind me. "Madonna, I did not wish you to see . . ."

Perhaps I ought to have feigned some sort of feminine sensibility, but I found I could not bring myself to just then. "Turn him over," I ordered Luca.

"Madonna?"

"Just do it, Luca."

Casting me a curious glance, he seized his oar from the gondola and rather ungracefully managed to flip the man over onto his back.

It was not Dioniso Secco; I had known that much simply by the size and shape of the body. I had hoped I would not know the man, but alas, I did.

It was one of the men who had come to take away Secco's body, the man with the scar across his face, still visible even though his flesh had started to bloat. The man I had recognized since he had done work for Malatesta before.

And now he was dead and floating outside my palazzo after having completed his last task.

"Alert the authorities," I said to Luca, then turned and went back inside.

Let those charged with keeping the city's peace do with this man's body what they would. I understood the message that had been intended.

A few days later, another body was found, a much more noteworthy one this time: the body of Dioniso Secco surfaced in a back canal in Cannaregio, near the Jewish ghetto. He was identified soon enough, and gossip was rampant in the city as to what had happened to him. With no obvious wounds or marks of violence, there was some question as to whether he had indeed been the victim of any foul play or had perhaps simply stumbled drunkenly into a canal and drowned. Such things happened.

In the days that followed, I thankfully heard no more from Malatesta. However, the amount I'd specified as double Secco's yearly fee had been delivered to me, as promised, and in gold, no less.

Yet the gold did not stop me tossing and turning at night, on those rare nights when I had a bed to myself, as I replayed Secco's last words over and over again, replayed the conversation where Malatesta had told me to kill him, turning each word this way and that and looking for things I might have missed. Some nights I looked for proof that my suspicions were correct, and that it had been Malatesta alone, not on behalf of the Council of Ten, who had sent me after Secco. Surely the fact that one of the men who'd removed the body had been found floating outside my door was proof enough of that? No doubt his accomplice was dead elsewhere in the city. Other nights I sought to reassure myself that Malatesta had been in earnest, that Secco had indeed been a traitor to Venice and had deserved to die, and that perhaps his henchman's death was unrelated, no more than a strange coincidence. On the nights when I managed to convince myself of the latter, I slept much better. Those nights were few and far between.

But I heard nothing for the rest of that month, nor the next—not from Malatesta nor from any other member of the Ten. And that suited me just fine. There was plenty of excitement and intrigue to be had for me in seeing to my various lovers and clients, managing their interests and their jealousies and their affections. I was relieved to be able to turn my attention to that for a time and, as summer drew near, to planning the two months I would spend at my villa with Ginevra and—for part of the time, at least—with Bastiano.

For two months, I would escape the stinking heat and humidity of Venice in the summer; would leave behind Malatesta and the Council of Ten and their conspiracies and bloody intrigues. I could be free of it all, if only for a short time. I could enjoy the peace that so much blood had wrought.

I could try to forget. I could look into my daughter's face and know that her life would never be marred by the evil and violence that my own had been. And I could, perhaps, forgive myself.

CHAPTER 13

"Mamma, up!" a small, bright voice demanded imperiously.

I looked down from where I stood near one of the villa's windows and laughed at Ginevra's impatient expression as she held her arms up to me. "Yes, of course, cara mia," I said, bending to scoop her up into my arms.

"What looking at?"

I pointed out the window at the river that wound through the countryside and past the villa, the entire scene tinged in gold in the late afternoon light. "The water. See all the colors in it as the sun sets?"

"Where it go?"

"It flows eventually to the sea," I explained. "To the Adriatic." I sighed. "In a few days it will take Mamma home to Venice."

"Why?"

"There is where I live, my sweet," I said. "There are things I must do there."

"Why?"

"So that I might continue to help you grow up strong and happy," I said.

"Why?"

I could not even be exasperated with Ginevra's constant questioning, a habit Bastiano and I had become very familiar with of late. How could I when I had such precious little time to spend with my daughter? I had thought it nothing less than a miracle that she remembered me; that after being prompted only once, she recalled that I was "Mamma."

I kissed the top of her head, inhaling the clean scent of her hair and skin, for she was fresh from the bath. "Because that is the most important thing in the world," I whispered.

A slight sound made me glance up to see that Bastiano was leaning against the doorway, watching us. "Yes," he said softly, as if in reply. "Yes, it is."

"Papa!" Ginevra shouted, and she squirmed to get out of my arms. I let her down, and she ran across the stone floor to Bastiano. He had arrived a week ago, his second visit of the summer, and would stay until it was time for me to return to Venice. Then he would make the journey back with me after Sonia Abate and her husband arrived to take Ginevra back to their farm.

It had been a blissful summer, just like the one before, perhaps even better. Ginevra could talk now, in full sentences, and seemed to love being with me and with Bastiano when he was here. I had explained that Bastiano was her papa, and that Sonia and her husband, whom she called "Zia" and "Zio," were there to take care of her when Papa and I couldn't. It made enough sense in her young mind, which was all that mattered to me just then. In the years to come, there would be more explanation needed—much more—but I would handle that when it came. For now, I simply reveled in every moment I could spend with my daughter.

"I've a gift for you, figlia mia," Bastiano said as Ginevra threw her arms around his waist. He withdrew a hand from behind his back and produced a doll, beautifully made of fine fabric and wearing a satin dress.

Ginevra squealed with glee and eagerly accepted the doll, running her little fingers over the hair, face, dress, and hands. "Mamma, look!" she cried, holding up her prize to me.

"I see," I said approvingly. "She is very beautiful."

Ginevra immediately flopped onto the rug at one end of the room to commence serious study of her new toy, murmuring to herself—or perhaps to the doll—as she did so. Even at a young age, Ginevra had such moments of introspection, where she liked us to be near but did not need us to be paying immediate attention to her. I had been ever thus as a girl, and it did something strange to my heart to see a trait of my own in my daughter.

"Wherever did you get that?" I asked as Bastiano drew near to me at the window, both of us smiling as we observed Ginevra.

"In Venice," he replied. "I had it made and brought it with me. This seemed like a good time to give it to her."

"Why now?"

He shrugged. "I don't know. It just seemed right."

I nodded, needing no further explanation than that.

He drew me against his hip and kissed the top of my head, neither of us looking away from our daughter. "Maybe we should bring her back to Venice with us," he said softly.

I pulled away from him. "Absolutely not."

"Why not?"

"We have been over and over this, Bastiano. Venice is not safe for her."

"You do not think we can keep her safe?"

"I think it is a wonder we can keep ourselves safe, most days."

"Valentina." Bastiano placed his hands on my shoulders and forced me to look him full in the face, his expression solemn. "Do you truly think that the Ten could not find her if it suited their purposes to do so?"

"If Ginevra was not in the room right now, I would slap you," I spat through gritted teeth. "How can you say such a thing? How can you even think it?"

He lowered his hands. "It is an unpalatable truth, I readily admit, but it is true all the same."

I could not engage with that idea any further, so I ignored it. "And even if we did bring her to Venice with us, where would she live, hmm? Certainly not in my palazzo, where I am fucking a different man every night of the week. Will your parents welcome her at the Bragadin family palazzo, then?"

Bastiano fell silent at this. "I have not spoken to them of it," he said at last. "They know Ginevra exists, and no more than that. But—"

"But what? You will show up there in a few days with your bastard child in tow, and they will welcome her with open arms? I think not."

"They may . . ."

"And if they don't? Then we have taken Ginevra from the only home she has ever known for nothing." I took a deep breath, raising both my hands as if to physically bring the argument to a halt. "No. No. She stays in the country with the Abates for the time being."

Bastiano was silent for a long while. "You're right," he said at last. "I do not like it, but you are right."

"I do not like it either, but this is the way of it." I sighed heavily, looking back down the room toward Ginevra, oblivious to our argument as she chattered to her new doll. "This is the way of the world we live in, Bastiano. And neither you nor I can change it, much as we might want to."

"Would that we could," Bastiano said softly, also turning his attention back to Ginevra. "Would that we could."

I could not bring myself to refute his romantic nonsense as I usually did, not then, not that day. And so I said nothing.

* * *

Giving Ginevra back over to the care of the Abate family a few days later was more painful than I'd remembered. It was only from years of iron-hard control—and my own personal suspicion that I had spent all the tears I possessed earlier on in my life—that I did not cry when Ginevra sadly called, "Bye, Mamma!"

"Goodbye, Ginevra," I'd called back, my voice catching in my throat. "Be a good girl for Zia Sonia, and I will see you soon. I love you."

And then she was gone as the Abate farm cart rattled down the drive from the villa.

* * *

Back in Venice, the Bragadin barge let me out at the water entrance of my palazzo. My servants, having been duly informed in advance of my arrival by letter, hurried out to unload my trunks as Bastiano helped me out of the boat into the chill, gray afternoon.

I turned to face him. "Stay tonight," I murmured to him.

His face crumpled slightly. "I cannot. I have . . . business to attend to."

"Already? But how?" Cold fear clutched my insides. "No one from the Ten sent you a letter at the villa, did they?"

"No." Bastiano gave a cursory glance around us, as if making sure all the servants were too far away to hear. "This does not have anything to do with the Ten. It is business on behalf of my father."

"What business?"

"I cannot say."

I drew back and studied his face. This was the second time he had mentioned business for his father and not elaborated as to what precisely that meant. He was tasked with overseeing most of the Bragadin family's mercantile interests, and he usually had no hesitation in speaking of such things. What was this, then? And why did it suddenly seem as though both Bastiano and Malatesta had some sort of secret agenda of which I could know nothing?

Venice was a city of secrets, most certainly. Only I was used to being privy to many of them.

"I did not know that trading in silks had become so mysterious," I said at last, an edge to my tone.

He sighed. "Valentina. I would have thought you'd understand that anything I don't share with you is for your own protection."

My blood boiled at those words. Here, again, was a man thinking I needed to be protected. Putting himself in harm's way, but wanting me protected.

"What danger are you in, Bastiano?" I whispered.

"Don't ask me that."

"Very well," I bit out. "I will see you some other time, then." I turned away from him.

"Valentina." He caught my hand and drew me tight against him, capturing my mouth in a heated, almost punishing kiss, right there on the dock for anyone to see. And damn him if my knees, beneath the skirt of my traveling dress, did not go a bit weak. When we broke apart, he was grinning.

I rolled my eyes and shoved him away. "You are an insufferable rogue," I said, making my way toward the palazzo.

"That's what you love about me!" he called after me.

I did not look back until I reached the door, and by that time he had climbed back into the barge and was out of view.

Love. Indeed.

CHAPTER 14

Even as I settled back into my routine of seeing clients, Bastiano's evasiveness of late bothered me. I knew I should not think on it. This was hardly the first time—nor the last, no doubt—that Bastiano was involved in something that could get him killed should it go sideways.

Yet something about the whole situation was troubling me. Was it truly only business for his father? I did not know the Bragadin patriarch well—my only encounters with him had been an introduction Bastiano had made once at a salon, when I was rather frostily received, and crossing paths with him at one other gathering, where he ignored me altogether. But from everything Bastiano had told me about his father over the years, he did not seem the type to involve himself in any sort of intrigue. He was a conservative sort, conservative in business and in politics. So what could Bastiano possibly be doing on such a man's behalf that warranted such secrecy? Unless the elder Bragadin was not involved at all, and that was simply a fiction Bastiano had given me. But I did not think he would lie to me quite so brazenly.

So I could, perhaps, take his words at face value. But that did not assuage my concerns at all, for it seemed to beg the question: Was whatever Bastiano was doing something that could cause him to run afoul of the Council of Ten?

The whole thing had me on edge in a way I could not remember being in years, not since I had first started working for the Council of Ten. I quickly realized that, if I traced this feeling back, it had begun the night I killed Dioniso Secco, when he had protested his innocence and mentioned Malatesta's name, and had only grown since then because of both Bastiano's evasiveness and the discovery of the body of one of Malatesta's associates floating outside my palazzo.

Something was off in Venice—I knew that much. Something was not as it appeared to be, as it had been represented to me. Perhaps more than one thing. There was too much in my life that wasn't adding up, and I didn't care for it. Not one bit. And it was quite difficult to enjoy a hedonistic life of costly clothes and rich food and fine wine and good sex under such circumstances.

So, one night I did something that I was not proud of.

Bastiano arrived at my palazzo for an evening together, which we had arranged. But he arrived in a rather foul mood. He kissed me somewhat distractedly, then flung his cloak and a worn leather satchel over the back of one of the chairs in the dining room. I poured wine for us both, yet as we waited for Lauretta and Bettina to serve dinner, he kept rising from his chair, pacing the room, and running his fingers through his hair with tense, irritated movements.

I watched him from my seat at the head of the table, over the rim of my wineglass. "Bastiano, what is wrong?" I asked finally.

He shook his head, not meeting my gaze. "Nothing."

"Clearly something," I said, irritated myself now. Did he think I couldn't see he had worked himself into a right state?

"It's not important."

"Then why is it troubling you?"

He sighed and finally stopped in his pacing, facing me. "It is nothing," he said again. "Just . . . some bit of business not going as I had hoped."

I waited for him to elaborate, but he did not.

"Very well, then," I said. "If that is all, then do not let it ruin our evening."

He sighed again and sat down in the chair beside me. "You are right, amore mio." He leaned forward and kissed me softly. "We do not get enough time together as it is. I should not spoil what time we do get with this . . . this nonsense."

He said nothing further about it after that, and indeed his mood improved, though it seemed as though it took a bit of effort on his part. But we passed a pleasant meal, complete with dessert and dessert wine, then adjourned to my bedchamber, where our lovemaking was much more than pleasant.

Soon after, Bastiano fell asleep, but I did not. I lay awake, staring up at the velvet canopy above the bed, struggling with myself.

I had noted that Bastiano had brought his leather satchel with him into the bedchamber, rather than simply leaving it on the chair in the dining room where he'd tossed it along with his cloak. Why? He had never done that before that I could recall. Why the satchel and not the cloak? And why not simply leave them both where he'd put them initially until he left in the morning?

What was in the satchel that he did not wish to let out of his sight?

In truth I wrestled with my conscience for only a few minutes before silently slipping from the bed and crossing the room to the satchel, on a chair against the wall.

This was a violation of Bastiano's trust, and I knew it. If he were to snoop among my things in this way, I would likely find it difficult to forgive him. But I found I could not help myself. I was certain that he was involved in something dangerous, and I could no longer live with not knowing what it was.

With one last glance over my naked shoulder, to make sure Bastiano was still asleep, I lifted the flap of the satchel and reached inside, withdrawing a sheaf of papers.

Slowly, carefully, I flipped through them, trying to do so silently. The page on top was written in code of some kind. I did not know much about codes and code breaking, even if I had the time to sit down and attempt to decipher this one. Encoded missives were how the Council of Ten communicated with diplomats and other assets abroad, and indeed they had rooms full of code creators and code breakers within the Doge's Palace, developing new codes for their use as well as attempting to break the ciphers of rival nations. Since I received all my instructions from the Ten in person, there had never been a need to provide me with any sort of key or instruction in deciphering encrypted messages.

So I set that page aside, able to discern only that it had not been written in Bastiano's hand. It could be from anyone, about anything. From the Ten or someone else.

The next page was blank, save for what looked like an address scribbled on it. A house on Giudecca, by the look of it. I set that aside as well, careful to mind the order the pages had been in so that I could replace them correctly.

Another check to ensure that Bastiano was sleeping soundly—he was—and then on to the next pages.

The following two were also written in code. Presumably the same code as the first, but I was not even certain of that much.

Then yet another page in code, but this one in Bastiano's hand. I tapped a finger against my lip thoughtfully. Curious indeed.

Could this be . . . surely not espionage. Surely Bastiano Bragadin, of all people, was not colluding with some foreign agent or agents against Venice? No. Impossible. He knew better than anyone what befell traitors to the Venetian state, knew that they rarely succeeded in their nefarious plans.

The next page, at last, was written in Italian. It was short, and scrawled in a rough hand, as though the writer did not have much occasion to write at all: *Contact at 10 knew nothing of DS. Says they did not order it. Proof of treachery only if written.*

The missive was signed simply "FC".

I began mentally flipping through all the people of my extensive acquaintance with the initials "FC." Felicita Cavazza? I paused there for a moment. I had seen her in a clandestine exchange of information with that man at Ottaviano Lotti's home. She could well be involved in intrigue. But I discarded this possibility, for the handwriting on the note seemed distinctly masculine.

Then I gasped, clapping a hand over my mouth to stifle the sound, as the meaning of the rest of the missive sunk in. So distracted had I been by who FC could be that the obvious had escaped me until then.

"10" was certainly the Council of Ten. And DS was certainly Dioniso Secco.

They did not order it.

Whoever this mysterious FC was that Bastiano was corresponding with had a contact on the Council of Ten, and this person claimed that the Ten had not ordered the assassination of Dioniso Secco. It was exactly what I had feared and suspected.

Proof of treachery.

But of whose treachery specifically? Yet as soon as the question formed in my mind, I realized the very obvious answer.

Ambrogio Malatesta. The man who had personally given me the order for Secco's assassination, and who had, I now knew for certain, been acting outside of the Ten's purview.

Only if written.

Well, there was the problem, wasn't it? Malatesta had given me the order in person, as he always did. There was never any written communication between the two of us. And I knew Malatesta well enough to know that he would never commit something like this—something so far beyond the bounds of his authority, for his own devious ends, whatever those might be—to paper. He was too smart for that. He had to be.

And by having me kill Secco, he had implicated me in his plot, whatever it might be.

I heard Bastiano stir behind me, and I quickly shoved the papers back into his satchel, only barely remembering to put them all in the right order. I stood and turned toward the bed, but luckily he was still asleep.

Heart pounding, I returned to the bed and slid in beside him. But there was no hope of sleep now.

So Bastiano was investigating Malatesta. Had it been my assignment to kill Secco that had made him start to question? Surely he couldn't have known when I'd first told him of the assignment that the Ten hadn't truly sanctioned it; surely he would not have let me go through with it had he known. So perhaps it was after that that he began to wonder. Especially as Secco had been an unusual target for the Ten: he had been vastly wealthy, very powerful, and influential—and had equally powerful and influential friends. He was perhaps not as powerful as someone like Bastiano's own father, or even Niccolo Contarini and others of the oldest and noblest Venetian families, but his political and social weight was—had been—formidable, nonetheless. I had wondered at it myself, and surely Bastiano had as well.

So was that what had prompted this . . . whatever he was involved in? But if so, why had he not shared it with me? It had been I who had killed Secco, after all. I was involved up to my neck already. But I had never shared my doubts and concerns, along with Secco's last words, with Bastiano, nor had I told him about one of the men who'd removed Secco's body turning up dead. No doubt Bastiano thought to protect me, as I sought to protect him; no doubt he did not want to let on that I had done anything wrong until he was sure. Until he had proof of what Malatesta was doing and why.

Or was this in fact what he was looking into on behalf of his father? Was the Bragadin patriarch somehow in Malatesta's sights, either politically or otherwise?

Anything was possible. And I likely would never know.

I could just ask Bastiano, of course. Confess what I had done, that I had violated his trust and his privacy, and demand to know what was afoot. Of course, there was a very good chance that he would be even *less* inclined to tell me after my snooping, and trust me less in the future.

No, I decided reluctantly. I could not ask him, even as my worry for him had now been doubled rather than assuaged.

Oh, how I wished I had never looked in his satchel! How I wished I knew nothing of this when I was powerless to help or learn more.

Such was the punishment for those who meddle where they don't belong.

* * *

I must have fallen asleep at some point, for I woke in the morning to the crackling of a fire in the grate opposite the bed. I opened my eyes blearily and sat up, only to see Bastiano, dressed in breeches and a loose shirt, crouched before the grate, tossing something into the flames. Papers of some kind.

"A fire, Bastiano?" I asked, my voice gravelly with sleep. He jumped slightly, startled, and whirled to face me. "Is it that cold?"

"Ahh . . . I awoke with a bit of a chill and thought I would warm the room," he said.

I noted the satchel at his feet and understood that he had burned at least some of the papers within. Perhaps he had meant to do it the night before but had gotten distracted by the food and wine and lovemaking. I studied his face carefully. Did he know that I had looked at the papers? Had he been able to tell somehow? But there was no accusatory gleam in his eyes, no anger or doubt when he looked at me. His face was smooth, his expression impassive.

I had resigned myself, the night before, to not learning more about his activities. I both wanted to know more and didn't at the same time. Like a child who learns not to touch the stove only after they've been burned, I finally accepted that whatever Bastiano was doing, it likely *was* better if I did not know.

"There are much more enjoyable ways to keep warm than that," I said, reaching out for him. "Come here."

Chapter 15

I put Bastiano's intrigues out of my mind as best I could in the next weeks. I saw clients, passed time with Amalia, corresponded with Sonia Abate about Ginevra, ordered new gowns and shoes for winter, saw Bastiano when I could.

Fortunately, I did not hear anything from Malatesta. I might have tried to put from my mind what I had learned, but I could not forget it. What would I do when next he called on me to kill a man he deemed a threat to the Republic? How could I be sure that that was in fact true, and not merely in service of whatever Malatesta's own aims were?

I would decide what to do should that moment come. There was nothing else I could do. But every day that I did not hear from him or anyone else on the Council of Ten was a relief.

I let the intrigue fade from my mind, let myself believe for a time that I was nothing more than a successful and highly sought-after courtesan.

It almost worked. It did work for a time, until a night about two weeks into October, when Bastiano once again showed up unannounced at my palazzo.

This time I was, alas, with a client. Alvise Gasparo was asleep in my bed when I heard a tapping at the door. I got up immediately, wrapping myself in a velvet robe against the chill. All of my servants knew well to never interrupt me when I was with a client, so something must be terribly wrong indeed if one of them was doing so anyway.

I cracked open the door to find Marta peering back at me. "I am so very sorry to disturb you, Madonna," she said in a whisper, "but I did not know what to do. He insists on seeing you immediately."

I stepped out into the hallway, closing the door behind me, hoping that Gasparo would sleep through the whole thing. "Who, Marta?" I demanded.

"Bastiano Bragadin. He is downstairs—and quite beside himself too, saying he must see you this instant. I told him you were with a client, but he would not be deterred."

Fear clutched my heart. Bastiano would never do this except in the gravest of circumstances. "Send him to my upstairs sitting room," I said, already moving toward the stairs. "Then return here and wait outside the door. If Gasparo awakens and looks for me, just tell him there is some household issue I had to attend to . . . a small fire in the kitchen—I don't know; think of something."

"Sí, Madonna," Marta said, hurrying to do my bidding.

Once in the upstairs sitting room, I paced furiously, feeling as though an iron hand were constricting my chest.

"Valentina, thank God," I heard from the doorway, and I turned to see Bastiano standing there, dressed in dark clothing and a heavy cloak. He quickly shut the door behind him.

"Bastiano, what is it?" I demanded. "Is it Ginevra? Have you had word—"

"No," he answered immediately, and I almost crumpled to the floor in relief. "No, Ginevra is well last I heard. No, I had to see you because . . ." He ran a hand through his hair. "I haven't much time."

"In the name of Jesus Christ and all the saints, Bastiano, just tell me what is the matter!"

"I am leaving," he said. "Leaving Venice."

"And so?" I asked, with a prickle of annoyance now. "You come and go on your father's business all the time. Never have you made such a spectacle of it as coming here when I—"

"No," he said. "I am not leaving on business. I am going into hiding."

The words fell between us like a flaming sword. "You . . . what?" I managed.

"I am going into hiding," he repeated, "and do not know when I will be able to return to Venice."

"But why?"

"It is better if you do not know. Believe me, Valentina. I mean that with all of my soul. All you need know is that something I have been looking into has made me a target of someone very powerful. I need to disappear for a bit, in the hopes that I live to fight another day."

"Bastiano," I whispered, "you cannot mean . . ."

He shook his head. "I can say no more—for your own safety, my love. But I wanted you to know what had happened and where I am going. Only you will know, but you must not contact me. Only if you are in danger or something happens to Ginevra."

"Of course," I said. "Of course, I—"

"There's no time," he said. "I am going to Verona. I may still be able to do what I need to do from there. Here." He handed me an address, scrawled on a bit of parchment. "Memorize that and then burn it immediately."

"Verona?" I asked, taking the paper. "Should you not go farther? Leave the Republic altogether? Surely—"

He was already shaking his head. "That is what this person expects me to do, I think," he said. "Run somewhere abroad, like Constantinople, and I'm sure he wishes I would, for then he might paint me as a traitor of some kind. He will perhaps not anticipate that I will remain so close. And there are people here I must stay in contact with."

"Bastiano, what—"

He crossed the room to me and took my hands in his. "I must go, Valentina. I'm sorry." He took my mouth in a desperate, bruising kiss. "I love you."

And then he was gone.

I stayed where I was, standing alone in the middle of the room, trembling slightly.

I love you.

I looked down at the bit of paper in my hands, repeating the address over and over to myself until I remembered it as well as I did my own name. Then I moved woodenly downstairs to the kitchen and threw the paper into the fire in the hearth.

I took a moment there to collect myself, breathing in and out deeply, banishing the tears that had started to gather. I must return to bed with Alvise Gasparo and, if he was awake, play the part of the charming, carefree courtesan as though nothing were wrong. As though the man I loved were not in the gravest danger. As though I had not just bid that man goodbye knowing that I may never see him again.

At least I did not need to wonder why, what had caused Bastiano to take this extraordinary step.

Ambrogio Malatesta. Who else?

Part Two

The Shadow God's Bargain

November 1538

Chapter 16

It was impossible for me to put Bastiano's hasty departure from my mind. There was no word from him—nor did I expect any—and so I had no idea what had befallen him after he'd left my house that night. Had he been captured or killed somewhere along the way? Had he made it safely to Verona, only to be discovered there? Had he even made it out of Venice? Or was he safely ensconced in his safe house, the address of which was branded in my mind? I had no idea, and no way of knowing when I might learn Bastiano's fate. Either he would be killed by those who sought him—Malatesta, most certainly—and I would hear of it eventually through acquaintances, or he would turn up in Venice again one day, all danger behind him.

It could be weeks. It could be months. It could be years. I might never see him again.

Still, there was life to be lived, clients to see, parties to attend, money to be sent to the Abates for Ginevra's upkeep. So I did it all, carried on as I always had, even though this time my facade felt in more danger of crumbling than ever before.

* * *

It began as a day like any other: I rose, went to the market with Bettina to find something to make for Senator Querini when he came to see me that evening, and then spent the rest of the day sorting through and replying to correspondence.

That last task, however, was interrupted by Lauretta knocking on my study door. I sighed and called "Enter," laying down my quill.

"Begging your pardon, Madonna," the maid said as she sidled in, "but that patrician is here to see you, that older one, oh, I always forget his name . . ."

"Querini?" I demanded, laying my quill down. "He isn't due for hours yet. I've not even started getting ready. Send him away."

"Not that one," she said, giving me a significant look. "Malatesta! That's it."

My stomach curdled, and for a moment I was certain I would be sick.

Lauretta was watching me curiously. I had never felt the need to clarify or contradict for my staff the story that those in my circles knew, that Ambrogio Malatesta was one of my lovers, and so they had been led to believe the same as everybody else. They had always known, however, that something was not quite true in that tale. I never went anywhere with Malatesta, and when he came to call, I never insisted on being attired in my best. Nor was a meal ever prepared for him. We certainly never went into the bedchamber, nor did he stay the night. So whatever my servants thought, I could not say. But I was not about to disabuse any of them of their notions.

I sighed and rose from my chair. I had known all along that the day was coming when he would have another assignment for me; had known that I could not avoid him forever.

Refusing to see him would arouse his suspicions indeed, would all but confirm for him that I knew something I ought not. So see him I would.

"Very well," I said reluctantly. "Show him into the receiving room."

"He is already there, Madonna."

Of course he was. I sighed again and left my office. I used the few moments it took me to get to the receiving room across the hall to mentally don the armor I always wore when dealing with Malatesta, hoping it had some extra thickness and heft to it that day.

He looked much the same as ever, if a bit grayer and more drawn. Apparently seeing to the interests and security of the Republic—while also engaging in his own duplicitous ventures—was not an altogether restful job.

"Signor Malatesta," I said, taking the chair at an angle to the one in which he'd seated himself. "To what do I owe this surprise?" I deliberately did not use the word *pleasure.* "No word from you for some months, and now here you are, having invited yourself into my home once again. One wonders at the nerve."

He scowled slightly. On top of everything else, I had not forgotten our last encounter, had not forgotten his propositioning me, and while I was sure he had not either, he did not show it. "Valentina," he said shortly, "your hospitality leaves as much to be desired as ever."

"Oh, should I have sent for some refreshments? Wine, perhaps?" I asked innocently. "But then, I know far better than to think that you would ever accept a cup from my hand."

His scowl deepened, and I bit back a smile. He trusted me enough to do his bidding, but he did not trust me completely, and it was plain enough that needled at him, at least somewhat.

He decided to ignore this latest riposte and get right to business. "I am here on a very delicate and sensitive matter," he began.

"You always are," I observed. "In fact, that is all men ever come to me for, I've found. Sex and death: two very delicate and sensitive matters indeed."

It was perhaps too easy for me to slip back into the arrogant, irreverent persona I always used with Malatesta. One thing to be thankful for at least. If I were behaving any differently around him, he would mark it at once.

As I spoke, Malatesta's scowl was replaced with a look of boredom. "Are you quite done?" he asked. His tone held an edge of anger that belied his expression.

"I don't know," I mused. "This is an interesting thought that has just occurred to me. I may have much more to say on the subject."

"Enough," he growled. "I've no time for this foolishness. I'm here because I—because the Ten have a job for you."

I noted his slip, even as I was not entirely sure it meant anything. "It's been so long I rather thought you all had lost confidence in my skills," I said. "Or do you simply pay the whores on the Bridge of Tits to stick a knife in a man these days?" I shook my head. "Those desperate women will do anything for less, poor souls."

"Enough!" he said sharply, giving me pause. I had never seen Malatesta quite this agitated, which for him meant that his body was stiff with tension, so much so that it seemed as though too quick a movement would shatter him like glass.

"We have a job for you," he repeated. "It is one only you can complete, I'm afraid."

"Isn't it always? Very well. Who is the victim?"

"Target."

I rolled my eyes. "Now who is refusing to get down to business? Who is the *target*, then?"

"Bastiano Bragadin."

The room swam before my eyes just then. Malatesta seemed to shimmer before me, just like the light reflected by the canals onto the underside of a bridge. My entire body went icy, as though I had just been plunged into the cold waters of one of those canals.

Truly I should have expected this.

"I do not think I heard you correctly," I said faintly.

"You did. The target is Bastiano Bragadin."

"Is this some sort of sick joke?" I snapped, back in possession of myself. It was a lapse I could not allow to occur again.

While I could not recall Bastiano's name ever coming up in conversation between Malatesta and me, he certainly knew that Bastiano was my lover. All of Venice knew, but in that way they pretended not to whenever it suited them.

"It is not," he bit out. "I am in deadly earnest, Valentina. Do you think I come here to waste my time in jest with you? Do you think I've nothing better to do than toy with you for my own amusement?"

"I can think of no other explanation for what just came out of your mouth," I said in a clipped voice. By the Shadow God, why had Marta laced my dress so damned tightly? And how had I not noticed until just then? It was suddenly quite difficult to breathe.

"It is no joke. The Council of Ten has amassed evidence indicating that Bastiano Bragadin is a traitor to the Venetian state. As such, he must be eliminated."

I closed my eyes and clenched my teeth. This was a nightmare. This was *the* nightmare.

"You cannot ask me to do this," I said, my voice low. "You cannot be asking me to do this, Ambrogio. Tell me it is not so."

He flinched at my use of his Christian name, a privilege he had never officially granted me. "But I am. Because it has to be you. Who else could it be?"

I laughed, a harsh sound. "Who else indeed?"

"He is conspiring against the state, Valentina," Malatesta said again. "He has been for some time. We have proof."

"What proof?" I demanded. I did not doubt that Malatesta had proof that Bastiano was conspiring against *him*. That was certainly true. But against Venice herself? No. Never.

"It doesn't matter what—"

"The hell it doesn't," I blazed, rising from my chair.

"Mind your tongue," Malatesta snapped, and began to say something else, but I cut him off. He was lucky I did not cut his throat right then and there and end the entire mess at once.

"You cannot expect me to agree to this," I said.

"You wish to hear the proof?" Malatesta asked, rising from his own chair. "Fine. I do not know what difference you expect it to make, but fine. Bastiano Bragadin is involved in—at the center of, actually—a conspiracy against the Venetian state. It involves selling both Arsenale secrets and other military secrets to the Ottoman Empire."

Lies, all of it. "You expect me to believe that?" I said incredulously.

"Why shouldn't you? He goes to Constantinople several times a year at least. Certainly that would indicate that—"

"What—that he is a Venetian merchant?" I said. "This city is full of merchant sailors who are back and forth between

Venice and Constantinople regularly. And you expect me to take that as proof of Bastiano's supposed treason?"

"Interesting. The validity of the evidence has never bothered you before," he commented.

I wanted to scream, and nearly did, but did not want to attract the servants' attention. "Your word was enough for me once," I spat. "But no more. You are asking me to murder, in cold blood, the one man who . . . Of course this is different, you heartless bastard. Of course it is!"

"Not so cold-blooded a killer as you pretend to be, are you, Valentina?"

"I am not a monster. Not like you."

"Aren't you?" he shot back. "You take men to your bed and then kill them. You poison men who are paying for your company, men you have lain with. You've never cared before from whence my evidence came, or whether the men I've sent you after are even truly guilty of what I've claimed they are. I might have been using you to eliminate my personal rivals all this time, for all you've cared."

"Is that truly what you think of me?" I asked, horrified. Horrified at the idea, horrified that he was so brazenly saying what I now knew he was, in fact, guilty of. At least in the case of Dioniso Secco.

"Of a woman who not only sells her body, but also kills for money? Of course. Should I have a rosier view of who you are and what you do, my dear?"

I took a step back as though his words had physically struck me. For a moment I saw myself, perfectly clearly, through Malatesta's eyes. I was a whore in every way. I sold my body, sold my skills as a killer, and so I sold my soul. A woman who would do such things had no scruples, none at all. And so why not ask her to kill the man she loved? For such a woman could not know what love meant—not truly.

He saw me as the monster I had always insisted, even if just to myself, that I wasn't.

"You are wrong," I said, struggling to keep my voice even. Struggling to keep him from seeing that, deep down, I'd always feared that the things he was saying were true. "You are wrong about me. I do what I need to do to survive. To protect others."

He gestured at the room around us. "This is just what you need to survive, is it? The big house, the fine clothes, the costly furnishings? This is protecting others?"

"You are wrong," I said in a whisper. "I am not who . . . I am not what you think I am."

He laughed mirthlessly. "Keep telling yourself that, Valentina, if it helps you to sleep at night."

"You need me," I flared. "You look down on me so, think I am such a monster, but without people like me, who will do your bidding?"

"Don't flatter yourself. There are thousands more like you, who will do what you do, for the right price. Most people will do anything for the right price, in fact."

"Then get one of them to do your evil deeds," I said. "For I won't do it anymore. I will not do this."

"But it must be you," Malatesta said. "Do you take me for a fool? I know that Bastiano Bragadin has fled Venice, and I know that you know where he is."

The floor seemed to tilt beneath my feet, but somehow I managed to remain standing. "I do not know what you are talking about," I said, my voice sounding faint even to myself.

"Enough of your lies, Valentina," he said. "Let us be honest with each other for once, hmm? I know that Bastiano fled—fled the justice he knew was coming to him. I also know—because I know him, and I know you—that if there is one person in this city whom he told where he was going, it is you. You can get to him when no one else can. And so it must be you."

"I don't know anything of this," I repeated. "I have not seen Bastiano in some time—that is true. And I do not know where he is."

"You can get word to him, then. You can lure him back to the city to complete this task. He will return for you."

"I will not do it!" I cried. "Even if I knew where Bastiano was, or how to reach him, I will not do this! You must have gone mad, Malatesta, to ask me such a thing, to expect me to obey. You may believe there is nothing I will not do, no sin I will not commit, but you are wrong. I will never harm Bastiano—never!"

He sighed, sounding as though he were very disappointed indeed. "I had thought you might say that. I had hoped that I was wrong and that it would not come to this."

"Come to what? You cannot force me to do this. You'll have to send one of your other hired thugs after Bastiano, and only hope that I haven't managed to warn him first." My voice grew in confidence as I spoke. "You've shown me your hand now, Malatesta. How did you ever think I would agree to this?"

"You have a daughter, do you not?"

My sharp retort to whatever I'd expected him to say froze in my throat. My heart seemed to stop. "I . . . what?"

"Yes. Ginevra is her name, I believe. And Bastiano Bragadin is her father. It is well enough known in much of Venetian society, as you must know."

"Leave Ginevra out of this," I snarled, "or so help me—"

He sighed, shaking his head piteously. "I so wish that I could, Valentina. Truly I do. The Council of Ten is not usually in the business of threatening children. A most distasteful business it is." He wrinkled his nose as if in disgust.

The room swam before me again, the shades of a nightmare threatening to choke me. *Wake up, Valentina, wake up!* "You . . . you wouldn't," I whispered. "You wouldn't dare."

"For the safety and security of the Venetian state, I surely would."

"For the safety and security of your own position, you mean," I spat.

He shrugged. "There is little enough difference."

"Why, you arrogant—"

He held up a slender, aristocratic hand. "Spare me your useless threats," he said. "I suppose I shall have to spell it out for you, then, as you seem quite resistant to the subtleties. You will either kill Bastiano Bragadin, or your daughter will be the one to pay the price. Is that clear enough for you, Valentina?"

"You are the monster," I hissed. "Not me. You."

"Again, spare me."

"You'll have to find her first," I said. "She is not here in Venice. Not with me and not with Bastiano. Your threat is an empty one."

"Oh?" he asked. "Then I suppose the names Vincenzo and Sonia Abate mean nothing to you?"

This time I did have to collapse into a chair.

"Ah," he said, watching me closely, "I thought they might. Did you truly think the Ten did not know? We know all, my dear. We know everything."

"You monster," I said, past my constricted lungs. "You unutterable bastard, you who would threaten an innocent child . . ."

He crossed the room to me, placing his hands on the arms of my chair, trapping me in place. "I do what I must," he hissed through clenched teeth, his face just inches from mine. "I do what I must to keep the Republic and her people safe. You are nothing more than a tool I use to that end. It is best you do not forget it."

I moved quickly to strike him across the face, but he grabbed my wrist in a vise grip, stopping me. His grasp was painful, and it felt as though the bones in my wrist were grinding against one another. But I'd be damned if I would so much as wince.

"You are out of options, Valentina," he whispered. And, damn him, but was that a flare of desire I saw in his eyes? As though my trying to strike him aroused him. "And you and your threats and your rather common brand of violence do not frighten me." He released me and straightened up, smoothing his senator's robes as though we'd simply been having a friendly chat over a glass of wine. "But I am not the monster you name me," he said, his voice once again back to normal: urbane, polished, secure in his own power, and a touch bored. "You may have some time to acclimate yourself to the task ahead of you. And I expect it will take some time for you to make contact with Bragadin and convince him to return to the city, or whatever you need to do."

I slumped in my chair and closed my eyes. I could not stop the tear that slid from beneath my eyelid; I could only hope he had not seen it. "How much time?"

"Let's say until the end of the month," he said. "By the end of November, the deed must be done. Or there shall be those rather unfortunate consequences we spoke of."

"The devil take you, Malatesta," I spat. "If I do not cut your throat myself first."

He shrugged. "As I said." He moved toward the door to take his leave. "It isn't all bad, really," he said, almost as an afterthought. "Think of it this way, Valentina. At least you can make his end painless. Well, as painless as possible. I've no doubt you have your ways. Someone else I might send would very likely show a great deal less mercy."

"Burn in hell, Malatesta."

He shrugged again and turned to leave. At the door, he turned back and said once more, "The end of November, Valentina. Do not fail."

Then he was gone, and I let out a scream of fury and sorrow in his wake.

Interlude

Somewhere in Tuscany, June 1527

"You're quiet."

I glanced up to find Fernando Cortes watching me from the other side of the campfire. "I suppose I am."

He didn't reply, simply continued to watch me as he sucked the meat from the bones of a rabbit he'd trapped and roasted over the fire for us.

His silent scrutiny made me squirm. "What of it?" I retorted. "You're not exactly loquacious yourself."

"Don't know what that means."

"What *what* means?"

"Loquacious."

I sighed, irritated. "It means someone who talks a lot."

He nodded. "That's true enough. I'm not. Never have been."

"Then why pick at me for it?"

He shrugged. "I just thought maybe you'd want to talk about it. Thought you would have talked about it by now."

Panic began to prickle the back of my neck. "Talk about what?"

"What happened to you. What you're running from."

I looked away from him, down at the few scraps of greasy meat before me. Any appetite I had was suddenly gone. "Surely you know what I'm running from. Or you can guess. You were there, weren't you?" This last was spoken with a note of accusation in my voice; I couldn't help it. Cortes was Spanish, and it was mostly the troops of the Spanish Holy Roman Emperor who had sacked Rome. That much I had learned by then, and why: the pope, once an ally of the emperor and of Spain against the French, had switched his allegiance to France when it seemed expedient. The emperor, outraged, had invaded the Italian peninsula and, when his troops eventually realized he had no money with which to pay them, had sacked Rome to get whatever riches they could. Anyone who tried to stand in their way was cut down, along with plenty who didn't.

If the whispers and rumors we'd begun to hear from those on the road were true, those who had simply been killed outright—like my family, like Massimo—had been the lucky ones.

I had known nothing of this as it was unfolding, as the imperial troops made their deadly march toward Rome. My father always held that politics were not fit for young girls, and so I'd always lived in complete ignorance of what went on in the world outside our villa on the outskirts of Rome. My whole life had ended in a storm of blood and fire, and I hadn't had any idea of the reason why.

So when I'd met Cortes, his Spanish-accented Italian had made it plain enough who—and what—he was. Yet he was headed away from Rome, in the same direction as me, so I'd decided to take my chances with him. But now I eyed him carefully, wondering if perhaps I'd made a mistake.

He nodded. "I was there," he admitted. "And I was horrified by what I saw. Stripping the wealth from rich merchants and preening prelates seemed like a good idea at first. We received no pay for months of marching and fighting." He shrugged. "Certainly the Church would say it's wrong, but that's the way of war." He took another bite of rabbit meat and chewed thoughtfully.

"What I saw, though . . . the slaughter of innocents, the torture for sport, the rape . . ." He glanced at me apprehensively and coughed. "Erm, well. It disgusted me. And so I deserted."

"You could have stopped them," I spat, horrified to find tears welling behind my eyes. I had not cried in all these days on the road, had not shed a single tear since finding the savaged bodies of my loved ones. Why must I cry now? "You could have stopped your fellow soldiers from doing these terrible things."

He gave me a stiff, crooked smile. "How was one man meant to stop legions of soldiers?"

"You could have *tried*." A single tear rolled down my dirty cheek, and I quickly swiped it away.

"They'd have likely killed me too, for trying to interfere in their fun, and I'd no interest in dying over it." He shrugged and tossed a few bones into the fire. "I never said I was as noble as all that."

I looked down, tears making the ground before me swim as though it were a river of mud.

He took a swig from the skin of wine he'd traded for at a town we'd passed. "Now you."

"Now me what?" I demanded, letting anger drive the tears away.

"I told you what happened to me. What I did. Now tell me your story."

"I . . ." I looked away again. "I can't."

"Yes you can."

"I don't *want* to!" I cried. "I don't ever want to speak of it!"

He watched me through the flames for a moment, his gaze so steady that I was finally forced to meet it. "Not healthy to hold it all inside like that," he said. "Maybe you'd rather not speak of it. I don't blame you. But you should."

There were a few moments of silence after that, the crackling of the fire the only sound to be heard.

Then I drew a deep, shuddering breath. "I'd fallen asleep in the stables. With Massimo, my betrothed . . . after we . . . well." I blushed.

"I can imagine. I was young once. Go on."

"And we woke up," I went on, "and heard shouts and screams, and something outside was on fire. And Massimo . . ." My eyes filled with tears again. "He made me promise to stay put until he came back for me. And he went out there, and I did as he said. Until the morning, when . . . when I finally went out."

I told him the rest, in as few words as I could, reliving it as I went, feeling as though I was walking the grounds of our villa again, seeing Massimo's mutilated body, finding the bodies of our servants and my parents, all butchered. I told him of losing consciousness and coming to in the blood-spattered upstairs hallway where I'd fallen, who knew how long later. I told him of chopping my waist-length hair short and hiding it under a cap, and of dressing in men's clothing. And of leaving, walking north, away from Rome, headed nowhere in particular except as far away as I could get, wanting only to leave that horrible scene behind me.

By the end of the tale, I was sobbing, sobbing so hard my head ached and I felt I was going to vomit, so hard I could scarcely breathe, all the pain I'd carried and locked away inside me finally, finally coming to the surface. Cortes came around the fire and settled himself beside me, awkwardly patting my back. And when I flung myself into his arms, scarcely knowing what I was doing, he simply held me and let me scream and howl my pain and rage into the night.

Chapter 17

I do not know how long I stayed in the receiving room. I had broken a set of glass goblets and overturned the chairs and side table in sheer rage, causing the marble top to crack. I could feel the traces of tears on my face, though I could not remember shedding them. They were tears of rage, and as such they had not landed so heavily on my heart as did tears of sorrow.

But those would surely come later.

How had it come to this? How? How had I let this happen? How had I thought I could have my clients, and my lover and my daughter, and commit murder on behalf of the Council of Ten of Venice, thinking that there wouldn't someday come a reckoning?

No, that wasn't entirely true; I had always known a reckoning would come. I had always known that the day would come when I would have to pay for the deeds I committed at the Ten's behest, in one way or another, regardless of whether I believed them to be for the greater good. That was why I had kept my daughter far away, was it not? So that she might never factor into this accounting of blood and allegiance and sin.

And I had failed. She was in harm's way despite all I had done, and I had ultimately failed to protect her, the one person truly worth my protection.

Foolishly, I had thought distance would keep her safe, just as I'd foolishly thought that amassing money and influential lovers would insulate me from the reckoning to come. But now it was here, and there was no way out that I could see. No way but the unthinkable.

I had to assume that Malatesta's threat to Ginevra was not a bluff. Ambrogio Malatesta did not bluff, not when it mattered. Malatesta had issued this threat to ensure that I did his bidding, and would no doubt follow through if I refused—his killing a man who had likely been loyal to him for years was proof enough of his ruthlessness. I knew Malatesta. And oh God, how I wished I didn't. How I wished I'd never heard of him. How I wished I'd had old Fernando Cortes leave me in Florence instead when we'd passed through all those years ago. How I wished I'd never accepted Cortes's offer to bring me to Venice, where he himself had been headed. How I wished I had stayed in that city of mud and dirt and brick nestled among the Tuscan hills, and never come to this floating city, hanging suspended precariously by lies and deceptions and blood. And truly then did I know how desperate my situation was, if I was longing in any way for my broken past, for those days when I had lost everything.

I had not thought life—or the Fates, Fortuna, God, or whomever you please—could be so cruel. I had foolishly thought that having lost everything once before, surely I could never come to such a sorry pass again.

Oh, how they were laughing at me, whatever those powers that be.

I was startled from my furious, anguished reverie by a knock on the door, followed by Marta opening it and sticking her head in. "Madonna Valentina, are you—Madonna!" she gasped, taking in the condition of the room. "What has happened? Are you all right?"

I laughed hollowly. "No. No, Marta. I am not all right. Not at all."

She stepped tentatively into the room. "What . . . what has happened? Was that Malatesta . . . was he violent with you?"

I laughed again, the same empty, soulless sound. "Was he violent with me. Yes, after a fashion. Not in the way you are probably thinking, though."

Marta hesitated, staring at me aghast.

I sighed. "I am unhurt physically, Marta," I said dully. Other than the bruises on my wrist from Malatesta's fingers. "Leave me. Please."

"But Madonna . . . begging your pardon, but Senator Querini will be here in not two hours. You must ready yourself."

"Fuck Senator Querini," I spat, appreciating but not commenting on the irony that that was exactly what he was coming to me for. "I will not see him tonight."

"But Madonna, it is arranged—"

"I will not see him tonight!" I all but shouted. "Send him a message telling him I am indisposed. Tell him whatever you want. But I will not receive him. I will not receive anyone. Not tonight. Is that quite clear, Marta?"

"Yes, Madonna. But what—"

"Good. Get out."

She hastily scurried away, closing the door behind her and leaving me to stew in my rage and despair and the ruin of my receiving room. Poor girl. She deserved better treatment than this. None of this was her fault. Sometime in the future, perhaps, I would apologize. But just then I did not feel capable of any emotion but rage.

He had me well and truly trapped, did Malatesta. And so cruelly. Despite everything Malatesta had spouted about how it had to be me, how I was the only one who knew where Bastiano was, was the only one who could reach him, the only reason was cruelty. To show me he had me completely under his thumb. To punish not only Bastiano but me as well. Malatesta surely had other spies and assassins at his disposal, under the auspices of the Council of Ten, who could track down Bastiano if need be. But no, he much preferred to torment me.

I remembered that flash of desire in Malatesta's eyes as I'd tried to strike him, as though the idea of me being violent toward him aroused him. And perhaps it did. I remembered the feeling of his cold fingers on my cheek at that party at Flora's, the way he'd lowered his voice intimately and stepped close to me, the way he'd propositioned me. The anger in his eyes when I'd refused him. When I, a courtesan available to any man in Venice with the coin to pay me, had refused Ambrogio Malatesta, a prominent patrician and member of the Council of Ten. And I remembered feeling as though his eyes were boring into my back as I'd walked away from him.

This was his revenge. This was why he had made it so that I could not refuse. One did not spurn a man as powerful as Ambrogio Malatesta, a lesson I should have learned by then.

And there was no way out.

For a moment, I considered: *Had* the full Council of Ten sanctioned this assassination? I knew Bastiano was no traitor, but he had certainly been working against Malatesta. It was possible that there was some proof that Malatesta had been able to lay his hands on. Had he twisted it to make it look like Bastiano was truly part of a conspiracy against the Venetian state?

Was he playing the Council of Ten to his own advantage as well?

I was inclined to think not, to think that the rest of the men of the Ten would surely see through such treachery and might at the very least balk at ordering the assassination of a son of the Bragadin family. But—and my heart twisted with anguish yet again—could I be completely certain of that? Certain enough to stake Ginevra's life on it?

And I had no proof of what I knew to be true of Malatesta, and no idea where I might get any. My stomach twisted almost painfully at the realization that even if I dared go to someone else on the Council of Ten, or even in the Senate, with what I suspected, it would likely do me more harm than good, for I was implicated in the whole plot. Malatesta had used me to kill Dioniso Secco, so it would look like I was his coconspirator, turning on him for reasons of my own.

I could flee, or try to, but surely Malatesta would find me. And there was no guarantee I could get to Ginevra before Malatesta's henchmen. Oh God, maybe he had someone watching her already, ready to strike should I try to weasel my way out of this hellish state of affairs in which I found myself.

But . . . if there was even a chance, should I not take it?

No, I realized. And the realization sent me to my knees on the floor. No. Not when it was my daughter's life I would be gambling with. No chance was worth that.

And Bastiano, I knew, would offer up his own life in exchange for our daughter's, if it came to that.

It was that thought that finally unleashed the tears of sorrow.

Chapter 18

When I awoke the next morning, for a few blissful moments I enjoyed the luxury of thinking that everything that had passed the day before had been an evil dream. Something so awful could not have been real. Surely not, and surely now it would remain confined to the realm of nightmares, where it belonged.

Yet all too soon the truth of the matter came screaming back, shrieking in my ears like a demon come to foretell of death. Death that I must soon bring about.

I sat up in bed and drew my knees to my chest. It was real. All too real.

I would have to either kill my lover or let my daughter be killed in turn. And no doubt I'd be killed as well, for I would be of no use to Malatesta if I could not carry out his orders. It was an unthinkable choice that was no choice at all.

"The end of November, Valentina. Do not fail."

Well, there *was* the obvious way out. Had I had my wits about me the day before, when Malatesta was here, I could have done it then, and the whole thing would be over. But, I excused myself, I had been receiving some devastating information. It was perhaps to be expected that I was not as sharp as

I would normally have been. But today, with the shock having receded, the answer presented itself. Before I could think better of it, I rang for Marta and had her dress me in a plain gown.

There were plenty of reasons this was a terrible idea, of course. Murdering a patrician from an old family, a current member of the Council of Ten, would rock the Republic to its core. I'd certainly be executed—if I was caught, that was. And I rather thought that with my considerable skill set, honed after so many years of doing Malatesta and the Ten's dirty work, I might be able to evade detection, though getting past his servants would likely be the difficult part. Because surely a man who sat on the Ten had plenty of other enemies. And if Bastiano was able to get his hands on hard proof of Malatesta's scheming and bring it to light, perhaps there would be less zeal for his murderer to be found and brought to justice.

But it didn't matter, ultimately. If I could ensure both Bastiano and Ginevra's safety, then what happened to me wasn't important.

Once I was dressed, my hair bound back in a simple braid, I dismissed Marta and went to a small chest in my dressing room that I kept locked. In it were an assortment of daggers and knives, lengths of cord, my poison ring, and a few vials of poison. I slid a dagger into the pockets sewn into the lining of my cloak, and another into my boot.

I knew where Malatesta lived, of course; had made it my business to know when I'd first started working with him. His family palazzo was farther up the Grand Canal, smaller than those of families like Bragadin or Contarini, but respectable, nonetheless. Because of its location, it had a dock and water entrance right on the canal, but I certainly wouldn't be entering through the front door. I'd have to make my way to the rear entrance.

I left my palazzo on foot, winding through the streets of Venice to the Rialto Bridge so that I might cross to the other side. I had found Malatesta's palazzo on foot once before, but it had been some time ago, so I had to do a bit of doubling back and squinting up at the back of buildings before I found it again. Luckily, it being broad daylight, there were plenty of people out and about, thus making stealth less important. Everyone was about their own business and did not care about me or mine.

I lingered a street away from Malatesta's palazzo, in a spot where I could view the back door. All was quiet and still, with no one going in or out. I had expected to see more servant activity, as there often was at the grand palazzi of the city. Yet Malatesta lived alone, so far as I knew, and he certainly did not entertain much. So likely there was not a great deal of work for his servants.

Then there was, of course, the matter of whether Malatesta was even home, should I manage to gain entry. It was early yet, but perhaps he was already off and about his business, either the government's or his own. But that didn't trouble me overmuch. If he was not in, I would lie in wait.

I wanted this over, done with.

A woman emerged from the door. In her middle years, she was, I assumed, the housekeeper. She walked away without locking the door behind her, off into the warren of streets.

This was likely my moment. Hopefully someone on the other side of the door had not locked it after she'd left. Once she was out of sight, I darted along the street to the door. I had just put my hand to the knob when a voice behind me asked, "What are you doing?"

I winced inwardly. So much for my confidence in my own abilities, but I could blame my eagerness to get this particular job done. Yet all was not lost, and no assassin went into a situation without a backup plan. I turned to see the woman who had just left the palazzo, perhaps returned for something she'd forgotten. *Stupid, stupid, Valentina,* I chastised myself. I ought to have waited a bit longer for just that reason. I gave the woman a smile. "This is the home of Ambrogio Malatesta, is it not?"

"Who wants to know?"

"I bring a message from one of his associates," I said, banking on the fact that Malatesta's work for the Ten involved much delivering of messages from varied persons.

My assumption seemed to be correct, for the woman didn't seem perturbed in the slightest. "He's not at home," she said. "You can leave the message with me."

"I'm afraid I can't. My orders are to give it to the signore himself—no one else." I shrugged. "I'll have to come back later, then. Perhaps tonight?"

"He'll not be here, then, either. You'd best seek him at the Doge's Palace. He'll be staying there for some time, so he said."

I wanted to scream in frustration even as I felt disbelief that this woman was so indiscreet as to give me so much information about her master's whereabouts. Yet what difference did it make? I'd not be able to infiltrate the Doge's Palace, nor would anyone else. Which was no doubt exactly why Malatesta had chosen to ensconce himself there after giving me this latest assignment. He'd known I would come after him before I even knew it myself. And so he'd put himself entirely out of my reach.

I managed another smile. "Very well, then. To the Doge's Palace I go. Thank you." I turned and left, and only when I was a good distance away did I let a litany of curses fall from my lips.

I should have known it couldn't be so easy.

* * *

The next morning found me lying in bed, staring at the ceiling and turning over my options. Was there a way I could perhaps lure Malatesta out of the Doge's Palace? I could try, I supposed, but he'd certainly be suspicious of any message asking him to depart. If he'd holed himself up there for his own safety, he'd not stir forth again readily.

So where did that leave me?

I took a deep, shuddering breath and sat up. Surely there was a way out here, one that I was not seeing. Surely, after everything I had been through, everything I had survived, everything I had learned, and all the ways in which I had hardened my heart and sharpened my mind and my instincts, surely Ambrogio Malatesta could not have me so completely trapped, so utterly cornered into doing his heinous bidding.

I mulled this over as I rose and summoned Marta to dress me, barely speaking a word to her. She remained silent, which was just what I needed: silence, in order to puzzle out how I might go about defeating Malatesta. For he could be defeated, of course. He was only a man, after all, albeit a powerful one. And no man was without weaknesses, even the men of the Council of Ten. Who knew that better than a courtesan?

I had just reached for a pair of earrings sitting on my dressing table when that thought struck me, and I froze mid-reach, my hand hovering over the pearl baubles as though suspended in time. And indeed, it felt as though the world had stopped spinning around me, just for a moment.

"Madonna?" Marta asked, noticing my aborted motion. "Is everything all right?"

"Yes," I breathed, scarcely hearing my own reply. "Yes, Marta. Just fine." With that I completed the task of picking up the earrings and putting them into my ears, hardly aware of what I was doing.

Who indeed knew the weaknesses—and secrets, scandals, and foibles—of men better than courtesans? No one. No one in Venice, and no one in the rest of the world either, I'd wager. That was why I was so useful to Malatesta, to the Ten. Why courtesans made the perfect spies. I was certainly not the only one pressed into service as such, as my observation of Felicita Cavazza and Anzolo Balbi at Lotti's party had proven.

The Council of Ten were the masters of secrets, yes. But they could not do everything themselves. There were those they employed to do their work for them, much of it dirty and bloody. For this reason, there were many people in Venice who knew, who must know, the same secrets the Ten did. And whether it was because they were involved themselves or because they bedded the men who did, I knew that a great deal of those people were surely courtesans.

Bastiano had been investigating Malatesta's activities before going into hiding, and he had been working with others. The papers I'd found in his satchel proved that. There were others who knew what Bastiano had known, or at least suspected it. And if I could find proof, proof that Malatesta was misusing his authority for his own personal gain, proof that Malatesta was the traitor, then I could use it to entrap *him* in turn.

And if there was anything to know about Ambrogio Malatesta, anything that might damn him, anything that might render him powerless, anything that I could use to fight back against what he was trying to do to me and to those I loved, it would be my fellow courtesans and my fellow women of Venice who would know it.

I smiled broadly at my reflection in the Murano glass mirror as Marta slid the last pin into my hair. "Feeling better, Madonna?" she asked, noting my expression.

"In fact, I am, Marta," I said, my smile widening. "I very much am."

* * *

As luck had it, I was set to accompany Agosto Zorzi to a salon hosted by a fellow courtesan that very evening. Zorzi was a newer client of mine, one I had just begun seeing that year, and so far I had found him quite delightful. He was in his late thirties, charming, amusing, and desperately handsome. We had become fast friends, and he was thorough in the bedroom. I was glad I had decided, rather on a whim, to accept his initial invitation all those months ago.

Of course, such a gathering would mean that plenty of other courtesans would be in attendance. It was time to learn what I could about Ambrogio Malatesta.

Agosto came to call for me in his gondola, and we chattered genially on the way to the party. It was admittedly hard for me to focus on anything—even the handsome man beside me—with Malatesta's ultimatum hanging over my head and knowing that this could not simply be another night of leisurely entertainment and pleasure for me, as it sometimes was with my favorite clients. But a courtesan—and an assassin too, come to that—was an actress first and foremost. And I had not survived—and thrived—this long by being anything less than a master performer. I made sure that Agosto suspected that nothing was amiss even as I considered who might be in attendance that night, whom I would approach and how.

Upon arrival at the palazzo, owned by a courtesan named Stella Molino, we circled the room, greeting Agosto's friends and acquaintances. As I'd expected, there was quite the crush of people in attendance, with many of Venice's well-connected men present—quite a few of them with courtesans on their arms.

Luckily, there were several women in attendance with whom I was friendly, including Amalia, who was on the arm of one of Senator Tron's sons. She threw me a wink from across the room when our gazes met, and I returned the gesture. Perhaps Amalia knew something of Malatesta, for what I did not know about the rich and powerful in Venice, she usually did. I was reluctant to involve her, but surely asking her some casual questions at some point could do no harm. I would speak to her when next she came to call or when I went to call on her, I resolved. But first I would see what I could learn that night.

When we entered the room, I fancied that I could feel numerous eyes on me, more so than usual. I remembered the man who'd followed Bettina and me at the market, the man I knew worked for Malatesta. Were there indeed eyes on me everywhere I went? Or was I simply being paranoid, especially given what I was hoping to accomplish that evening?

It didn't matter. I would sparkle and shine as a courtesan was expected to, and I would be the soul of discretion in my inquiries.

In our first pass of the room, Agosto and I were hailed by a pair we both knew: a patrician and member of the Great Council by the name of Angelo Collari, who was a friend of

Agosto's, and the courtesan on his arm, Margarita di Mazi, a woman with whom I was friendly. Like most courtesans, Margarita was a raving beauty, with a full figure, plump lips, and cascades of light brown curls.

"Wonderful to see you, Agosto," Angelo said.

"And you, Angelo."

"I've been meaning to ask you, your investment in the salt company . . ."

Margarita caught my gaze and subtly rolled her eyes. I grinned, and we drew nearer to each other, leaving the men to speak of business. I usually didn't mind such talk—it was all information, and information of any kind could be useful, whether to me in navigating the upper strata of Venetian society, or to one or the other of my clients. But investment in salt wasn't the sort of information I was looking for that evening.

"You look lovely, Margarita," I said. "New gown?"

She glanced down at it carelessly. "It is," she said. "There is a new seamstress over by the Rialto. She is fabulous. I must give you her address."

"Please do," I said. "I also wonder if you may have some gossip for me."

Her eyes lit up. "For you, Valentina, always."

"Have you heard anything of late about Ambrogio Malatesta?"

She looked slightly surprised, then thought for a moment. "Hmm, I do not know that I have," she said. "If I am calling to mind the right man, that is. In his fifth decade, perhaps? Tall, slender, graying hair?"

"Yes," I said.

"He is on the Council of Ten currently—I know that," she said, clearly consulting her prodigious knowledge of Venetian society. "And so a senator before that, of course . . . widowed some years ago and never remarried."

"Yes, that's right," I said. Malatesta's wife had died long before my acquaintance with him. No doubt death was a preferable state to that of matrimony with Ambrogio Malatesta.

A smile curved Margarita's lips. "Why ask me, though?" she said. "From what I've heard, you would know him far better than I." She winked at me.

I smiled and hoped she could not tell it was forced. "The gossip is quite correct, as usual. But even so, I wonder what you may know of him, since . . ." I sighed and shook my head. "He has been rather mysterious of late, and I wish I knew why."

"If he is on the Council of Ten, I'm sure he has much to be mysterious about," Margarita said.

"Yes, that's true," I said, then launched into the explanation I had prepared for why I was asking about Malatesta. "It will sound petty, I'm afraid, but he has long been a client of mine, as you say, and then he rather . . . disappeared. Or disappeared so far as I am concerned, at any rate. He was a rather . . . frequent visitor for a time." All of that was at least somewhat true. I shrugged. "It all seemed most curious, is all. And so I wondered what I ought to make of his behavior, if anything at all, and thought I might endeavor to see what gossip there is about him."

Margarita grinned and opened her lace fan. "I must say, I am surprised that you are so bothered over his absence. He always seemed like a bit of a cold fish to me."

I laughed. "As I said, a bit of pettiness on my part—nothing more. If he has strayed to another, I should like to know who, so I might outshine her."

"Hmm." Margarita eyed me for a moment, as if she didn't quite believe me. "Allora, now that you mention it, I think I did hear a rumor once that he preferred male company. I think it began simply because he never remarried after his wife's death, though surely he could have made a good match, and he is never seen in public with a courtesan. And if he is one of your clients, then that puts paid to that rumor. Unless, I suppose, he is one of those men who takes his pleasure wherever he finds it." She frowned. "Although from what I've seen of him, he does not seem like one who takes pleasure in anything."

"Yes, I don't believe that is true," I said. Damn it all. There was nothing in this whole conversation that was of any use to me.

"You could always ask Aretino, if you are curious," Margarita added. "He would certainly know if *that* particular rumor were true, and would likely know anything else worth knowing about the man. He always does." She glanced around. "He is here tonight, I know, though I don't know where he's gotten to."

I grimaced. Pietro Aretino was a writer and satirist who was a frequent guest at many literary salons and parties in Venice. A man who made no secret of his preference to bed other men, he had also written a number of verses satirizing and attacking the courtesan's profession. His acid tongue—and pen—and his ability to spread gossip made many wary of him, even as they courted his favor. While I did admire some of his writings that boldly critiqued the mighty and powerful, I had always steered clear of him. There was a great deal I would not want him to discover about me, after all.

"I do not think there is any gossip for which it is worth it to sell one's soul to that man," I said.

Margarita laughed. "I quite agree with you there."

"Valentina," a voice at my side said, and I turned to see Agosto smiling down at me. "Shall we continue our turn about the room?"

"Of course," I said with a warm smile. I nodded to Margarita. "Lovely to see you, Margarita. And thank you for the gossip."

"Of course, my dear."

Margarita had not known much of use. But surely, I thought, scanning the glittering assembly, someone here did. I would just need to be careful to ask the right person.

Agosto and I continued to move through the gathering, greeting everyone he knew, which was a great many people. Unfortunately, Amalia always seemed to be on the opposite side of the room from us.

After another round of the room, Agosto drew me into a group of men who immediately began speaking of their business ventures. Beside me in the circle was none other than Felicita Cavazza, who smiled upon seeing me. "My dear Valentina," she said warmly, leaning in to kiss my cheek. "Lovely to see you."

"And you," I said. "Are you enjoying yourself this evening?"

"We've just arrived," she said, indicating the man beside her, a patrician whose family name I knew was Boscolon. "And so have you, I believe?"

"Yes, not so long ago," I said, inclining my head toward Agosto.

"I believe we are both in need of refreshment, then," she said. She turned to her patron for the night. "Tommaso, if you will excuse me?"

He waved her off, barely hearing her, engrossed as he was in the conversation. Agosto did much the same, though he did give my waist an affectionate squeeze as I drew away.

Felicita and I threaded our way through the throng, seeking a refreshment table. "I am glad to have encountered you," I said, ready to begin again as we each picked up a glass of wine. I subtly drew her a bit away from the table. "I am in need of some gossip."

A smile curved her lovely lips, tinged pink with just the right amount of rouge. "Who isn't, in Venice?" she asked, lifting her glass to those lips. "About someone in particular, then?"

"Sí," I said. I kept my voice low, but not so low that she would think anything was truly amiss. "Ambrogio Malatesta. Do you know him?"

A shadow passed over her face, so quick I was not quite sure I had really seen it. "I do," she said, a somewhat guarded note in her voice. "Curious."

My interest was piqued. "What is?"

"Why is everyone so interested in that man all of a sudden?"

I took a sip of wine to avoid showing my surprise, though beneath the fine Burano lace on my bodice my heart had begun to beat faster. "Who is 'everyone'?" I asked, with what I hoped was no more than a passing interest.

She glanced around us, then lowered her voice a bit. "Senator Gritti is one of my lovers," she said. I nodded once; I already knew this. "He asked me a week or so back what I knew about Malatesta. Apparently . . ." But just as Felicita spoke, our hostess entered the room, inviting everyone to be seated for some recitations of poetry that were about to take place. I felt frustration rise in me.

Felicita nodded once, as if deciding something. "It would be better if we spoke of this in private, in any case. May I come call on you tomorrow?"

I could scarcely breathe past the anticipation. "Yes, of course," I said, struggling to keep my voice neutral.

"Bene. You still live over in San Marco, sí? Between the piazza and the Rialto?"

"Yes."

"Bene," she said again. "I will see you tomorrow, then—perhaps midday?"

"Perfetto," I said. "I will have my cook prepare us a light luncheon."

"Lovely." She smiled and raised her wineglass to me. "Until then."

Then she melted back into the crowd.

I did the same, though Agosto had since moved on and was speaking to someone new. I continued to play the role of the perfect courtesan, the perfect mistress, for the rest of the night: made jokes, laughed at Agosto's witticisms, joined in discussions of politics, and even recited a few poems when asked. But my heart was not in it, and indeed I was scarcely thinking about what I was doing and saying. My mind was a whir, wondering what Felicita could possibly have to tell me. And if it would be enough.

Chapter 19

Felicita arrived promptly at noon the next day, and Lauretta showed her to my sitting room, where I was waiting with some crisp white wine; plates with cheeses, cold meats, and white bread; and some pastries. Felicita was gracious with Lauretta as she showed her in and took her cloak. Felicita then settled herself onto the divan at an angle to my chair.

"Thank you, Lauretta," I said as she took up her position by the door. "That will be all."

She looked surprised for a moment. Often, when I entertained a friend, Lauretta stayed on hand in case we should need anything. But she quickly bobbed her head and departed, closing the door behind her.

Felicita turned to me with a smile. "Grazie, amica mia," she said. "I'm sure your servants are quite discreet, but it is best no one overhears this conversation, I think."

"As discreet as any courtesan's, I suppose," I said. And much more discreet than Malatesta's; I had reminded them all, after my visit to his palazzo, that if anyone ever came calling for me when I was not home, they were never to reveal my whereabouts. I paid well; more, I knew, than many patrician households, and so I was as certain as I could reasonably be of their loyalty. "And yes, given your wish to speak privately last night, I thought we'd best have no listening ears." I laughed, a bit uneasily. "Though I confess I've become a bit nervous at what I might learn from my casual inquiry."

Felicita sighed. "It may be nothing, what I'm about to tell you," she said. "Or it may be . . . something. Quite something. That's why it wouldn't have done for us to be overheard last night."

I waited for Felicita to ask me why I wanted to know, why I was asking about Ambrogio Malatesta at all, but thankfully, she didn't. Instead, she simply launched into her recitation.

"So, as I said, and as you no doubt already knew, Senator Gritti is one of my lovers," she began. "He asked me to tell him whatever I knew about Ambrogio Malatesta, and hinted that if I could learn more, that might be very beneficial to him."

"How so?" I asked.

She lowered her voice, likely out of habit, as we were behind closed doors in my own home. "Apparently," she said, "since his tenure on the Council of Ten began, Malatesta has begun amassing a great deal of power and influence."

"Is that so unusual when a man sits on the Ten?" I asked.

"No," Felicita said, "but in Malatesta's case, it is apparently an unusual amount of influence. More than most men in government have."

"Malatesta?" I asked incredulously. "He is not . . . much of a charmer." I decided to leave it at that.

"No," she agreed, "not that I know him well. But apparently, in the halls of power he is passionate, an excellent debater, a persuasive reasoner, and sharply intelligent. It has led many men to respect him and to follow where he leads."

That was all it took, I supposed. And Malatesta was wily and ruthless enough to exploit such gifts to the fullest. That, perhaps, was the difference between him and other men who were also persuasive, intelligent, and all the rest.

"And according to Gritti," Felicita went on, "Malatesta's level of influence has grown to such a level that the doge himself is rather discomfited by it."

That made me sit up straighter. "Really."

"Yes."

Interesting. *Very* interesting. But how to use it?

Yet Felicita was not done. No, far from it.

"I did not turn up much gossip about Malatesta at first," she went on. "But then Gritti told me something else. Apparently Malatesta plans to introduce legislation to abolish the term limits for serving on the Council of Ten."

I gasped. This—this was shocking. There were term limits everywhere in the Venetian government, save for those pertaining to the doge himself, and the ones for the Council of Ten were the strictest: a man could serve only one year—and then never again. It had all been designed that way specifically to prevent any one man from becoming too powerful, too popular. Venetians detested nothing in their politics so much as a cult of personality; almost as much as they detested things like the plague or economic unrest.

"Yes, I know," Felicita went on. "Apparently members would still need to be elected to the Council each year, but the same men could be elected as many times as they choose to enter their name into the running."

"But why would anyone even consider this?"

Felicita hesitated, but only for a moment. "Apparently, Malatesta is working on uncovering evidence of a great conspiracy by the Turks to overthrow the Republic," she said. "The Ten as a whole is involved, of course, but he is the one who first became aware of it. I don't know how. His case for this legislation, then, is that he must be allowed to stay on the Council to continue investigating and to continue sniffing out anyone who may be involved, within Venice or without. And by extension, in the future, should such plots be uncovered, the men of the Ten could have the opportunity to see them through and make any response more seamless."

"He goes to Constantinople several times a year," Malatesta had said of Bastiano. Did he truly think Bastiano was somehow involved in this Turkish conspiracy, then?

If there even *was* any such conspiracy.

It was plausible, certainly. The Ottoman Empire was both Venice's greatest enemy and most important trading partner. It was safe to assume that the Turks were always plotting *something* to Venice's disadvantage.

But . . . an overthrow? From what I knew—and I knew a great deal—they weren't likely to be capable of such a thing. The Ottoman Empire was vast, and maintaining it left them with few further resources for conquest, especially of a state as wealthy and well defended as Venice.

There would be many, both in government and without, who would believe it, though. Hatred and fear of the Turks was not uncommon in Venice. It would take little enough to convince the right people that such a coup attempt was coming, especially if it was a member of the Council of Ten who was sharing that information. It would make people afraid, and people who were afraid would do all sorts of terrible things. Including dissolve one of the most sacred precepts of their government—and perhaps create a tyrant in the process.

I was making a lot of assumptions, of course. Perhaps too many. But Dioniso Secco's dying words came back to me, as well: *"Malatesta . . . he wanted . . . I wouldn't do . . . he thought I would agree to . . ."*

Had Malatesta tried to involve Secco—rich, influential Secco—in some conspiracy of his own? And had I essentially killed Secco for refusing?

I didn't know. I could not, perhaps, ever know for sure. But the leaden feeling in my gut made me think it was so, that this was what had not felt right from the beginning about Secco's assassination. It had nothing to do with Murano glass. It was about Malatesta's political power.

It was becoming clearer now. Bastiano—or those with whom he was working—had uncovered Malatesta's plot, and so needed to be eliminated before he could present proof to the rest of the Council of Ten. And that would solve two problems for Malatesta: remove the meddling Bastiano Bragadin and get me firmly under his thumb all at once.

Felicita had been studying me silently as I worked through all of this in my head. "I see that I have told you what you were wishing to know," she said.

"Yes," I said. "I . . . did not quite comprehend exactly what I wished to know, really. But yes. This was it."

"Gritti has asked me to find out who supports Malatesta's legislation, who would vote for it," Felicita said. "And it has support. From men belonging to old and powerful families. More than I would have thought."

"Who?" I asked.

"Cornaro, Tron, Corner, Gradenigo, Morosini, Querini," she listed, naming some of the most important Venetian families. I was startled—but not truly surprised—to hear the name of my most odious lover on the list. "There are others who have said nothing about it as yet, like Loredan. Not that anyone knows of, anyway. Gritti is opposed, of course," she added, almost as an afterthought. "That is why he is using me to get information, that he might undermine Malatesta's efforts."

"Are any other powerful men opposed?"

"According to what Gritti hears, the doge is not in favor," Felicita said. "That wouldn't matter if the Senate voted for it, though, of course. Let's see . . . Bembo is opposed, as is Barberini. Foscari has expressed disapproval, but Gritti fears he might be swayed. Bragadin seems opposed as well but is mostly keeping his own counsel." She arched an eyebrow at me. "But you would know Bragadin's thoughts better than I."

Further proof, then, that Bastiano's father was working against Malatesta. But I replied lightly, "The senator? No. We are not truly acquainted."

"Ah. Just the son, then. The third son, yes?"

"Yes. Bastiano."

"Yes. Him, you are very well acquainted with, I believe." She winked at me.

I laughed, but my mind was whirring again as the pieces clicked into place. Malatesta's conspiracy, then, was indeed what Bastiano had been looking into on behalf of his father. Senator Bragadin was opposed to the legislation and suspected that something else was afoot. He had tasked his son with finding out more, and now Bastiano was in hiding. It was all of a piece.

Oh, Felicita was well informed indeed. For a moment my mind flitted back to the initials on the letter I'd found in Bastiano's satchel. Perhaps "FC" had been Felicita, after all. But she was very clearly working on behalf of Senator Gritti; would she have any reason to be corresponding with Bastiano herself? I did not know that they were acquainted. And besides, I could not rid myself of the near certainty that the handwriting on that letter had been a man's.

"And then there is Dioniso Secco," Felicita said.

My head snapped up. "What of him?" I demanded.

"He was a client of yours, was he not?" she asked. "Surely you heard what happened to him."

"Of course," I said, guilt twisting my insides. "Awful. But what of it? I heard it may have been an accident." I felt guiltier still, lying to Felicita so boldly, but what choice did I have?

"Maybe," she said reluctantly. "But his death alarmed Senator Gritti greatly. Secco had been vocally opposed to Malatesta's proposal. And then he turned up dead."

I forced a laugh, which sounded even to me too high and shrill. "Surely you're not suggesting . . ."

She shrugged. "I suggest nothing. I am merely saying that Senator Gritti thinks there is something suspicious about Secco's death. Make of that what you will."

Oh, I would make more of that than Felicita could ever possibly know. Secco had died for Malatesta's own ends, and he had used me to do it. Bastiano and his associates, whoever they were, had discovered that to be true. But, at least as of when I'd discovered Bastiano's papers, they had no hard proof of it.

Perhaps it was a ridiculous notion, given that Secco had died by my own hand, but I thought that if I could somehow destroy Malatesta before he destroyed me, Secco's death might at least be avenged.

"And where does Anzolo Balbi fit into all this, for you?" I asked aloud, on a whim.

She looked sharply up at me, and I could see the calculations going on behind her eyes: wondering how much I knew and how I knew it. Then, like the dawning light of morning, I saw her recall the party at Ottaviano Lotti's palazzo and how I had spied her and Balbi having a whispered exchange in the corner. "Ah," she said. "Ah yes."

I could not resist a smirk. "You are good, Felicita, but a bit more discretion might be warranted. Believe me, I know."

She looked somewhat startled at that, at what I was admitting, but then acknowledged my advice with a quick nod. "You are right," she said. "But Balbi . . ." She looked away. "That is a . . . separate intrigue, and not relevant here."

"I see," I said, and let the matter drop. I felt much the same as I had the night I'd witnessed her and Balbi together: both angry and sad that the courtesans of Venice were used by its wealthy men in such a way, beyond the scope of our profession. Truly men saw us as tools to be used, and nothing more, even as Malatesta had said.

I realized, however, in thinking over all I had learned that day, that in doing so, they gave us more power than they knew. They gave us their secrets and were fool enough to think that we would not use them.

"I must thank you, Felicita," I said. "Truly and sincerely. You have told me everything I could have wanted to know, and more."

"It is no trouble," she said. "You have fed me and given me wine, after all." Her face turned serious again. "You did not hear all of this from me, though."

"No. Of course not."

Our talk turned to other things then, more casual, frivolous gossip, and much as I enjoyed Felicita's company—and she did have some truly hilarious stories—I could not help but wish to be left alone, that I might better consider what I had learned and how I could use it.

When, the better part of an hour later, she rose to take her leave, I put a hand on her arm, stopping her for a moment before I summoned Lauretta. "Felicita," I said, "there is one more thing I wish to know."

She regarded me slightly warily. "What?"

"You never asked me why I wished to know anything about Malatesta," I said. "Why? Why tell me all this when you don't even know my reasons?"

She looked at me a bit incredulously, as though she couldn't quite comprehend why I was asking. Then she shrugged. "Your reasons are your own, and I assume they are good ones," she said. "I count you as a friend, Valentina, and certainly wish to help you if I can." She hesitated a moment. "And," she added, "if you wish Malatesta some ill, then I assume you have a good reason for that as well. With everything I now know about the man, I would not be surprised if you did. And that, too, is your business." She smiled, but it was a smile with a jagged edge. "We courtesans must look out for one another, when all is said and done. No one else will if we do not."

The Council of Ten and the Senate might run Venice and their own corner of Europe, but I realized that at the same time there was a council of women behind them, in their shadow, who had pieces of the mosaic of power but did not often have occasion to put them together.

But now we would, now that we had reason to. Now *I* would.

I was surprised to find tears stinging my eyes, but I quickly blinked them back. "Thank you, Felicita," I said, taking her hand and squeezing it. "Truly. And if there is any way I can ever return the favor, then do not hesitate to ask."

"Oh, I won't," she said, her breezy, fun-loving personality back. She grinned. "You may count on it, in fact."

Chapter 20

The next day, while I was still sorting through all the information Felicita Cavazza had given me, Amalia dropped by. She swept into my sitting room, dressed in a pale pink day dress I had never seen before and sporting a beautiful strand of pink pearls to match, with her dark hair braided and pinned up on her head.

"Amalia," I said, rising and kissing her on both cheeks in greeting. "You look like a spring day on this autumn afternoon."

She laughed. "That is a great deal of whimsy from you of all people," she remarked. "In a fine mood, are you?"

I was not, of course, but I had to pretend that I was. "As fine as ever," I said lightly, as I rang for Lauretta to bring us some refreshments. "Especially now that you are here. It has been too long, I fear."

"It is always too long," she agreed, sitting down and settling her skirts around her. "My clients seem to be feeling as though it is spring as well." She waggled her eyebrows. "My schedule has been quite full, even more so than usual."

"I did not think your schedule could get any fuller," I observed, pouring some wine.

"Nor did I, but it seems to have happened," she said with a sigh. "That Ottaviano Lotti keeps me busier than most."

"Does he?" I asked. "And his attentions remain pleasing to you, then?"

Her eyes sparked. "Oh, most pleasing. There is something he does with his tongue that I never even imagined . . ."

She went on to detail just what the apparently divine Lotti did with his tongue and what it did to her in turn. I laughed and giggled just as though this were any other conversation we were having, on any other day, when we compared notes on our lovers and shared tips and tricks of the trade. As though the lives of the man I loved and my daughter did not hang in the balance.

Once we left the topic of Ottaviano Lotti, the conversation moved into some gossip Amalia had heard at a party a few nights ago, about how a certain patrician had utterly lost his head and asked his courtesan mistress to marry him. The courtesan in question, a woman of both of our acquaintance named Simona Poselina, had turned him down flatly, though he had apparently been back to her palazzo many times since to insist she accept.

"Simona told him that she makes more money in her current profession than she would ever have access to as his wife," Amalia reported. She laughed. "Can you imagine?"

"Good for her," I said, momentarily diverted by this story that I had not heard yet. "I'm sure it's true."

"Of course it's true. Simona is much sought after these days."

"I suppose she is," I said, thinking back. "She's been at every gathering I've been at for some months."

"Indeed. And his family would never accept her, not for a moment. She'd spend her married life never hearing a civil word from any of his relations. Why turn her back on everything she has for a life of misery and less money?" Amalia shook her head at the very thought. "She's a smart woman."

"And skilled, apparently," I said. "Perhaps we ought to be asking her what her tricks are, that she has patrician men proposing marriage to her."

"Neither of us needs help from the likes of her," Amalia said. "Besides, as we see, patrician men proposing marriage are more trouble than they're worth. I'd rather make my own money. After all, what is a wife but a modestly dressed whore who owns nothing of her own?"

I could not argue with that—at least not based on what I had seen of Venetian patrician marriages.

A lull came over the conversation then, and before I could think better of it, I decided to bring up the topic most on my mind. "Speaking of gossip," I said as casually as I could, "I wonder if you might have some for me about a particular man."

"Oh! Who?" Amalia demanded, leaning forward. "A new client?"

"Not exactly," I said. "I was just curious about something I overheard recently . . . and, well, what do you know of Ambrogio Malatesta?"

Amalia froze—just for an instant, but I saw it, nonetheless. Anyone else would have missed it, but not me. "Ambrogio Malatesta?" she asked, her tone as falsely casual as mine had been a moment ago. "Why do you ask?"

"Oh, Niccolo related something interesting he heard about him, and I wondered if it was true," I said airily. "That's all."

"Hmm," she said, sitting back, as if to buy herself time. "I know what everyone else knows, I suppose: that he is very ambitious, currently a member of the Council of Ten, keeps mostly to himself, is not much out in society. And widowed too."

My heart sank as I realized she had nothing more to say about the man—not because she didn't know anything else, but because she did not wish to share it, for whatever reason. And I noticed she did not point out, as Margarita had, that Malatesta was allegedly one of my lovers, and therefore shouldn't I know more about him than she did? I had never discussed Malatesta with her before in any capacity, for obvious reasons, and yet it was almost as though she knew he was not really my lover. What I made of that, I wasn't sure, but I marked it all the same.

"That is all I know as well," I said. I heaved a fake sigh. "Ah well."

"Why do you ask?" she said again. "What was Niccolo's gossip?"

"Oh, nothing exciting," I said, waving a hand. "Just a bit of political intrigue; something that I thought might help Agosto Zorzi. Think no more of it."

I reached for one of the bits of cheese on a small platter on the table, ready to turn away from the subject as if it were indeed of no real import, when Amalia put her hand out and caught my wrist. I looked up at her, surprised, and found that her lovely, usually warm brown eyes were rather severe. "Ambrogio Malatesta is a dangerous man, Valentina," she said softly, her eyes never leaving mine. "Whatever you are up to, whatever you are seeking to learn about him, for whatever reason—leave it."

I withdrew my hand, and she let me. "I can't imagine what you're thinking, Amalia," I said, my light tone belying the churning in my stomach. "It was just a bit of political gossip I was after, nothing more."

"Leave it," she repeated. "It isn't worth crossing him—not for Agosto, not for Niccolo, not for anyone. Whatever it is isn't worth it. Just . . . don't, Valentina."

"You know something you aren't saying."

She looked away from me then. "Perhaps," she said. "But it isn't anything I can repeat."

"Amalia, tell me."

She looked back at me. "Just stay away from Ambrogio Malatesta, Valentina. Please."

A chill settled over me at the certainty in her voice, at the trace of fear in it. "Very well," I lied. "I will."

CHAPTER 21

I tossed and turned much of that night, sleep eluding me. At least I was alone, thank goodness, even as my traitorous body and heart yearned for Bastiano beside me, to wrap me in his arms and soothe me.

I did think, more than once, that perhaps I *should* take the risk of contacting him, letting him know what Malatesta had asked me to do and how long he'd given me to do it. We could then both put our rather impressive minds together and find a way out, find a way to solve the problem.

But time and time again, I returned to the realization that I could not do any such thing. Not yet. Maybe not ever. He would try to do something brave, something rash. And I could not take the risk of Malatesta finding out that I had told Bastiano of his order. Ginevra's life was surely forfeit if I did.

Everything I had done, all that I had sacrificed to try to protect my daughter had been for naught. She had been drawn into the danger of my work for the Ten just as I had always feared she would be. But there was nothing for it now. The only thing I could do was try to find a way out of this web of conspiracy Malatesta had me trapped in, as labyrinthine as the dark and winding canals of Venice herself.

Nor could I risk that my sending word to Bastiano would reveal his location to Malatesta. No doubt he had henchmen watching me; he might even be hoping that I would try to contact Bastiano or go to him in person, thus revealing his hiding place and letting Malatesta send another assassin after him. Then he needn't wait to see if I would actually kill my lover.

But hopefully such measures were not necessary. Felicita Cavazza had given me plenty of information, more than I'd dared hope. All that remained now was to determine how best it might be used to my advantage, something I was still not quite certain how to do.

That Malatesta was ambitious was clearly well known to all, but trying to change such a long-standing and dearly held aspect of the Venetian government as the term limits for the Council of Ten was very bold, bolder than I'd ever thought he would dare be.

And yet it *was* being entertained, and by some very powerful men—that much was plain. Zuan Gradenigo, head of yet another very powerful, very old Venetian family, was rumored to be serving as one of the Tre Capi, the Three Heads of the Ten, this month. Each member of the Ten took turns serving as one of the heads for a month at a time, and during that month those men were forbidden from leaving the Doge's Palace, for fear that they might be compromised by opposing interests during their tenure. Such was the power the Capi held. So if Gradenigo was in favor, along with the patriarchs of all those other powerful families that Felicita had named, then it most certainly had a chance.

And that terrified me.

And then there was Dioniso Secco, of course. Dead because he had opposed Malatesta, or so Senator Gritti suspected.

And he was right.

Secco's last words, which would never truly leave me, came back in force: *"Malatesta . . . he wanted . . . I wouldn't do . . . he thought I would agree to . . ."*

As I'd pointed out to Malatesta when he'd first given me the assignment, Dioniso Secco had been a man with considerable influence and powerful friends. What if Malatesta had asked Secco not only to support his proposed legislation but to persuade his political allies to do the same?

And when Secco had refused, Malatesta had sent me after him, had decided that the man needed to die for his refusal to cooperate and for his potential to thwart Malatesta's plans. In the end, as Secco lay dying from the poison, he had known Malatesta was behind it.

That explained everything. And it confirmed that Malatesta had used me, used me as though I were a mindless killing machine to eliminate his political opponents. And I had gone along with it, had swallowed the story he'd fed me about Secco meaning to betray the secrets of the glass to the French.

I had, in fact, killed an innocent man, one who was likely trying to *protect* the Venetian Republic, not harm it.

I closed my eyes and let the guilt burn through me. I had gotten so lost in my desire to protect those who needed it that I had allowed that desire to become twisted, to be used against those who meant to help and not harm. I had asked hardly any questions of Malatesta; had perhaps doubted but had shoved those doubts aside.

Was it any wonder Malatesta thought me a remorseless killer, a monster who would not ultimately balk at killing her own lover?

But no more. I was not Ambrogio Malatesta's creature anymore.

What of Senator Gritti, then? What if I went to him with what I knew? He was clearly working against Malatesta himself.

If I gave him the missing pieces he did not yet have, perhaps he could bring Malatesta up on charges of treason and whatever else he deemed fit. I could let the state I had fought so hard to protect now protect me and mine.

But of course I, too, was implicated in Malatesta's conspiracy by the fact that I had killed Secco. I could not confess that Malatesta had given the order for Secco's assassination without also confessing that my hand had administered the poison. And then what would become of me? Could I expect that Gritti, that the Council of Ten, would simply look the other way and not see me punished for murder? Would it matter that I had thought I was doing the Ten's bidding?

I honestly did not know, and I did not want to find out.

And even if the Ten themselves didn't punish me, Malatesta had made it quite clear, by having the body of his henchman left outside my door, what he did to those who knew too much and were no longer useful. Maybe he'd decide my access to Bastiano was no longer quite so convenient and have both me and Ginevra done away with. I couldn't take the chance.

But clearly Malatesta had other enemies besides me. Enemies within the halls of power. Enemies who might be able to help me, wittingly or unwittingly.

"Supposedly the doge himself is a bit discomfited by Malatesta's level of influence," Felicita had said.

"Ambrogio Malatesta is a dangerous man, Valentina. It isn't worth crossing him," Amalia had said.

Somehow, eventually, I fell asleep, with these words and my own ruminations gnawing away at my mind, like a rat with a crust of bread.

And when I woke up, I had an idea.

Chapter 22

I sat at my desk in my study, the parchment in front of me covered with sharp, spiky letters. I had tried as best as I could to disguise my handwriting. I wished I could have had Marta or Lauretta copy the letter for me, but that would have involved them learning its contents, and I couldn't have that. No one else could know what I was doing, what I was about to do.

I would place this letter in a bocca di leone. Bocche di leone were carvings in the shape of the lion of San Marco, that great symbol of Venice, located in various locations throughout the city, including one in the courtyard of the Doge's Palace. The lions' mouths gaped open, leading to a locked box where letters could be placed and later collected by one of the servants of the Ten. If one knew of some illegal activity or some plot against the state or any of its agents, one could slip a letter into a lion's mouth, to denounce the individual or individuals involved. And then could rest assured that the matter would be looked into. Letters slid into the lion's mouth were received and reviewed by the Council of Ten, who would take whatever action they deemed necessary. It was a rather ingenious way to allow and encourage Venetian citizens to monitor and police one another, and certainly true danger had been averted at times by letters put into a bocca di leone. It had also always seemed to me a good way to get revenge on anyone against whom one had a personal grudge, though one assumed many of the submitted letters were easily revealed to be petty nonsense. But now, for the first time in my life and hopefully the last, I would make use of it.

I read over my words once more, trying to see them with an objective eye, trying to judge whether they sounded convincing. Not only Bastiano's and Ginevra's lives but likely my own as well depended on this letter being as convincing as possible.

Esteemed signori of the Council of Ten,

I am a citizen of this our Venetian Republic, and as such feel it my duty to inform you of an act of treachery of which I have recently become aware. It grieves me to report that the perpetrator of this act is one who has professed to serve our Most Serene Republic and to put his interests before its own. Alas, in this sacred obligation he has fallen gravely short.

I have learned that one Ambrogio Malatesta, current member of the Council of Ten, has yielded to the basest self-interest of mankind and is seeking to undermine the authority of His Serenity, the doge, as well as of your good Council. Just a few months past, he authorized the assassination of Venetian citizen Dioniso Secco without approval from any other authority.

I have come to understand that he committed this act out of a desire to cover up his own treachery and double-dealing. Ambrogio Malatesta seeks to increase his own power at the expense of others on the Council, and of the doge himself, thus making him the true power in Venice and subverting the architecture of the Venetian state. He has invented a conspiracy by the Ottoman Empire against Venice, to try to increase his own power and pressure members of both the Great Council and the Senate to agree to extend the term limits for those on the Council of Ten, himself of course included.

This was a gamble. I did not know *for certain* that there was no Turkish conspiracy. There might well be. But that did not change the fact that, real or invented, Malatesta was trying to use Venice and Venetian's fears of our greatest adversary in his attempt to seize power. It was diabolical. I continued to read over my words.

In furtherance of this aim, he has also recently ordered the murder of the son of an old Venetian patrician house, who has learned information about Malatesta and his conspiracy that Malatesta does not wish to be known. And so Malatesta has abused his authority by attempting to eliminate a man whom he sees as a threat to his position and his quest for power.

If Ambrogio Malatesta is allowed to continue unchecked, I fear, from what I know of him and his actions, that he will stop at nothing to eliminate those who oppose him, which may include yourselves, his fellow council members.

I beg you, esteemed signori, to investigate these claims I have laid before you, and to put a stop to Malatesta's deadly abuses of power. He cannot be allowed to continue unchecked and put Venetian citizens—and Venice herself—at risk.

I signed the letter, not with my name, but simply *A Venetian.* This, too, was a gamble. It was known that the Ten took letters of denunciation less seriously when they were unsigned. But I hoped the nature of the accusations, and of the man I was accusing, would at least give them pause, would compel them to at least ask a few questions.

I only needed to make them doubt Malatesta, which, given that there was already opposition to him within the government, shouldn't take much doing.

I read it through once more and could think of nothing else to say, no better way to say it. There was plenty here to get the rest of the members of the Ten to at least ask questions. To look at their colleague in a new and less favorable light. Certain anonymous letters had raised suspicion with even less information, if all the things I'd heard over the years were to be believed. And I knew for a fact that I had killed more than one man whose name had first come to the Ten's attention in a letter slipped into a bocca di leone.

I folded the letter carefully and sealed it with a bit of wax. I would have to wait until nightfall. I had already canceled my client for that evening, a member of the Great Council who was of no particular consequence and not especially generous, in bed or out of it.

Was it a half-mad scheme? Yes. Was it desperate? Yes. Was it rather foolishly reckless? Again, yes.

But I had to try. I had to roll the dice, even with everything dear to me hanging in the balance, and hope that I rolled the winning numbers.

⋆ ⋆ ⋆

It was just before midnight when Luca pulled the gondola up to one of the docks at San Marco. I parted the curtains of the felze and looked around but did not see anyone nearby. Luca offered me his hand, and I stepped out onto the dock. "Wait here," I said to him in a low voice. "I will be back very soon."

He nodded, not replying.

I crossed the stretch of cobblestones between the docks and the Doge's Palace, the massive pink-and-cream stone facade dwarfing me, its Gothic arches and stonework looking menacing as jagged teeth in the darkness.

My heart pounded as I slipped through the entryway and into the courtyard, glancing furtively about from beneath the hood of my cloak. *Swiftly and quietly, Valentina,* I told myself. *No one will ever know you've been here.*

I did not know why I was so nervous. I had cut a man's throat in the middle of a crowd and been less nervous.

Once the letter left my hand, the situation would spin out of my control—more so than it had already. If this did not work, then I did not know what I would do. It was not a feeling I cared for, not when so much of my life had already been dictated by circumstances outside of my control. But I did not see that I had a choice.

I had to try.

I clung to the shadows of the colonnade that ringed the courtyard, knowing there would be the eyes of guards on me, that I'd not be able to advance farther than this courtyard should I try. I glanced up at the staircase that dominated the space. The traitorous doge who had tried to overthrow the Great Council and Senate, Marino Falier, had been executed at the foot of those stairs a few hundred years ago. I allowed a small smile to touch my lips as I imagined a similar fate for Ambrogio Malatesta.

It was a satisfying image, yet not nearly as satisfying as the thought of killing him myself.

Along the wall, I found what I sought. I realized then, as I took in the grotesquely carved lion with its gaping maw, that I had never set eyes on this particular bocca di leone before. Yet it was an object of such legend in Venice that everyone was certain they had seen it at one point or another.

I stood before it and withdrew the letter from an interior pocket of my cloak. I held the parchment tightly between my fingers, thinking through what I was doing and all the possible outcomes—and everything that could go wrong—one last time.

Then I thrust the letter into the lion's mouth, where it was swallowed into the darkness and taken somewhere out of sight. Hopefully into the hands of someone who could, and would, help me. And help Bastiano and Ginevra. And Venice.

I turned around and left swiftly, back the way I'd come, and only exhaled once I was back on the dock and Luca was helping me into the gondola.

The die was cast. I could only wait and see if my gamble had paid off.

Interlude

Florence, June 1527

Fernando Cortes and I sat atop our horses. Cortes had stolen one on the road for me, and I was thankful my father had insisted I learn to ride when I was younger. We looked at the city of Florence spread out in the valley below us, baking under the hot summer sun. Nestled among the rolling emerald hills of Tuscany, it looked rather charming: red tile roofs all spread around at the base of the enormous Duomo, its dome towering over everything.

It was an impressive structure, true, but I knew that St. Peter's Basilica in Rome would someday surpass it when it was finally completed. But would I ever get to see it? Did I ever even want to return to Rome?

I shoved those thoughts away. No point in dwelling on where I had come from. It was where I was going that mattered, and that was what Cortes wanted to discuss just then.

"It seems a lovely place," he was saying. "Florence. I'm sure there's a fine convent here that will take you in, and it's not so very far from . . ." He trailed off.

I wrinkled my nose. Cortes was determined to leave me in the care of a convent, and he was correct in that it was the only respectable place left for me. That did not mean I had any desire to be locked away behind a convent's walls. Never to attend a banquet again, or wear fine clothes or jewelry, or make love . . .

Perhaps, given all that I had lost, the thought of losing such things shouldn't have bothered me. But it did. Shouldn't I be able to keep some of my former life, at least? Why should every little thing I had once enjoyed or taken pleasure in be forbidden to me? I had survived while everyone I loved had died. Did I not owe it to them, and to myself, to make the most of my life?

"I'd rather keep going," I said in response to Cortes. "On to Venice."

He glanced sidelong at me. "Are you sure? Your journey could end here, you know. You could begin to move on."

"My journey isn't over," I said. "And I told you, I've always wanted to see Venice." It was true. My father had traveled there many times on business, and I'd always begged him to take me, but he'd always refused. Massimo had promised to take me for a visit once we were married, but . . . I'd be seeing the city without him. I pushed that thought away as well. "A city that floats on water . . . who wouldn't wish to see such a sight?"

"If you're sure," he said.

"I am," I said. I reached over and playfully shoved his shoulder. "And besides, you've not finished teaching me to fight. If I stay here, I'll never learn enough to beat you."

A smile tugged at his lips. "Yes, that's true," he said. "Very well, then. I've got a bit of coin; we'll spend the night in an inn. Get a proper night's sleep for once." He clucked to his horse.

I was hardly about to argue with that after weeks of sleeping on the cold, hard ground. As we began to ride down the hill toward the city, I noticed that the smile had stayed on

Cortes's face—a rare sight. "You are glad I'm staying with you," I said, part incredulous, part teasing. "You'd miss me if our ways parted here, wouldn't you?"

"Never said any such thing," he said gruffly.

But still his smile remained.

CHAPTER 23

The next few days and nights went on very much as usual. I was, as always, frequently engaged, and saw a client each night, including Niccolo once. I went to parties and dazzled rooms with my wit and conversation and recitation of poetry, had fine meals prepared for my lovers, and made love with all the skill and enjoyment I could muster. Yet I spent each conversation, each turn about a room, listening carefully for any trace or hint of the gossip I was hoping to hear: that Ambrogio Malatesta had fallen from favor, that he had been removed from the Council of Ten. That he was being investigated and his palazzo had been searched. That he had disappeared. By the Virgin, even that he'd left the Doge's Palace in a huff one day. Anything. Anything that might clue me in that my letter, my desperate gamble, had worked.

But there was nothing, and I did not dare ask anyone for further word or gossip of him. I had done as much of that as I dared, and it wouldn't do to draw too much notice from those in power. More than I already had, anyway.

I had known, somewhere in the back of my mind, that this was how this particular gambit was likely to play out. I would not know for some time if it had had any effect whatsoever, if I would ever know for certain. If my letter had done what I hoped it would, I would need to wait to hear the whispers in a crowded drawing room, or innuendos around a dining table. If Felicita heard something, I had no doubt that she would tell me. But perhaps she hadn't or had but couldn't discreetly tell me.

I had known the waiting, the limbo, would come, but living in the reality of it, living in the uncertainty, was a different matter altogether. I could not live with the not knowing forever, not when my daughter's safety was at stake.

But for the time being, I went about my business, on edge the entire time but putting up a facade such that no one would ever have known. Because I had no choice.

Perhaps a week after dropping my letter in the bocca di leone, I was in my dressing room, wearing only my underthings, as Marta pinned up my hair for a night out.

Without warning, the door to my dressing room burst open, flung with such force that it crashed against the wall. Marta shrieked, and I jumped up from my seat at the dressing table, eyes flying to a chest of drawers across the room, in which was housed the nearest weapon. Could I get to it before the intruder was upon us?

But then I saw who had stormed into the room, face filled with a wrath to rival one of the old Olympian gods: Ambrogio Malatesta.

He had emerged from the protection of the Doge's Palace. And he had walked into the lioness's den, as it were. I *had* to get to that knife.

"How dare you," he seethed, his breath coming in heavy pants, as though he had run to my palazzo from whatever corner of hell in which he dwelt.

But first, I had to make sure my servants were safe. Behind him, I saw Lauretta cowering in the doorway. "Madonna, I'm sorry! He pushed past me, knocked me right over, he did, and I cannot find Luca," she babbled.

"It's all right, Lauretta," I said. "Go." I glanced over at Marta. "You too."

Marta's eyes were wide with fear, but even so she gave me a look that clearly said, *"I do not wish to leave you."*

"Go," I repeated, and she scurried around me, past Malatesta, and out the door with Lauretta.

Malatesta thankfully ignored the two women completely, his eyes locked on me as he approached. "How dare you," he said again. "You deceitful whore."

"How dare *you*?" I spat, my chin raised defiantly as I met his eyes. Though I wasn't much given to modesty, I was suddenly aware of how thin and sheer my underthings were, and I wished dearly that I were dressed properly for this confrontation. But it could not be helped. "How dare *you* come storming into my home and my private room without permission, and how *dare* you lay hands on one of my maids." I reached out and shoved him away, and he was surprised enough, even in his rage, that he stumbled back. "I've killed men for less, as you well know."

"Don't you presume to lecture me, you treacherous bitch!"

Had this been any other time, had there been less at stake, I would have commented acidly on the fact that men seemed low on creativity when it came to insulting women. *Bitch* and *whore* were all they were ever able to come up with. And as I cheerfully acknowledged being both, it was rather less than insulting.

Malatesta brandished something in my face. "I know what you did. Did you think I would not? Did you think I would never find out? Are you truly that stupid?"

I recognized the piece of parchment as though it were an old favorite handkerchief.

My letter. The letter I'd slipped in the bocca di leone. He had it.

By the Shadow God, I thought I'd planned for everything, or at least the most likely outcomes. I had no idea who collected the letters from the bocca di leone, but I'd never dreamed it was Malatesta himself. Or even if it hadn't been, that a letter denouncing him would make its way to his hands. There had only been a slim possibility that the letter would end up with him, or so I'd thought. I had been willing to gamble on the odds that there were enough other members of the Ten that one of them might see it first.

Yet clearly I had lost.

But I'd be damned if I'd admit that I was beaten. I needed to keep him talking, needed him to relax his guard so that I might cross the room and get to my dagger. I snatched the letter from his hand and read it over—or pretended to. My heart was pounding loudly, and I was filled with so much dread that I could not focus on the words on the page; could barely see them. But I let my eyes skitter over the page as if I were reading, and after a moment I looked back up at Malatesta. "What is this?" I asked coldly, handing it back to him pinched between my thumb and forefinger, as though it were a dirty rag.

He snatched it from my hand, so roughly that the edge tore slightly. "Don't pretend you don't know, you lying slut. You *wrote* it."

Ah yes, *slut*, the third insult always flung at women. How had I forgotten? I ought to have known that one was coming as well. "I wrote no such thing," I said, my voice dripping with disdain, as though I were a queen receiving a particularly rude petitioner. "Is this the reason you forced your way into my home and manhandled my maid? To accuse me of writing some nonsense?"

Malatesta let out a bark of laughter. "Oh, you are a fine actress, truly, Valentina," he spat. "A lesser man would be fooled entirely. I can well see how you bewitch all those poor bastards who flock to your bed."

"Rich words coming from you, who wanted to be one of the poor bastards in my bed," I shot back.

Utter fury flared in his eyes, and for a moment I was certain he would strike me—or try, anyway. I rather wished he would, that the altercation would finally become physical, for I knew I would best him, and how I would relish it. But he only began to speak again, his rage barely leashed as his voice came out low and tight, hissing through clenched teeth. "Let us dispense with any further pretense that you know nothing of this letter. You wrote it. Do not insult me."

"I have no damned idea what you're talking about, but—"

Malatesta slammed a hand down on my dressing table, causing the various bottles and hair implements to jump and clatter back into place. I flinched at the sudden motion; I could not help it.

"You thought you could outwit me," he jeered, drawing close, thrusting his face near mine. I did not back away, but met his gaze squarely. "You thought that you, a whore who sells her body and her soul for money, could outsmart a patrician of the Venetian Republic. A member of the Council of Ten. And what's more, you *dared.* You dared try to betray me, to ruin me." He crumpled the parchment in his hand and threw it to the floor. "You failed. You were always doomed to fail. Surely even *you* realize that."

I was done holding my tongue, done pretending, "Surely even *you* realize," I blazed, "that you could not command me to kill the one man I love and that I would just meekly do your bidding. Surely you know me better than that, Malatesta. Surely *you* were not so foolish and shortsighted as to think I would take this lying down."

"Isn't that how you always take things, Valentina? Lying down?" He laughed harshly. "Or on your knees or from behind, I suppose—"

"Fuck you, Malatesta," I said, shoving him back, trying to edge around him. "Get out of my house."

"I will not," he snarled, advancing on me again. My legs bumped against my dressing chair, and I stumbled and found myself sitting in it. I moved to stand, not wanting to be at any disadvantage in this confrontation, but Malatesta swiftly closed the remaining distance, placing both his hands on the arms of the chair and trapping me there. I glanced longingly at the chest of drawers that held a dagger. I could see the large vein in his throat, pulsing beneath his skin with rage, such an easy target . . .

"I could have you killed for this," he growled. "I could haul you to the prisons beneath the Doge's Palace, have you tortured and executed, ruin that pretty skin and face, break that beautiful body . . ."

"Do it, then!" I spat.

"I could kill you here myself, and no one would ever know," he went on. I shifted in my seat slightly, made uncomfortable not so much by the things he was saying as by the way he was saying them. As though sharing with me some long-held fantasy. "No one who mattered, anyway. I could wrap my hands around your throat and choke the life from you. What's one dead whore in a city filled with thousands of them?"

"What's stopping you?" I challenged. "Afraid I'll manage to kill you first? I could, you know. I could, and yet you're too stupid to be afraid of me."

Because we were so close, I could feel the change in his breath as it came shorter and faster; could see his eyes darken as they bored into mine. His grip tightened on the arms of the chair, as though he were trying to hold himself back from something. His eyes traveled over me, as though finally noticing the flimsy shift I was wearing.

My stomach soured and my skin crawled. I could feel his gaze on me like a physical touch. That thwarted lust was as much a part of what he was doing to me as anything else.

He swallowed, and his eyes met mine again. I didn't flinch, didn't look away. "Touch me," I whispered, "and I will kill you."

He remained where he was for a moment, as if transfixed. Then, suddenly, his gaze cleared, as though a spell had been lifted. "I could also," he continued, returning to our previous conversation as though nothing had happened, "have your daughter killed right now. Today. And why shouldn't I, since you've proven yourself most uncooperative?"

I lashed out, raking my nails across his face. He cried out in pain and stumbled back, and I sprang across the room to the chest of drawers. I wrenched open the middle drawer and pulled out the dagger from where it was hidden, grinning like a madwoman as I wrapped my fingers around the handle. I whirled to find Malatesta already advancing on me again, three bloody scratches marring his face. I raised the dagger, and he stopped in his tracks.

"Vicious bitch," he said, raising his hand to his face and scowling as it came away bloody. And then, knowing I was out of reasons not to kill him, he turned and ran. I sprinted after him, dashing out into the hallway, only to see him shove Marta, who'd been coming up the stairs, back down the staircase. I heard her cry of pain as I reached the steps just in time to see Malatesta descend out of sight. I hesitated for just a moment, but I couldn't simply leave Marta lying there, not even for this. I cursed loudly and ran to her side.

Chapter 24

"Marta," I said, dropping the knife as she sat up, looking dazed. "Are you all right?"

"I . . . I think so, Madonna. Just bruised." She winced as she shifted her position. "And you? Did he hurt you?"

"Do not worry about me," I said, helping her to her feet. "Come, let's have you lie down."

I had Marta lie down in the parlor and called Bettina to attend to her. She truly seemed fine, other than the distress and a few bruises; she had not hit her head, which was the important thing. Once she was settled, I called Lauretta and had her help me set my dressing room to rights. That done, I dismissed her and sat down heavily at my dressing table. I needed a moment alone, to think.

I thought back to the words Malatesta had used when he'd first stormed in here with the letter. *"You treacherous bitch . . . You dared try to betray me, to ruin me . . ."*

Never once had he disavowed what I'd written in the letter. Never once had he said any of it was untrue, nor denied it. He might have implicated me in his plot, but he also could not take the risk of handing me over to the Ten. He couldn't be sure they wouldn't believe what I might tell them, just as I couldn't trust them not to side with Malatesta.

But before I could consider any of this further, Bettina appeared in the doorway.

"What is it?" I asked her. "Is Marta all right?"

"She'll be fine," Bettina said. "Something else I wished to speak to you about."

I sighed, not sure I had the energy for whatever this conversation was going to be. "And that is?" I asked wearily.

"I know his maid," she said conversationally. "One of them, anyway. Quite well."

I shook my head. "Whose maid?"

She nodded toward the door. "The man who just stormed in here and then out again. Ambrogio Malatesta, yes?"

I sat up straighter in my chair. "Yes," I said. "Yes, it is."

She nodded. "Yes. Tomasina is her name. The maid who works for him."

"Why are you telling me this?"

Bettina shrugged. "She hates him," she went on. "Her master, that is. Says he's sour and unpleasant, and he strikes her if she displeases him. His staff all hate him, sounds like."

"Interesting," I said, for it was. "And not terribly surprising. But again I shall ask, Bettina—why are you telling me this?"

I had a good idea as to why—was pretty certain, in fact—but I wanted to hear her say it. Wanted to make sure we both understood each other.

Bettina looked hard at me. "I am telling you," she said, "because if you would like information to harm that man, then Tomasina will get it to you."

"Will she?" I breathed, now scarcely able to believe my luck. "And how do you know this?"

Bettina shrugged again. "She's been waiting for a chance like this. Trust me."

"And . . ." My mind quickly began to consider all the possibilities. What did I need? More importantly, what could I *use*? "Can she read?" I asked.

"And write," Bettina said.

Was Malatesta foolish enough to have committed any part of his conspiracy to writing? Certainly he must be sending letters to *someone*; even if they were in code, that might be a place to start. But was there enough time?

It didn't matter. I would take whatever I could get. I had no choice.

But . . . but Tomasina had a choice. And I wanted her to make it for herself. "If she can get me any letters," I began, "I could use anything about Council of Ten business, anything about a conspiracy by the Turks, anything about extending term limits for the Ten." Bettina looked surprised at this last request, but she nodded. "But, Bettina," I added, "only if she wants to and only if she can do so safely. I would not have her put herself at risk."

Bettina waved this away. "She'll do it," she said. "She's long been waiting for a chance like this. If she finds anything of note, she'll bring it to you."

"How can you be so sure?" I demanded, not wanting to get my hopes up.

Bettina smiled slightly. "Tomasina is my daughter."

Interlude

Somewhere in the Veneto, July 1527

I stumbled backward, landing square on my ass in the dirt. Before I could so much as blink, Fernando Cortes's dagger was leveled at my throat.

"And now you're dead," he said in his gruff voice. "Again." He sheathed his dagger in one smooth motion and extended his hand. "Up."

I scowled at him before reluctantly taking his hand and letting him haul me to my feet. I brushed off the seat of my breeches, as if they weren't already filthy after weeks on the road. We were nearing Venice; the river we were sparring beside eventually emptied into the lagoon within which the floating city was ensconced, or so Cortes had told me. We were close, close to the city I'd always wanted to see and a future I'd never wanted. But I'd deal with the looming shadow of the convent later.

"I don't know how you ever expect me to best you," I complained. "You're a soldier. You've been doing this all your life. Everything I try, you have some move to counter it—"

"Excuses," Cortes interrupted. "You're quick enough; you can block a strike and you've learned well enough how to wield that dagger. But you mustn't forget you're a woman."

I glared at him. "If I were likely to forget, I'd remember at least once a month when I start bleeding," I spat. "But if my being of the weaker sex makes me so incapable, then I wondered that you bothered to attempt to teach me at all."

"You're a woman," he went on, as though I hadn't spoken, "and so any man you're fighting against is likely to be bigger than you, and probably stronger as well. You can't keep trying to get into a wrestling match, because you'll lose."

I scowled again; if I kept this up, soon my face would freeze in one of these unbecoming expressions, as my mother had always threatened. But it hurt too much to think of my mother, so I didn't. "What do you mean?"

"I keep telling you, girl. You likely won't win any contests of strength. You've got to use your attacker's strength against him." He gestured to me with his dagger. "Like just now. You blocked my strike, and then you tried to push me away. That's when I knocked you on your ass.

"But," he went on, "if you used my force against me, diverted it and sent it in a different direction . . ." He trailed off, raising his eyebrows at me. "Do you understand?"

I frowned, thinking through what he'd said, going over our last sparring match in my head. Slowly I nodded. "I think so."

"Good. We'll try it again." He took his position, a few feet away from me on the mud-churned grass, getting into a fighting stance. I did likewise, watching him carefully.

He ran at me again, this time going for an overhand strike. I blocked him, and in the instant where I felt his weight begin to bear down, attempting to force me to the ground, I crouched down and spun away to the side, causing him to stumble to his knees. I came up behind him and put the blade to his throat. "Now you're dead," I said softly, pride tinging my voice.

I withdrew the dagger, and Cortes rose to his feet and turned to face me. When he did, I saw a new respect in his eyes, and I felt a warmth beneath my breastbone. For whatever reason, I wanted to impress this gruff and blunt-spoken old solider. It mattered, somehow.

But when he spoke, his tone was as businesslike as ever. "Good. Exactly what I meant. Now do it again."

Chapter 25

"Go," I urged Luca in a low voice once Amalia was settled within the gondola and the curtains of the felze closed around us. "And keep to the back canals."

"Sí, Madonna," Luca replied, and pushed away from the dock, steering us away from the Grand Canal.

This was no pleasure cruise, as Amalia and I were sometimes known to indulge in. For one, it was the dark of night—after midnight, in fact. And for another, Amalia looked a bit miffed and confused at why I had insisted on this meeting.

"I've the Spanish ambassador asleep in my bed," she informed me as Luca steered us through the warren of back canals of San Marco and into Cannaregio. "I should very much like to be back before he wakes up."

"I'm sorry, amica mia," I said. "I would not have insisted you join me if it weren't urgent."

"And I would not have come if I did not know it must be urgent," Amalia said. "And"—she gestured at the closed felze and the darkness of the night beyond—"rather delicate, I should think, given the hour."

"Indeed it is," I said, though my brain only just then seized on what she'd said moments before. "I didn't know the Spanish ambassador was one of your lovers."

"He is. He has been for a few months now."

"You'd best be careful," I advised. "Should he be found to be passing information back to his king that the doge and Senate do not wish Spain to have, you could be implicated."

Amalia made an impatient gesture with her hand. "You think I am not aware of that?" she said. "You need not worry. The only information being passed is from him to me, to—" She broke off abruptly. "Never mind to whom."

I sat back, shocked. Amalia was spying? Passing Spanish secrets to . . . someone? But I should not have been so surprised, I knew. Amalia was canny, intelligent, and as accomplished an actress as any courtesan. Who better to be an informant?

Whom did she report to, I wondered. But I shook my head slightly, clearing it. It didn't matter. There was no time for that just then.

"Now what is this about?" Amalia demanded.

"I have something to tell you," I said, lowering my voice so that Luca might not overhear. Gondoliers were bound never to reveal anything they overheard in their gondolas, and their brother gondoliers would slit a man's throat and dump him in a canal if he besmirched the honor and discretion of his position. But for Luca's own safety, it was better that he knew as little of what I was about to tell Amalia as possible. I wished I need not tell her anything, but I dearly needed her help. "I . . ." I squeezed my eyes shut and began again. "I recently received a visit from a member of the Council of Ten."

"Who?" she demanded sharply.

"Shh," I hushed her. "It doesn't matter who. All you need know is that it is someone with whom I have worked in the past, on whose behalf I have . . . gathered and passed along information."

Not a complete lie. I had passed my share of information to Malatesta and others over the years, in addition to my other . . . duties.

But even now, I could not bring myself to tell Amalia the whole truth. Mostly for her own safety, but also so that I need not face the judgment and horror with which I was certain she would greet such news. I could not bear for her to name me as the monster that Malatesta thought me. As the monster that perhaps I was.

Amalia was silent as she considered what I'd said, and I wondered if she would put the truth together—that Ambrogio Malatesta was the member of the Ten to whom I referred. It would not be such a leap for her to make—not after I had so recently asked her what she knew of him. But I could not worry about that. She could guess at whatever she wished, and so long as I confirmed nothing, she would be safe. I hoped.

"This time, though," I went on, "he asked me for much more than information. He . . . he asked me to do something for him. For the Ten." Oh, saints, this was much harder to say aloud than I had thought it would be.

"What did he ask you to do?" Amalia whispered.

"He . . . he asked . . ." I swallowed, my mouth dry. "He *told* me to kill Bastiano Bragadin."

Shocked silence filled the gondola, the only sound the lapping of water against the sides of the boat and the buildings that pressed in around us.

"This is a poor jest, and an even poorer time for one," Amalia said coldly.

I might have laughed at her words, so like my own when Malatesta had first told me what was required of me. "Oh, would that it were a jest, Amalia. My God, how I wish it were a jest."

More silence.

"I wish it were too," Amalia said aloud, "but I know you certainly didn't drag me out onto the canals at night in November to play some ill-considered joke on me."

"I did not."

Amalia took a deep breath. "This is real. This is true, what you are telling me."

Tears pricked my eyes; hearing Amalia speak of it indeed made it real in a way it hadn't been before, somehow. And now there was no hiding from it. But I resolutely shoved the tears back. Crying had never solved any problem for me, and it would not do so now. "Yes. It is."

"Why would this member of the Ten come to you with this task?" Amalia asked, businesslike as ever, even in the face of such a shock. It was one of the many things I loved about her, even now, as she came close to my deadliest secret. "You are close to him, true, but surely the Ten have professional assassins to carry out such deeds?"

I was silent just an instant too long at that, just one revealing instant. Hurriedly, Amalia went on. "Never mind that. I do not want to know . . . never mind. But regardless . . . why the cruelty of having you do it?"

"The cruelty is the point with this man in particular," I said savagely. "And he wishes . . . Well, there are other reasons why that do not ultimately matter. But Bastiano . . . Bastiano is in hiding, never mind why. I am the only one who knows where he is."

"I had no idea, but I suppose I have not seen him out and about, now that you mention it," she said. "But it is well known that you and Bastiano are lovers. How could any of the Ten expect you to agree to do it?"

"They—he—never expected me to agree," I said darkly. "They intend to force me. They have made it so that I do not have a choice. And so I am trying to find any way out that I can."

"By the Virgin," Amalia exclaimed, "how on earth could they possibly force you to kill the man you love?"

I was silent.

"Valentina?"

"How else?" I asked bitterly. "By threatening the only life for which I would forfeit Bastiano's." This last part I found I could not bring myself to say aloud. Not even to Amalia.

She understood, nonetheless. Shock and horror filled her face. "No," she whispered. "No. Not . . . not Ginevra?"

I nodded once.

She sagged in her seat. "They'd never," she said. "Not even the Ten. Not an innocent little girl. Surely not."

"They are not bluffing," I said. "At least, not—not the man who gave me the assignment."

"Surely that is too far—"

I laughed, a touch hysterically. "You do not know this man, Amalia. He needs Bastiano Bragadin dead badly, and he needs—wants—me to be the one to do it. I am in no doubt whatsoever that the threat to Ginevra is in earnest."

Amalia was silent, considering all this. "And how long has he given you?" she asked quietly. "When must you have . . . when must the deed be done by?"

"The end of the month."

Amalia swore under her breath. "That is less than two weeks."

"I am aware."

"And so what are you going to do?"

"I don't know!" The words burst from me in an anguished cry. "I am faced with an impossible choice! I would do anything to keep my daughter safe. Anything. But this . . . it is impossible for me to . . . to *kill* Bastiano. I . . . I could never—" I broke off, taking a deep breath and just barely stopping myself from breaking into sobs.

Silence fell again, so that all that could be heard was the sound of Luca's oar dipping in and out of the water as he propelled the gondola forward.

"What does Bastiano say?" Amalia asked, breaking the silence.

"I have not told him."

"What?" Amalia gasped. "Not any of it? Not when it is his life and his daughter's life at stake?"

"I can't take the risk of contacting him," I said. "Not when it might lead someone right to him. And if he knew, he—" I broke off, biting my lip. I could not speak my last fear, not even to Amalia. A small part of me worried that if Bastiano learned of the bloody task that had been set for me, he might well take his own life to save Ginevra and spare me the choice. And I would not be able to bear that either.

"What is it you need from me?" Amalia asked, her tone gentle yet somehow also as unyielding as steel. "I assume you have told me all this because you believe I can help in some way. And I will do whatever is in my power—I'm sure you know that."

I sighed. "I . . . I don't know, precisely," I said. "I am at my wits' end, Amalia—truly I am."

"I can imagine," she murmured.

"And so I . . . I am sorry to have burdened you with this knowledge," I said. "Saints, I should never have told you at all."

"No," she said immediately. "Do not say that. I am here for whatever you need. You know that. What is it you would like me to do?"

I sighed again. "I don't know," I repeated. "I don't know that there is anything you can do, but I . . . I had to tell someone, someone I trust. I have been over this and over this in my mind until I feel as though I am going mad, and I cannot see any way out. I suppose I was hoping that maybe you would see something that I have not. That I cannot."

"Hmm." Amalia tapped a finger against her plump lips, thinking.

"And is there . . . Christ, isn't there someone we know between the two of us who might help? Who might do something?"

"Is there anything Francesco might do?" she suggested. "Would the Church's influence be of any use? He wields much more than he used to, now that he is vicar general."

"I don't know if the Council of Ten takes much heed of the Church," I said. "If I thought Francesco or his contacts in Rome would be of any use, I would have tried that already, believe you me. But if I am found to have solicited help from Rome, I'll likely be branded a traitor of some kind myself."

"What of this man who told you to kill Bastiano?" Amalia asked. "Is there anything you know about him that you might use against him?"

I laughed harshly. "I tried that. I believe . . . I am certain it is he who is the true traitor. That he is working for his own ends, and the rest of the Ten know nothing of it. But my plan, it . . . it backfired. Rather spectacularly."

"But you know something he does not wish you to know?" Amalia asked, leaning forward.

"I . . . I do," I said. "I am quite certain I do. But . . ."

"Then use that! Threaten to tell others what you know and—"

"I have no proof!" I cried. "He all but confirmed what I suspected, and yet I have no way to prove it. Nothing in writing, no one else who overheard him. And you know the way of the world, Amalia. I am a woman, and I am a courtesan. I will not be believed. Not without proof."

"Who is he, Valentina? If I knew that, I might see what I could learn about him. I would be better able to help."

"I can't tell you, Amalia. It . . . it would put you in too much danger."

"Valentina." She lowered her voice. "I . . . I know a man on the Council of Ten. I am . . . intimate with him. If you tell me what you need to know, I may be able to find it out for you."

"No," I said instantly. "I cannot have you asking such a man anything for me, Amalia. It's too dangerous. I cannot . . . God, I could not go on at all if I thought you were putting yourself in danger for my sake."

She threw up her hands. "Then what can I do?"

I shook my head. "Take us home, Luca," I called, raising my voice. To Amalia, I said, "I am sorry, amica mia. As I said, I should not have told you. Just . . . if you think of anything else, anything at all that might help, please tell me. I . . ." I bowed my head, blinking back tears. "I do not know what else to do."

She reached out and embraced me, drawing me against her, and I relaxed into her. "Oh, Valentina," she said. "I am so sorry. I am so sorry you have been put in this situation."

I drew back and smiled weakly. "I brought it on myself, I suppose," I said. "I have toyed with danger, and with dangerous men, for too long now."

Amalia's face hardened. "I do not think that is true," she said. "I think these dangerous, powerful men think they can do whatever they like, and that they can use the rest of us to do their bidding. I do not think it matters much what we do or do not do."

"No doubt you are right, but what are the likes of us to do to stop them?"

She sighed. "That is the question, is it not? I will think on this, Valentina. I will try my hardest to think of something that might help. There must be a way out of this." She reached out and squeezed my hand. "And if your telling me only unburdened you a bit, then that is good."

I squeezed her hand in turn. "Thank you, Amalia. Thank you."

"You need not mention it. You know I will do anything I can to help you." She closed her eyes briefly. "Good God, the evil of men," she murmured. "Does it know no bounds?"

"From what I have seen," I said, "I do not think it does."

What I could not tell Amalia, not even then, as the gondola slipped through the darkened canals toward home, was that I could not rid myself of the belief that all this was naught but a punishment for my own sins. For all the evil I myself had done.

Chapter 26

While unburdening myself to Amalia *had* made me feel a bit better and less like I was alone in my own private hell, in some ways I felt more desperate after talking to her. Perhaps a part of me had believed that she would know something, have some idea, that would allow me a way to escape this whole hideous situation. But of course, what could she do? I believed that she would try to think of something, would try to see a way to disentangle me from this mess, but was there one? We were running out of time. I had less than two weeks, as Amalia had pointed out. Short of Tomasina finding a detailed, written plan of the conspiracy in Malatesta's own hand, I was not sure there were any chances left.

Less than two weeks to find an impossible solution or commit an impossible act.

The night after I spoke with Amalia, Francesco came to see me. I had dinner served, as usual, but pretending that everything was normal was proving difficult, even for me. I tried to follow all the things Francesco was telling me over dinner, all the church politics and gossip and scandal, but I could not focus, could not remember all the names of the people he was telling me about, could not bring myself to speak any witty repartee. I could tell that Francesco noticed that something was different, that I was not myself, but he let it pass. At least, until after dinner.

We adjourned to the bedchamber, and I closed the door behind us and turned to him, waiting to see his preference as to how to proceed. Francesco was usually quite clear about what he wanted.

Yet I found that he was standing near the bed, simply watching me. "What is wrong, Valentina?" he asked.

"Wrong?" I said brightly. "Why, nothing."

"You might have a bit more respect for my intelligence," Francesco said, arching an eyebrow at me. "I can see that you're not yourself. I know you rather well, after all."

I laughed mirthlessly, suddenly done with pretending. "You know me in the biblical sense, certainly," I said. "But that is not all there is to me."

He watched me carefully. "Of course it's not. I never thought it was."

"But that is what you are here for." I gestured to the bed. "Let us get on with it, then."

"Valentina." This time he crossed the room to me, cupping my face in his hands. "It is not only your body I come for." A half smile crossed his face. "Though I certainly enjoy and appreciate it. But I also enjoy your company. I enjoy speaking to you. I enjoy hearing your thoughts on politics, on what is happening in the Republic and the world. Surely you know that."

I sighed. "Yes, of course I do." Why had I ever started this conversation?

"And so I think I've gotten to know you rather well over these past few years." He studied my face. "And I believe that you have let me get to you know. Am I right about that?"

"Yes," I conceded. "More . . . more than most."

He withdrew his hands. "I think I am right, then," he said, his voice gentler than I had ever heard it, "in saying that I can tell something is troubling you."

I wasn't sure if it was his words or the terribly tender way in which he said them, but I broke then. I drew away from him and buried my face in my hands. "Oh, Francesco," I gasped, trying desperately not to dissolve into sobs. "If only you knew. If only you knew!"

He laid an arm across my shoulders and drew me toward the bed, where he had me sit on the edge of the mattress before sitting beside me himself. "What is it, Valentina?" he asked softly.

I shook my head. "I cannot say."

"I am a priest, you know," he said. "And we are not in a confessional, but . . ." He shrugged. "Whatever you say to me now can be considered to be said in the spirit of confession, I think."

I looked up at him, at his handsome and familiar face, as though I had never seen him before. And I realized that somehow he was right. For the first time in a very long time, I did need a priest that night. Whoever would have thought it?

I looked away from him again. "Francesco, I . . ." I closed my eyes and drew a deep, shuddering breath, trying to summon the right words. "I have never thought of myself as an evil person."

"I do not think you are either. For whatever that is worth."

"But you do not know all the things I have done."

"What have you done, Valentina?"

"What haven't I done?" I cried. "And yet none of that torments me so much as what I . . . what I am afraid I might do.

Might *have* to do. What I am thinking of doing." I looked up at him beseechingly. "Is even thinking of committing a terrible act a sin?"

"The Church would tell us so, yes," Francesco said, a trace of reluctance in his voice. "But what matters most to God, I think, is the intent of the thing. Do you intend to do evil, Valentina?"

"No!" I burst out. "No. I contemplate this evil act, this unthinkable act, only to avoid one that is worse."

I waited a moment, certain that Francesco would begin to ask me questions, would ask me to explain the riddles I had just told him. But to my surprise, he asked nothing. He did not even speak for a long while.

When he broke the silence, finally, his voice was soft and understanding. "Sometimes we must choose the lesser of two evils," he said. "Human nature makes it so that we are sometimes put in such positions, whether through our own actions or those of others. God sees this, and He understands. Or so I have always believed."

I considered this.

He leaned forward and kissed my forehead. "Kneel," he whispered.

I did as he said, sliding to my knees on the floor before him—and not for the usual reason. The Valentina of weeks ago would have quipped as much. But I did not know where that woman was. She was gone, broken for the last time, perhaps. Yet at that thought, I felt her flare back to life within me. *No!* Ambrogio Malatesta would not be the thing that broke me at long last, not after everything. I would put myself back together again somehow, no matter that the pieces might never fit together just right. I would join as many of them together as I possibly could, even if the Valentina they would assemble was different yet again from the one who had come before her.

I had been broken and remade before. I could do it again.

Francesco placed his hands on my head. "Ego te absolvo a peccatis tuis in nomine Patris, et Filii, et Spiritus Sancti. Amen."

I let the familiar words, words I had not heard in a very long time, wash over me: "I absolve you of your sins, in the name of the Father, the Son, and the Holy Spirit." The traditional benediction did not specify which sins, I noticed, nor when they were committed. I knew the Church would not see it in quite that way, but it gave me comfort in that moment, nonetheless.

"Amen," I whispered, crossing myself.

"Rise," Francesco murmured.

I did, and he stood as well. "There is no sin of which God cannot absolve you, Valentina."

I smiled, a trace of my old jaunty, irreverent grin. "I've heard that. But, Francesco . . ." My smile faded as I searched his eyes. "What if I cannot forgive myself?"

"If God in His wisdom believes you worthy of grace, then so you must be," he said. "It can be hard to remember that at times, but it is true. And not only does God believe you worthy of grace, Valentina, but so do I."

He kissed me again, this time on the lips. And then he left.

Chapter 27

The next day, I dressed and had Marta pin my hair up in a simple braided knot. I then went next door to Amalia's palazzo. I had woken up that morning with only the certainty that I needed to see my friend, to speak to her. About what, I didn't know as it mattered; I just wanted to be in her company and let her reassure me.

A part of me had the idea that I would also ask her for absolution, in a way. Francesco Valier, the newly made vicar general, had assured me of God's forgiveness, no matter what the sin was. Yet I felt as though I also needed the absolution of someone I truly loved, as well; perhaps it was ludicrous of me, but I somehow wanted to know that if I did this thing, committed this horrible, unthinkable act for the pure reason of saving my daughter, Amalia would still be able to look me in the eye.

And if she could not—and I would not blame her if that was the case—would that make a difference to me, or simply make the deed I might well have to do that much harder? I tried not to think about that.

Or maybe, I reasoned, grasping desperately for a bright thought within the pitch blackness of my mind, Amalia would have thought of something or someone that could help. Maybe.

One of Amalia's maids opened the door for me. "Madonna Riccardi," she said, surprised to see me there unannounced. "I do not think my mistress can receive you right now. She is—"

I pushed past the girl and into the entryway. "I must see her," I said. "It is rather urgent."

"She is with a gentleman caller."

That drew me up short. It was late enough in the morning that her client of last night should have left; I had timed my visit just so. Perhaps there was a man she saw during daylight hours as well? That would be unusual, but not unheard of.

But it didn't matter. I could not leave until I had spoken to her. I did not have much time left. Bastiano did not have much time left. "I will wait for her, then," I said, walking up the stairs to the piano nobile, where Amalia did her entertaining. She had organized her palazzo in a similar way to mine.

"Please, Madonna Riccardi, I do not know if—" the maid called, hurrying up the stairs after me.

"Tell your mistress I am here, please," I said to her over my shoulder. Yet when I reached the top of the stairs, I stopped short at the sight that greeted me.

Amalia materialized from her dining room, her hair loose and tousled and with a silk dressing gown draped carelessly over her lush figure. She was smiling, as happy as I had ever seen her, looking lovingly at the man who had emerged from the dining room at her side.

Ambrogio Malatesta.

For a moment, I could not comprehend the strangeness of it, how out of place Malatesta looked in Amalia's palazzo of cream marble and rose-colored curtains and gilt-framed mirrors. Surely I was mistaken. Surely this man, who had come to be the embodiment of the devil for me, could not be smiling down at my dearest friend in all the world. Surely this was some sort of strange, upside-down dream.

But no, it was him, in the flesh, and once my mind caught up to my body, I marked my physical reaction to his presence. My hands curled into fists at my side, and the fingers of my right hand itched for the small dagger I kept tucked into my boot, at the ready whenever I left the palazzo on my own.

Yet in my instant of bewilderment, Malatesta glanced up and noticed me standing there, no doubt looking like some avenging goddess of old. His entire demeanor changed when he saw me, from relaxed and contented to tense, hard, on edge. He straightened a bit as he met my eyes. "Valentina Riccardi," he said coldly. "How surprising to see you here. Especially when you've so often chastened me for turning up at your home uninvited."

I did not reply, merely shot a glance over to Amalia, asking her with my eyes what this man was doing in her palazzo. At her shocked, resigned, and slightly angry expression, I finally realized what I had not thus far, like an utter fool.

Ambrogio Malatesta was Amalia's secret lover. The man with whom she had a true relationship, the man she really loved. I had often wondered idly who he was, tried to get her to tell me once or twice, only to have her insist that he did not wish anyone to know. I had always assumed she would tell me someday.

I had not expected this.

Inwardly I cursed to myself. In the name of the Shadow God, could this get any worse? Could anything about this entire nightmare possibly get worse?

Yet then, also belatedly, the fear seeped in. What had Amalia told her lover? Had she told him of our conversation in the gondola a few nights past? Oh saints, what if she had told him how I'd asked her what she knew about him?

I had always assumed anything I said to Amalia was said in confidence, as was anything she said to me. But how many times had I repeated something she'd told me to Bastiano in passing, a bit of gossip here or there about which I'd not thought twice? Bastiano was my lover, first and foremost. I trusted him.

Just as Amalia surely trusted Malatesta.

She would never knowingly betray me, but she might have done so inadvertently all the same. For, in the end, I'd not told her the name of the man on the Council of Ten who had ordered me to kill Bastiano.

Unbidden, I recalled the moment just days ago when he had burst into my dressing room, when he had flung the letter in my face and threatened me anew. I remembered when he'd loomed over me as I sat in my dressing chair, the arousal in his eyes, his breath. All the while he was my dearest friend's lover, whom she loved, while he—I assumed—at least professed to love her as well. Disgust crashed over me in a foul wave, and I nearly retched. I had not thought that I could loathe the man any more than I already did, but that memory made it so.

"Valentina is welcome here any time, Gio," Amalia said, looking up at him curiously. She turned her gaze to me, and I noted her slightly cool expression. "I do usually prefer a note first, though, just so I can be sure to receive you properly."

The rebuke in her words was clear, but I couldn't concern myself with that just then. "I . . . I am sorry, Amalia," I said. "I do apologize for the intrusion. I'll see myself out." I turned on my heel and made my way back down the stairs.

"Wait, Valentina," Amalia called, and I turned to see that she and Malatesta had drawn closer. "Ambrogio was just leaving. Stay, now that you're here, won't you?"

My eyes met Malatesta's cold, hard ones, and fear trickled through me. Not fear of the man himself, but fear of what this meant: for me, for Bastiano, for Ginevra, for Amalia. For Amalia and me. Fear of what Amalia might have told this man she loved about me and mine, not just since all this had started, but over the years. It would explain, I realized, certain things he'd known about me that I had never told him. I had always thought it was just that powerful men, and the Ten especially, had ways of knowing things far beyond those of which I was aware, which was no doubt true, but in my case, the explanation seemed to be a much simpler one, one closer to home.

No. I could not stay. I should never have told Amalia any of it. I cursed myself for a fool, for my weakness of needing a friend, a confidant. When would I learn? Everyone I loved had either died or left me, eventually. I trusted so few people, and even that small number had been too many.

"No, thank you," I said to Amalia, but my gaze remained on Malatesta. "I will go. I apologize for intruding." I looked at Amalia at last, but she was looking up at Malatesta with a quizzical look on her face. She looked over at me, a question in her gaze, but I turned away before any wordless communication could pass between us and descended the staircase back to the water entrance. I went back to my own palazzo as quickly as I could, back up to my bedchamber to pace and rage and dread the coming of the next dawn.

Without meaning to, I recalled that morning that I'd emerged from the stables of my family's villa on the outskirts of Rome, emerged to find my world utterly destroyed, to find that everyone I loved had been slaughtered.

That was the last time I had felt so alone.

INTERLUDE

Venice, July 1527

Venice in the middle of summer stank to high heaven as the waters of the canals ebbed low, and the waste and rubbish tossed into them reeked in the heat. It was not any worse than the city of Rome in summer, though. And at least Venice had a light breeze off the lagoon, carrying with it the scent of the sea, an aroma I found altogether intoxicating.

And now here I was, in a city not simply by the sea, but one that floated on it, as though suspended there by magic. *How did it not all sink into the waves?* I marveled. I could not imagine. Venice was even more beautiful than I had always heard it was, and in spite of all the blood and darkness and horror that I had just come through, I found myself utterly enchanted by the place that was to be my new home.

Yet it did not seem as though I would be given much of a chance to see it, to explore it. Not now, and likely not ever.

Fernando Cortes stood at my side before the door to the convent, looking up at the high stone walls. "You'll be safe here," he said, as he had several times in the last few days.

I snorted. "Safe, perhaps," I said. "Miserable as well."

"I wish there were another way," he said. "But where else is there for you to go? You've no family left, no friends to help. What other respectable place is there for a girl on her own?"

I looked down at the cobblestones of the street. "Why can't I stay with you?" I mumbled, embarrassed to be asking him for something more. For something so big.

He sighed. "I wish you could," he said, and beneath his usual gruffness I heard sincerity in his voice. "But I'll need to hire myself out as a bodyguard or paid blade or some such thing to make ends meet. That's no life for a young lady."

"Why not?" I asked. "Why did you bother teaching me to defend myself, only to drop me off at a convent?"

He shrugged. "I thought you ought to be able to get by on your own in case something happened to me on the road." He gave me a crooked smile. "And you may find a need to defend yourself from some bored and vicious nuns yet."

I laughed at that in spite of the fact that I really wanted to cry.

He turned to face me and put his hands on my shoulders. "You'll be safe here," he said again. "You'll be provided for. If there were any other options . . ."

I shrugged out of his grasp. "I know. I know."

He sighed. "I'm sorry, little lady. I am."

"You've done what you could. I . . ." I swallowed down a lump in my throat. "I'd never have made it without you. You . . . you saved my life."

"The least I could do," he said gruffly. "Well, I suppose this is where we part ways."

With that, he rang the bell at the convent's gate and then, with one last regretful look at me, turned and walked away.

The sisters that greeted me clucked at my appearance, at the filthy clothes I was dressed in and at the haphazard way I'd chopped off my hair. The latter didn't matter, though, they'd informed me; as a novice I'd have my head shaved. The Mother Superior was occupied that day and would be able to meet with me the following morning. I had no dowry? That was a shame, a shame indeed; without a dowry to my name, the best I could hope for was to be a lay sister.

I was not such a fool that I didn't know what that meant: I would be little better than a servant for the nuns who came from wealthier families, forced to clean up after them and do whatever menial tasks they requested.

The sisters bathed me and gave me a simple, clean dress, albeit one much too large for me, and fed me some fresh bread and cheese. They showed me to a tiny cell where I could spend the night until permanent quarters could be assigned to me the next day.

I was gone long before the bells tolled for Matins.

I knew Fernando Cortes had meant well, bringing me to the convent. I also knew that he was absolutely correct in that there was no other respectable place for a gently bred young lady like me.

I knew as well that I had not survived the hell and trauma and suffering I had lived through only to entomb myself behind stone walls and consign myself to a living death.

Everyone I loved had died. But I was still alive, and I wanted to live. I chose life. I chose *my* life, whatever it might be.

I roamed all over Venice that night, trying to remember where things were, even as I knew everything would look different in the daylight. Even as I knew that I had the rest of my life to learn every inch of this beautiful city. I could take my time.

I made inquiries of some people I met on my way, and soon enough I was directed to an establishment of the kind I sought, in San Marco. Even in the early hours of the morning, the brothel was brightly lit, and music and voices poured from within.

I knocked on the door and, when I said why I was there, was taken to the proprietress of the establishment. I told her why I had come as well as the fact that I was gently bred and well educated. She, a handsome, dark-haired woman of about my mother's age, listened carefully, her sharp eyes taking in all the details of my appearance as I spoke. When I'd finished, she had only one question for me. "Are you a virgin?"

This question, I understood even then, had a twofold purpose. The first was practical: if I was still a virgin, then my virginity could be sold for a very high price to the right client, a price that would profit both me and the proprietress greatly. As I would later learn, virginity could be sold for this substantial price whether a girl was truly possessed of it or not, so long as the man wanted to believe enough.

Yet there was just a trace of softness in the woman's eyes, eyes hardened by life, eyes that had seen not perhaps exactly what I had seen, but enough of life that she could well imagine. That she did not doubt what I had told her or why it had brought me to her door. And in that softness, almost tenderness, was the other side of her question: Did I know what it was I was getting myself into?

"No," I told her. "I am no virgin."

She nodded and rose from the chair behind her desk. "Very well. Luckily for you, one of my most popular girls just left, so there is a place for you. Got married, she did." The woman shook her head, as if unsure as to why anyone would voluntarily consent to matrimony. She scrutinized me again. "But we'll have to do something about that hair. And you'll need a different name. Maria Angelina will never do; you sound like a nun."

A nun was the last thing I wished to be, after all. And so Valentina Riccardi was born.

Chapter 28

I canceled on my client for that evening, Alvise Gasparo. I could not bear a night of following about on his arm, charming his friends and business associates and making inane conversation, being treated like an exotic bird who has been trained to speak. I couldn't endure it—not then, not when everything around me and within me was collapsing, and I could not seem to pull myself from the rubble.

I had already pulled myself from the wreckage of one life, managed to get back up on my own two feet again and start a new one. How could I possibly be expected to do so again?

Yet even having canceled my engagement for that evening, I found I also could not stay in my palazzo any longer, could not stare at the same walls that had once represented security and comfort and safety to me. Now the very building seemed to mock me, laughed at my misguided belief that I had ever thought I was safe. That I had ever thought I could stop running.

So I called for Luca to prepare the gondola and asked him to take me across the city to the Basilica di Santa Maria Gloriosa dei Frari, or as Venetians often called it, simply the Frari.

It was twilight, fading swiftly into darkness, and as we crossed the Grand Canal, I could hear shouts and laughter from the other boats on the waterway, music and the clinking of glassware drifting out of the windows of the palazzi that lined it. The world I usually inhabited, and indeed I should have been somewhere like that on that very night. Yet it felt alien, somehow; a place I didn't belong, had never really belonged, and would never belong again, perhaps.

And indeed, if any of the patrician men and their intellectual friends with whom I associated on nights such as this knew the truth about me, knew all the things I had done without flinching, they would cast me out in horror and fear.

Yet what hypocrisy, I mused as Luca guided the gondola down a smaller waterway that would eventually lead us to the Frari church. For the things I did, I had done at the behest of men very like them, to protect the very things they held dear. Money. Power. The security of the Venetian state that gave them both of those things.

No one wanted their hands dirtied, and yet the dirty deeds must get done nonetheless, so that all of Venice—all of the world—might stay afloat.

Someone had to keep the atrocities of war from Venice. I had decided long ago that I would do what I could toward that aim.

Luca drew the gondola up along a street, as close to the church as he could get, and helped me out. "Thank you, Luca," I said. "Wait for me here, please."

"Sí, Madonna."

I pulled up the hood of the cape I wore over my modest dress and crossed the piazza on which the church stood, dwarfing all the buildings around it. Out of the corner of my eye, I saw a shadowy figure round the corner of the church and disappear. Some henchman of Malatesta's following me? Or just my own fear and paranoia? I quickly pushed open the heavy wooden door of the church and let it close behind me. The sanctuary within was blessedly dark, quiet, and deserted.

I stepped softly onto the chessboard floor, blocks of white stone alternating with red. Columns lined the central nave, and above me I could see the vaults and beams of the ceiling disappearing into the darkness. There were candles lit within, in the chapels that lined the walls and in tall candelabras set along the aisle, the better to guide any late-night pilgrims. Thankfully, I was the only one.

I walked up the central aisle, stepping past the towering rood screen, topped with a crucifix in the center and various stone saints flanking it on either side. As I passed under it, its height and various figures looming above me in the dark sanctuary, I could not help but feel that it seemed more menacing than anything else; something that inspired fear rather than faith. Or perhaps all things of a religious nature were meant to inspire fear in a sinner such as me.

I moved past the choir stalls and toward the altar, where a few pews were arranged. Above the altar, dimly illuminated with votive and taper candles, was Tiziano Vecellio's magnificent altarpiece depicting the assumption of the Blessed Virgin. I had been to see it once before, on a quiet afternoon when the church was similarly empty. I so loved paintings, especially ones like this that made you feel as if you could simply step into them and a world of color and beauty and light, a world much better than this one. This painting made me feel that way, made me feel as though I were among the crowd standing below the Virgin's feet as she was carried up into heaven. The churches of Venice were havens for such art, though I would readily acknowledge that Vecellio's paintings were finer than most. But I made it a habit not to frequent such sacred spaces. And while there were many in Venice—and in the world—who sinned as much or more than I, and with equal or greater relish, and still went to Mass . . . well, that was a form of hypocrisy I did not much care for.

I had not attended a Mass since I'd begun plying the courtesan's trade, when I'd first come to Venice and begun working in that house in San Marco. I had stayed there, learning the finer points of my new profession, until I'd had enough money to set up on my own. And it was there that I had met Amalia Amante, another recent arrival to Venice, as full of life and the desire to appreciate it as I was. We had become friends instantly, as though we had always known each other, as though we had always been destined to know each other.

Most people would have expressed pity for me, forced by such horrible circumstances to descend into prostitution, to sell my body in order to survive. But it had been my choice. I had made it willingly, eagerly, even. The alternative had been the convent, drudgery, and an end to life before I'd really lived it. I didn't want that—had never wanted it. And while the courtesan's life wasn't without its dangers and troubles and annoyances, I liked it. I liked the life I had chosen. I had enjoyed making love with Massimo every time and had thirsted for it as much as he had. And so it had not seemed to my eighteen-year-old self like a bad way to earn a living. Quite the contrary; I liked making love and pleasing men and being able to have that power over them, sometimes the only power a woman got in life. I liked wearing fine clothes and going to lovely parties and meeting intellectuals and artists and poets and politicians; liked being applauded for speaking my mind and debating and claiming the attention of a room in the way "good women" were never allowed to. I liked that I was beholden to no one but myself. Had I the choice to make over again, I would not have chosen differently.

And yet, somehow, I had found myself beholden to the Ten, and to Malatesta. I had let my guard down after years of running my own life, years of answering to no one, and had thought that I could manage Malatesta before he managed me. I'd been foolish and arrogant and reckless. And I'd been wrong.

And all of that, for whatever reason, had driven me here.

I genuflected at the end of a pew, crossing myself, then sat down. I looked up at the wonder and peace on the Virgin's face as she ascended into heaven, considering it quietly.

I would not have chosen a different course for my life, but somewhere I had gone wrong. To say I should have declined the Council of Ten's overtures the first time they asked me for information—for that was how it had begun, with mere information and nothing more—was not so simple as it may have sounded. No Venetian—and certainly no transplant to Venice—was unaware of the Council of Ten, of who they were and what they did. And what power they wielded over the city and its inhabitants. Refusing what they requested of me was no simple task. Even if it didn't mean my life, it might have meant my livelihood. They would have wondered why I had refused. They would have wondered if I was myself hiding something. It had been safer, far safer, to acquiesce.

And in truth, I had not even thought of it in those terms. Providing them information, information I had easy access to thanks to my succession of lovers, made me a bit of extra money, and it gave me a sense of importance, of power, that I hadn't known before. At the time, I'd known of no reason to refuse and only reasons to agree.

And even when they began requiring assassinations instead of simply information, I was no more reluctant, not truly. Whatever could keep the people of the city I'd grown to love so desperately from enduring the horrors I had gone through was worth it, I was sure. Whatever could keep *me* from enduring those horrors again, I would do. And why not assure my own security, financial and otherwise, however I could?

And so I had used the skills Cortes had taught me to protect myself to protect a nation instead—or so I'd fancied. I would never again be the one left behind in the stable and told to stay put.

The first had been a man feeding information back to the Holy Roman Emperor, the monarch responsible for the slaughter of my family and the destruction of my home. Him I had killed with no qualms at all. And there had been others after him: a Genoese agent, a treacherous Arsenale worker, an Ottoman spy, a merchant sailor who was a double agent for the French, yet another Ottoman spy, a Roman assassin posing as a priest, another assassin in the pay of the sultan. The Spanish spy on Ascension Day.

And Dioniso Secco.

Then there was the man I had killed on no one's orders but my own, the man who had found me walking alone one night, late, and had attacked me and tried to force himself on me. He had chosen the wrong woman, and his death troubled me not at all. I liked to think that that one, at least, old Cortes would have applauded.

But in the end, whatever good reasons I had had at the time for all the blood on my hands, however many people I may have saved by doing what I'd done, I still found myself here. Still found myself alone, without choices, and at the mercy of a man who would destroy me. Everything I had fought so hard to avoid.

God—or Fortuna or the saints, or whoever one believed had charge of these things—must be laughing at me. And I could not help but wonder, there alone in the dark basilica, looking up contemplatively at the Blessed Virgin's face, if the church and the priests and the gospels were right. For what else could have brought me to this point but punishment for my sins?

Maybe I would not have made different choices. Maybe I could not have; maybe I was always fated to end up here simply by virtue of being the person I was. I had always justified it to myself along the way, no matter how much it had bothered me, but each assassination came to weigh on me more and more heavily. For the first time I asked myself: Could there be any innocent people in a nation that required this much blood to keep it safe?

Perhaps the fact that I was only now fully regretting the things I'd done, when I felt my actions might have brought me to this bad turn, spoke volumes in and of itself. It was all so complicated. And while I did not wish I could go back, not quite, I did long for the much simpler days when I was just Maria Angelina. Just a girl from a prosperous and pious Roman family.

I folded my hands, bent my head, and prayed, truly prayed for the first time in years. It was a brief prayer. I did not have much to say, nor did I think it likely that God had much patience to listen to me. Then I crossed myself, rose, and left the darkened church.

Chapter 29

The next morning, I had only just risen when Lauretta skittered into my bedchamber. "Amalia Amante is here to see you, Madonna," she said.

I tensed. "She's here? Now? At this hour?" I asked inanely, trying to buy myself a moment in which to decide what to do.

"Yes, Madonna. Shall I send up something for the two of you to break your fast?"

I let out an inaudible sigh. For the first time I could recall, I really did not want to see Amalia. It was best that she and I not speak further, at least not until this was over. And maybe, I realized with a sharp twisting pain somewhere in my chest, not even then.

But surely . . . surely I owed her an explanation of some kind, even if it was not the full truth. And surely I owed it to her to hear what she had come to tell me.

"Yes," I said at last. "Yes, send her into the parlor. I'll be in shortly."

Lauretta disappeared to do my bidding. I donned my velvet robe and braided my hair into one long plait that rested over my shoulder so that I did not look completely rumpled from sleep. If Amalia was going to call at so early an hour, certainly she wouldn't mind seeing me not quite dressed to receive.

Thus arrayed, I went into the parlor to find Amalia sitting and waiting for me. She rose quickly at my entrance, almost as if she meant to start toward me. She opened her mouth to speak and then closed it.

I shut the door behind me and leaned back against it. "Amalia," I said. "Are you well?"

"Well enough," she said. "I am sorry for the early hour, but—"

"No, it is I who should apologize," I interrupted. "I should never have come by uninvited yesterday. I am sorry if I made things . . . awkward."

She shook her head. "I suppose I always knew you would find out about Ambrogio, one way or another."

"Would that I had known sooner," I said. I did not explain my remark, nor did she ask me to.

"Indeed," she said uncomfortably. "Valentina, I—"

"Won't you sit?" I interrupted again, gesturing to the daybed she had been perched on when I'd come in.

"If you will," she said.

I entered the room fully and took a seat in the chair beside the daybed. I had never in all my years of knowing her felt so uncomfortable in Amalia's presence. And I hated it. Before, I had felt better able to face everything, anything, knowing I had Amalia on my side. Now I did not know on whose side she stood. But I had the feeling that I was about to find out.

"Valentina," she began again. "You must listen. I—"

Thankfully, this time she was interrupted again by a knock on the parlor door. "Come," I called, and Lauretta entered with a tray bearing a morning repast—some bread and cheese and cold sausage as well as some fruit—which she set on the low table before us.

"Is there anything else you require?" Lauretta asked, looking from me to Amalia and back again.

"No, thank you, Lauretta," I said. "That will be all."

Lauretta left, closing the door again behind her.

Amalia sighed, the sound tinged with frustration. "Valentina . . ."

"Eat something, won't you?" I interjected, gesturing at the tray.

"No!" she burst out. "I can't possibly eat anything until I've said what I came to say."

I bit back all of the retorts that entered my mind and simply said nothing.

Taking my silence for the acquiescence it was, Amalia began to speak again. "I do not blame you for coming by yesterday," she said. "You have ever been welcome in my home, as I know I am in yours. I meant it then and I mean it now. Yet I cannot help but wish that you had not come yesterday. That you had not seen . . ." She trailed off uncomfortably.

"Ambrogio Malatesta," I said, finishing what she had been about to say. "He is your secret lover."

"Yes," Amalia said. "Yes, he is. And has been for many years. Since I set up as a courtesan on my own."

Oh, if only I'd known. If only I'd known from the beginning.

"You love him," I said. Another fact I did not need her to confirm.

"Yes," she said again. "I always have."

"He is not worthy of your love," I stated.

She looked away from me, down at her hands, which were folded in her lap. Did I detect a faint tremble in them? "Perhaps you are right," she conceded, "but I love him all the same. I was so young when we met, and he was so charming . . . he always has been, to me at least. And he was so elegant and handsome . . . he still is, I think. He was this worldly and sophisticated man who truly listened to me, who cared what I thought and what interested me—or at least he pretended to. I had never experienced that before, not really, young as I was. And even as I grew older and a bit wiser, I suppose I . . . I never grew out of the habit of loving him.

"And," she added with a sigh, "I never felt completely secure in his affections, never could be quite sure that he loved me like I loved him. And that . . . that only made me want him more, in that contrary way the heart has sometimes."

I knew what she meant, even as I detested that she had been made to feel that way. "You deserve so much better than that, Amalia."

"Do I? Sometimes I wonder."

Silence fell over the room, neither of us looking at the other.

"Valentina," Amalia said after a moment, and I looked up to find her staring hard at me. "I know who Ambrogio must be to you."

I looked down. "I don't know what you mean," I mumbled.

"Do you take me for a fool?" she demanded. "I saw how you glared at each other; heard how you spoke to each other and what you said. It is plain to me that—"

"Have you never heard the gossip that Malatesta and I were lovers?" I asked desperately, in a last futile attempt to keep her from arriving at what she clearly already knew. "Would that not account for the animosity you saw between us? A love affair gone wrong?"

She gave me a rather derisive look. "I know there is no truth to it," she said. "I asked him once, years ago. I was jealous, and I let him see my jealousy, I admit. He told me that it was not true and that he had spread the rumor about the two of you himself so that no one might find out about me."

"And why was he so bent on keeping you a secret?" I asked, the question I had long wanted the answer to. "Why allow it to be said he visited one courtesan and not another?" I swallowed hard before saying what I had long wondered but had never asked, not wanting to hurt her with the thought, though I was sure she had asked the same question of herself more than once in this Venice of ours. "Is it because of your Turkish blood?"

She shook her head. "No. No. I . . . he . . . he said he did not wish anyone to know about me, so his enemies could not use me against him." I could see tears glistening in her eyes then. "It made sense to me at the time, and it makes sense now, of a sort. I always knew he was an ambitious man, a dangerous man who did dangerous work, especially since being elected to the Ten. Of course he had—has—enemies. Something about it still never sat quite right with me, but . . ." She trailed off and looked at me. "And I think that is all true, but also . . . yes. I also think there is some truth to what you have said. Or at least I have always wondered."

"And still you can love him?" I asked, horrified.

"I cannot help it!" she cried. "You know what it is like to be in love. To love a man so hopelessly."

I did, and yet I still could not quite believe the degree to which Amalia—Amalia, of all people!—had seemingly relaxed her razor-sharp mind, instincts, and pride for Malatesta. Malatesta, of all men. "Yes," I said, still trying to untangle Malatesta's web of lies and deceit. "But—"

"It doesn't matter," Amalia cut me off. "It doesn't matter now. I know he is not one of your clients and never has been. That was indeed a necessary fiction, as he told me years ago, but not for the reason he claimed. I know that he is your . . . what is the term used for such things? Contact? I know he is the one who told you—"

I got swiftly to my feet. "No," I said. "No, Amalia."

"You would deny it? Still?"

"It cannot be spoken aloud," I said. "I . . . no. No. Do not say it, Amalia. Do not speak of it. My God, how I wish I had never told you anything about it that night. How I wish neither of us knew what we know."

"But we do," Amalia said, rising to her feet, "and we cannot go back. We cannot undo the knowing."

"But we must," I said. "We must try. Otherwise . . ." I backed away from her, burying my face in my hands. "Otherwise, we are bound to hurt each other."

"Valentina," Amalia said urgently, "I can't—"

"I know," I said. "I know you can't. I know you can't help me without betraying the man you love. Just . . . just do nothing. Do nothing, Amalia. And forget everything I ever told you."

"How can you expect me to—"

"You have to try!" I said. I went to the door of the room and opened it, turning back to glance at her over my shoulder. Her lovely eyes were rimmed in red, and she looked devastated, yet somehow angry and defiant at the same time. "I must go, Amalia. I cannot speak to you of this anymore."

"Valentina, wait—"

But I left the room and closed the door behind me, cutting off whatever she'd been about to say.

⋆ ⋆ ⋆

I'd exhausted my options. There was no way out. In my desperation, I was willing to go to Senator Gritti or one of the other men who was working to undermine Malatesta. And whatever happened to me be damned, if it would save Ginevra and Bastiano. But I had waited too long. Who knew how long it would take them to use what I'd told them? They knew nearly all that I did, anyway, and still had yet to do anything. And I was almost out of time. Ginevra was almost out of time.

There was only the final choice to make. The choice that was no choice at all. The choice that had been both unthinkable and obvious from the beginning.

No one was coming to save me, to save Bastiano. Either Tomasina had lost her nerve for this game—for which I could not blame her—or she had not been able to find anything of use. But there were no further plays I could make.

Maybe young Maria Angelina Sartori should never have come to Venice at all, should never have fallen in love with this beautiful and deceptive city. Maybe she should have stayed in Florence when she and Fernando Cortes had arrived there. No doubt that was the only way this could ever have been averted.

But it was too late for that, far too late. And Maria Angelina was long dead. There was only Valentina.

And Valentina would make the choice Maria Angelina never could have.

I wrote a letter. And I sent it to Verona.

Part Three

Love's Dagger

November–December 1538

Chapter 30

Bastiano appeared just as abruptly as he had left, and in much the same manner: he appeared at my palazzo unannounced one night.

I was, thankfully, alone on the night that he appeared. I had been canceling on my clients more often of late. No sooner did I put up my facade than I could feel it crumbling. Once this was all over, I would have to try to rebuild everything somehow. But just then I couldn't handle parties and dinners and lovemaking. Not with such a horror hanging over me.

"Valentina," Bastiano said, stepping into my sitting room, Lauretta trailing behind him ineffectually and babbling that he had just walked right in.

I nearly jumped from my chair at the sight of him, as though he were a ghost. "Leave us, Lauretta," I said at once. She did so without question, shutting the door behind her.

Bastiano removed his cloak, coated with the dust of the road, and let it crumple to the marble floor. "Weeks apart, and that is how you greet me?" he asked, only the barest trace of humor in his voice. "*'Leave us, Lauretta'*?"

"I . . . I am surprised, that is all," I said. I frowned. It had been just two days since I'd sent my letter. And it was close, too close to Malatesta's deadline. "How are you here so soon? You could not have received my letter and made it back by now."

"What letter? I got no such thing. I was on my way back to Venice anyway." Then he grew alarmed. "Why did you send a letter? Is it Ginevra? What has happened?"

The letter had, in fact, said that he must return to Venice at once, for reasons I did not feel comfortable putting into writing. I had been mulling over what I would tell him when he finally arrived. Wondered if it mattered what I told him, in fact. So in the moment, I grasped for the first lie I could think of. "Oh . . . Sonia Abate wrote to tell me that Ginevra was ill," I said quickly. "She was most concerned, so I wrote to you, was hoping I might meet you there. But I've just had another letter that the fever has passed, and all is well."

Bastiano's face relaxed somewhat. "Well, that is a relief, then." He frowned again. "Hopefully no one followed your messenger, but . . . well, it matters not. I am here." He flopped into one of the chairs. "Please tell me you have something to eat."

"I'll run to the kitchen and have something prepared," I said. My heart pounded all the way down the stairs and all the way back up. Bastiano was here, tonight, before I was ready. Not that I would ever be ready.

"Why have you returned?" I asked him, once back in the sitting room. "Has the danger passed?"

He shook his head. "No, but I had to return, nonetheless," he said, leaving it at that.

"Bastiano, won't you tell me what—"

"No," he said again. "No, Valentina, I cannot. Do not ask me."

I did not say anything further about the matter.

We ate the meal that Girolama had quickly thrown together, rice with peas and bits of sausage. Our conversation was stilted; Bastiano was clearly exhausted, and I, for once, could not think of much to say.

"I will need to stay here tonight," he said after we'd finished eating. "And then I shall leave again in the morning."

I nodded. "Of course. Whatever you need."

"Right now I am most in need of a soft bed," he said, rising from the table.

I followed him into the bedchamber, leaving the dishes for the servants to clean up.

Yet once we were alone together, his tiredness seemed to fade away. He reached for me at once and, God forgive me, I could not resist him. He peeled off his clothes and then mine, and we were naked in bed together, and nothing else mattered. I may have been cursed to be a servant of the Shadow God, a bringer of death, but in that moment I felt alive again. Perhaps for the last time.

I drew Bastiano to me, my lips seeking his in the darkness, his short beard scratching my face. But I enjoyed the feeling of it, an intimate, pleasurable sensation. I let out a soft moan as he entered me, slowly and deeply, and as I moved fluidly with him, I forgot, for a short, blessed time, all the shadows and blood and conspiracy that choked my life. There was only this man I loved, only the passion between us. And when my pleasure came upon me, I lost myself completely, shattered and overcome in a way that had not happened for me in some time. I knew I cried out in ecstasy but did not know what I said; whether it was Bastiano's name or simply one long, primal cry. And when Bastiano met my eyes as he reached his own pleasure, as I felt it shudder through his body and threaten to tear him apart even as we were joined together, heard it in the way he groaned my name, I knew it was the same for him.

Maybe the pleasure was all the sharper because I wondered if this might be the last time.

I lost myself in it, wishing this moment of the two of us in bed together might last an eternity, and after, I tried not to let him see me cry.

Interlude

Venice, December 1531

I huffed a sigh of frustration. I had quite lost Amalia in the utter crush of people crammed into Piazza San Marco. It was the first night of Carnevale, and it seemed all of Venice had come out to the grand square: beggars and courtesans and patricians and everyone in between. I had no doubt the doge himself was among the crowd, well-masked for a night of revelry.

With so many people, I was not likely to find her again, but I was pleasantly drunk enough that I didn't truly mind. I would see where the night took me. Wasn't that the fun of Carnevale, really?

I had never seen anything like Venetian Carnevale. Oh, certainly there had been Carnevale celebrations in Rome as well, leading up to Lent, but nothing like this. Not that I had been allowed to attend any of the festivities; my parents deemed such things far too scandalous for a well-brought-up girl. Yet another boon of being a courtesan: when one became a purveyor of scandal, all the scandalous entertainments of the world become available.

But in Venice, Carnevale began on the day after Christmas and ran on for months, up until Lent. It did not maintain the intensity of the merrymaking of this first night, but still, for months at a time the city went about masked, and pleasure seemed to be the chief objective of many. During my first Carnevale in the city, I could scarce keep my eyes from popping out of my head at all the spectacles around me: the elaborate masks and costumes, the performers, the fireworks over the lagoon, the carts selling food and drink and sweets. Marcellina, the courtesan who had come out with me that first year, had laughed at my wide eyes, nudging me. "Careful, or everyone will realize you're a country girl," she'd said.

I hadn't even cared. I simply wanted to take it all in, breathe it all in, revel in the sense of utter freedom I'd felt that night, like nothing I'd ever felt before.

I would never have known such a feeling had I stayed at that convent.

That is one group of people not in attendance, I thought as I pushed through the crowd, still idly looking for Amalia. *Nuns.*

"Scusi. You dropped this."

I almost didn't hear the male voice at first, swallowed up in the noise of the crowd as it was. But soon it was accompanied by a tap on the shoulder. "Scusi, Madonna."

I turned to find a young man standing before me, a silver and blue half mask concealing the upper portion of his face. Yet what I could see of his face seemed most handsome indeed. "Yes?" I asked, arching an eyebrow above my own half mask, adorned with feathers.

"You dropped this," he said again, holding out a lace-edged handkerchief.

I eyed the handkerchief quizzically. "No, I didn't."

"You most certainly did. I saw it fall from your sleeve."

"You saw nothing of the sort," I said. "That isn't my handkerchief. I don't own one such as that."

His hand fell to his side. And was I imagining it, or was there a flush on his cheeks? "Oh," he said, a note of embarrassment in his voice. "My mistake. It . . . it must belong to some other lady."

"Why did you lie?" I pressed him, a half smile curving my lips. I had no shortage of men paying attention to me: young, old, handsome, ugly, rich, not so rich. But there was something about this young man, who seemed to be about my own age, that I found endearing.

"Lie? I? A gentleman?" he scoffed. "It was simply an honest mistake, my lady."

I crossed my arms over my chest, raising an eyebrow again.

He gave a sheepish laugh. "Very well," he said. "It's my own handkerchief. I saw you, beautiful as you are, and thought you might be more inclined to speak to me if you thought I was helping you."

"Indeed," I said, smiling now. "And how many young ladies have you met like this?"

"None!" he said quickly. Too quickly.

"Well," I said. "I commend you for your ingenuity. Now if you'll excuse me, I must find my companion—"

"Wait," he said, placing a hand lightly on my arm, to prevent me from leaving. "Don't go. I . . ." He bit his lip boyishly. "Might I at least walk with you? Prevent you from being jostled by the crowd? Buy you a cup of mulled wine?"

"You can barely see what I look like behind this mask. The piazza is full of women who need no subterfuge to win their attention. Why me?" I asked him bluntly.

I waited for him to repeat how beautiful I was, for him to say that he could tell, even though I was wearing a mask, that I was the most beautiful woman in the piazza that night—nay, in all of Venice. I had heard it all and more from more men than I could count. I had stopped counting long ago, in fact.

But he didn't say anything like that. Instead, his gaze met mine, and he said, "Your mask may hide your face, and your cloak your figure, but neither hides your eyes. And your eyes are full of fire, a fire that drew me in as soon as I saw you. It is a fire I find I must warm myself by or perish of the cold."

For just a moment, I felt myself hypnotized by his words; forgot, just for a second, the teeming crowd around us. I saw him and he saw me, and no one else mattered.

When I found my tongue again, I asked, "What is your name?"

His smile sparkled more than any of the fireworks over the lagoon as he took my hand and kissed it. "Bastiano Bragadin."

Chapter 31

After we made love, Bastiano fell asleep, holding me against him. He slept easily, deeply, and I both envied him and was grateful for it. If only I could fall into such a sleep and wake up years from now to see what course the world had taken without me. Would that not be easier?

Easier perhaps, but impossible.

I looked down at his sleeping face, feeling my heart break. Since the Carnevale night when we'd met in Piazza San Marco, there had been none dearer to me except Amalia. His bashful swagger that night had charmed me, but more than that, it had been the fact that he *saw* me. And even when I, eventually—weeks of secret meetings later—admitted that I was a courtesan, afraid that he would not wish to see me again, he had simply shrugged. "Your profession makes no difference to me," he said. "It is you I want. But I will not be your paying customer, Valentina. I would be more."

And so he always had been.

But there was no point in this nostalgia, not now. It would only make this harder.

The sooner I acted, the sooner it would all be over, and the sooner I could go about putting the shattered pieces of my life back together again.

I slid out from under Bastiano's arm and sat up, looking down at him as he slept. It was not the first time a man I'd shared a bed with had become an enemy—or, perhaps more precisely, that I had become the enemy of a man with whom I shared a bed. But the Shadow God and all the saints as my witnesses, it would be the last.

Would that it had not come to this.

I reached over and slid open the drawer of a small table beside the bed. Silently my fingers closed around the handle of the dagger that was concealed within, and I withdrew it from the sheath.

I crawled over toward Bastiano and straddled him, knees planted firmly on the mattress, and slowly brought the blade to his throat.

I squeezed my eyes shut for a moment, wondering if I could do it, if I could make the killing blow without looking, without having to see what I was doing, without having to watch the life leave his body. Why hadn't I poisoned his wine instead? Then it would already be done. Yet I could not rid myself of the image of Dioniso Secco's final moments, contorting and vomiting and writhing on the floor, just as other men I'd poisoned in the past had done. I could not bear to see Bastiano in such a state.

This would not be easier—quite the contrary—but it would be faster. And if I wished to make it as quick, efficient, and painless as possible, I would need to open my eyes and guide the blade surely so that his suffering was lessened.

I opened my eyes and pressed the edge of the blade to the large vein in his throat. My hand trembled, and I tried my best to steady it. Tears rolled from my eyes; I shuddered as I held in a sob.

I thought of Massimo, the first man I had ever loved, lying butchered in the courtyard. Once again the man I loved would be slaughtered, only this time it would be my hand that wielded the blade.

Everything I had tried to become, everything I had tried to escape, had been for naught.

Do it, Valentina. Do it and be done. Do it and save your daughter.

Would that I had died with the rest of those I loved that day in 1527.

Would, perhaps, that some other woman had caught Bastiano's eye in Piazza San Marco on that Carnevale night.

A tear slid down my cheek and landed on his.

He stirred beneath me, and instinctively I loosened my grip on the dagger, so he would not cut himself with the movement. Still trying to protect him, even now. *What are you doing?* that cold, resolute voice within me screamed. *Do it now! Hurry, before he wakes and realizes what is happening! Spare him as much pain as you can!*

"Valentina?" he murmured. I bit back a cry of despair as he slowly opened his eyes, groggy from wherever his dreams had taken him. His gaze remained hazy with sleep for a moment as he beheld me hovering over him, then went immediately alert, in less than a blink, when he realized what was happening. When he realized that there was a dagger at his throat.

His whole body went rigid, but he did not move, for fear of cutting his own throat open. "Dare I hope that this is some new tactic you are employing to heighten my arousal?" He gave a choked laugh. "Because if so, it is working."

I let out a strange sound that was a mixture of laugh and sob. "Oh, Bastiano," I whispered. "Would that it were."

"Ah," he said, his eyes going from my face to the blade in my hand, then back to me again. "I see."

"I . . ." My eyes flooded with tears, so that he blurred before my eyes. "I do not have a choice."

"There is always a choice," he said conversationally, as though we were having a civil debate over dinner.

"Not this time."

"Malatesta, I've no doubt."

"Who else?"

"Ah," he said again, and through my tears I could see the calculation in his eyes. "Yes, that explains a great deal. I had expected he would come for me, truth be told. I must admit I never dreamed he'd send you. Sadistic bastard."

"He . . . he told me you are a traitor," I said, as if any kind of explanation would help. "That you . . . you are conspiring with the Turks to destroy the Venetian Republic."

"And you believed him?"

"No. But I—"

"*He* is the traitor, Valentina. I am close to proving it. That is why he told you to do this. But I can defeat him—I know I can."

I shook my head. "It doesn't matter. I . . . it's too late now."

"It's not too late, Valentina," he said, a note of pleading in his voice now. "We can bring him down together."

I shook my head, my hand trembling even as I pressed the dagger closer. "We can't," I whispered.

"Don't do this, Valentina."

"I must!" I cried. "I must! If I don't, Malatesta will have Ginevra killed!"

I had not thought it possible for Bastiano to go even stiller, but he did just that. "He will do what?" he whispered.

"That is how he is forcing me to do this! He has someone watching her. He knows where she is, knows whom she lives with . . ."

"And if you do not kill me, Ginevra will die?" Bastiano asked, rage and despair all mingled together in his voice.

"Yes! Yes! Do you truly believe that there is any other reason that I would even consider . . ." I broke down in a sob, then tried to bring myself back under control. "I have tried everything to find a way out of this. Everything."

"Ginevra," Bastiano whispered. The room went completely silent, the only sound my gasping breaths as I fought to stop sobbing.

Then, to my astonishment, Bastiano tipped his head back, better exposing his throat to my blade.

"What . . .?"

"Do it," he said softly. "Do it. If there is truly no other way to save our daughter—and I well believe that you have tried everything else, fierce, splendid, determined, savage, and resourceful woman that you are—then do it."

It was at this that I finally broke. I began to weep, sobs wracking my body. I let the dagger fall to the mattress between us. I was aware of Bastiano picking it up and tossing it away; heard it clatter to the floor on the other side of the room. He gathered me in his arms, wrapping them around me tightly and rocking me as I cried. "I can't," I wept, barely able to form the words. "I can't, God forgive me."

"Shh," Bastiano soothed me. "It's all right, Valentina. It will be all right."

I drew back slightly, looking up into his beloved face. "How can you say that?" I whispered. "How can you say that when I just tried to kill you in our bed and when our daughter's life is forfeit if I do not do it?"

"I just need more time," he said. "A few more days, and I will have what I need to destroy Malatesta once and for all. That is why I came back to Venice."

I shook my head. "We do not have a few more days, Bastiano. If you are not dead by the end of tomorrow, Ginevra will die."

He swore softly. "That is not much time. But it is something." He rose from the bed. "I suppose that time is best spent getting to Ginevra, then, getting her to safety—"

"No," I said. "No, you mustn't. He has someone there, watching her, or so he's led me to believe. And people watching me—I've seen them before, felt them following me. If I leave the city, he will know."

"He cannot get word to his man before I get there," Bastiano said.

"Are you willing to risk it? Are you willing to risk our daughter's life?" I demanded. "Don't you think I would have gone to get her before now if I could have?"

He swore again, louder this time. "What can we do?"

"I don't know!" I cried. "I have been through all this, Bastiano. I have tried with all my might to find another way."

"You know this is just coming from Malatesta, don't you?" he asked. "Not the rest of the Ten. He is planning to make seats on the Council of Ten life terms, so he can amass more and more power. I believe his eventual plan is to overthrow the doge and make himself a king." He laughed shortly. "He learned nothing from Marino Falier, I see."

"I've gathered as much," I said, though that differed slightly from what Felicita had told me—she had never mentioned *life* terms. "I put a letter in the bocca di leone, denouncing him—"

"You did what?"

"We haven't the time for that now, but yes, I wrote a letter with some things I knew he'd done and some other information I'd gathered. I have no hard evidence, of course. I just thought that it would get someone's attention, and he would be stopped. But he got to the letter first, damn him, before anyone else, and when he came here to fling it in my face, he all but confirmed what I'd written."

"Then why did you not request an audience with one of the other members of the Ten? Or even the doge himself?"

"Why should they listen to me? Because I killed Dioniso Secco, which I know now the Ten did not order, so I am implicated in the plot myself. And even if I had not, I am a courtesan, and a woman. Why should they listen to me?"

"Wait. How did you know that the Ten didn't order Secco's murder?"

"I . . . Ah." Time to confess to something of which I was still ashamed, which felt silly now in light of the fact that I had been prepared to kill him. "I . . . found some papers in your satchel one night, saw a note confirming that the Ten had not ordered the assassination. I'd begun to suspect, but that confirmed it."

"So you knew then. Knew that I was working against Malatesta."

"I guessed as much, but after that I decided to stay out of it, as you bade me. When you fled Venice, I knew for sure, and when he came to coerce me into killing you—well, by then his trap had been laid. And tonight I . . ." I bit back a sob. "I was out of time. Ginevra . . ."

"I understand. I understand, Valentina. God, that fucking traitorous piece of shit. Would that I could kill him myself, but I hear he's ensconced himself in the Doge's Palace."

"It's true. I went to his palazzo to do just that, and one of his servants told me where he was. He no doubt expected me to come for him after he gave me his assignment. And when he came here . . ." I scowled, remembering how he'd pushed poor Marta down the stairs as I pursued him. "I'll tell you the story later, but he got away from me."

He ran his fingers through his hair. "Very well. There is a man here I must speak to, who has information. He will speak to none but me, and in person. That is why I returned to Venice; I was not making progress in Verona, so this seemed like a chance that needed taking. And I see I arrived at just the right time."

"What if the man doesn't show? Or he doesn't have the information you need after all?"

He shot me a look heavy with anguish and fury. "Then I will drown myself in a canal."

"No," I whispered.

"You said it yourself. What else is there to be done?"

"No, Bastiano. This is why I did not try to tell you at once. I knew you would do something stupid."

"What difference if I do the deed myself or you do it?" he asked. "Other than my saving you some of the pain."

I closed my eyes.

"Speaking to my contacts is our only chance, Valentina. There is another man here I have been working with; I will see him first, see if he has been able to find anything, and then I will meet our informant. It may all be for naught, but I must at least try."

I took a deep breath and opened my eyes again, grabbing on to a bedpost to steady myself. "Very well. Yes. We must try. Let me dress, and I will come with you."

"No," he said at once. "It's—"

"If you say it's too dangerous, Bastiano, so help me!" I flared. "There are few in Venice more dangerous than I."

He gave me a sardonic look. "I am well aware, and I would never dream of saying something so absurd to you," he said. "What I was about to say, before you insisted on an interruption that we do not have time for, is that it is better if I go alone, as the man I wish to speak to knows and trusts me. He knows you not at all, and we have no time to convince him to trust you as well."

"Would my very presence with you not lead him to believe that I can be trusted?"

Bastiano sighed, frustrated. "Perhaps, but again we have not the time to waste to convince him."

"I am not being left behind, Bastiano," I said, going to my wardrobe for a gown and my heaviest cloak, one with a large hood. "So convince him we shall."

Bastiano sighed again as he donned his own cloak and hat, knowing that there would be no arguing with me.

"Lace," I said, tugging on a simple, dark dress and turning my back to him so that he might do up the laces.

Thus attired, and with a dagger concealed in the pocket of my gown, we went down a floor and left via the secret staircase in my "public" bedchamber. No need to alert the servants to what we were about.

"Wait," I said as we made to pass Amalia's palazzo. "Just a moment. There is one thing I must do first."

"Valentina, we haven't the time!"

"For this we do," I said, and I ran to the back door of Amalia's palazzo, pounding on it. "Wait outside. Best if she doesn't see you."

Bastiano obliged, melting into the shadows so that I was not even sure where he'd gone.

It took a few moments—too long, in my mind—but then one of Amalia's maids came to the door. "Madonna Riccardi?" she asked, blinking rapidly. "I . . . I am sorry, but Madonna Amante is upstairs with a client, and—"

"Fetch her," I said, pushing past her into the kitchen.

"Madonna, I don't think—"

"This is urgent and will not take long."

Defeated, the maid left to do my bidding.

I paced the kitchen in the light of a single candle, waiting.

A few minutes later, Amalia appeared. She had obviously been asleep and looked a bit confused. "Valentina?" she said. "One of my clients is upstairs. This is—"

"I know, and I am sorry, amica mia," I said quickly. "I will leave momentarily. I just need you to promise me one thing."

"Anything," she said immediately.

And that was why I knew I could still trust Amalia, no matter what. Even now. "If something happens to me after today—if I don't return home in the next day or two—I need you to promise me you will take care of Ginevra."

"Valentina," she said, coming toward me. "What are you saying? What is happening? What—"

"Just promise me."

"Valentina, please do not take any unnecessary risks."

I laughed harshly. "Oh, it is all necessary, I am afraid. Just . . ." I lowered my voice. "Promise me, Amalia. Promise me that you will see to it that she is well cared for, that she never wants for anything, that she . . ." I cleared my throat, trying to banish the emotion lodged in it. "That she can make her own choices, when she is grown. And that she knows me. Please. Promise me."

"I promise," Amalia whispered. "Of course I do. But please, Valentina . . . please be careful."

I reached out and flung my arms around her, holding her tightly. "I will try," I whispered in her ear. I stepped back. "Thank you, Amalia."

Her face, as she looked at me in the dim light, was devastated. "Come back to me," she whispered. "Come back to Ginevra."

"I will do everything in my power. I love you, Amalia."

"And I you, Valentina."

Then I left.

"What was that all about?" Bastiano hissed as I joined him outside again and we made our way toward the lagoon.

I told him briefly what I had asked of Amalia, and he said nothing. He just nodded once.

And then our focus was back on the matter at hand.

"If we cannot get the information we need tonight," I said as we wove our way through the darkened streets, "then what?"

His gaze met mine, cool and level. "I've already said, haven't I?"

"No," I said. "No, surely—"

He looked away. "This is our last chance, Valentina," he said, his voice low and urgent. "If this fails, then I . . . I have to do what I must to protect our daughter. And you."

"You can't," I whispered.

He laughed incredulously and shook his head. "You had a blade to my throat in our bed not half an hour ago," he said. "You know there may not be another way out."

I could not argue further, as we had found a man sleeping in his gondola at the base of a bridge. Bastiano roused him and told him where we were headed, passing him a coin. Then we climbed into the gondola and were off.

We remained silent as the gondolier steered us out into the Giudecca Canal, seemingly headed for the island of Giudecca itself. I raised my eyebrows questioningly at Bastiano. "This is not where I usually meet this man," he acknowledged. "We've always met in the city proper. But he stays at a house on Giudecca when he is in Venice. I made it my business to find out as much as I could about him."

"Who is he?" I asked, my voice low.

"Spanish. An old mercenary, I believe. He's done quite a bit of . . . er . . . information gathering for the Ten over the years, or so I hear. That was how he got wind of Malatesta's plot. I ran across him when I started looking into Malatesta on behalf of my father." Bastiano chuckled darkly and shook his head. "My father asked me to do some digging into his old political rival to get to the bottom of this legislation he'd proposed, see if there was any truth to this supposed Ottoman conspiracy. I doubt he knew how far it would lead me."

"Or that it would send an assassin to your bed," I murmured.

"Indeed. My father was simply looking for some political leverage, and now we've uncovered a real plot against Venice—only one from the inside."

We fell silent after that, and I drew my cloak tighter around me, shivering in the cold November wind off the lagoon.

The gondolier brought us to a dock at the part of the island that Bastiano specified, and we quickly disembarked. "Do not wait for us," Bastiano called to the gondolier over his shoulder. Out of the corner of my eye, I saw the man shove off from the dock, guiding his craft back across the Giudecca Canal.

I followed Bastiano away from the water and to a modest, well-kept house, albeit one that was entirely nondescript. I stayed close to his side as he knocked on the door, loud enough to make himself heard, but hopefully not loud enough to wake any neighbors. "Come on—open the door!" he hissed. He ceased his knocking and put an ear to the door.

Nothing happened for a moment, and then I thought I heard footsteps within. A few seconds later, the wooden door creaked open.

"Thank God," Bastiano said to the man who'd opened it. "I need to speak with you immediately. Things have come to a head. This is—"

But when I saw the man's face in the flickering light of the single candle he carried, I gasped and staggered back a step.

After the life I'd lived, after everything I'd done, I had thought that nothing could ever truly shock me again. But this did.

The man squinted at me in the poor light. Then astonishment came over his features. "Maria Angelina," he said wonderingly.

Bastiano froze, recognizing the name I had been born with. I had only ever told the full story of my past to him and to Amalia. And to the man standing before us.

"Fernando," I said faintly. "Fernando Cortes."

Chapter 32

My hand shook as I lifted the glass of cheap wine to my lips. We were huddled around a fire Cortes had lit in the grate of his kitchen, and he had offered both me and Bastiano the wine to warm us after our journey across the open water. I found I could hardly take my eyes from the grizzled old soldier as he puttered about the room, finding chairs and adding more wood to the fire. When there were no more tasks that required his attention, he sat down himself and faced us. His eyes lingered on me, on my simple yet well-made gown and the heavy velvet of my cloak. His lips quirked into a half smile as he said, "I see you didn't stay at that convent."

I laughed. "No, I didn't."

"How long did you last?"

"Left the night you dropped me off."

He laughed outright at that, slapping his knee. "I might have known even those high convent walls couldn't contain you."

"I daresay the nuns are happier this way," I said, raising an eyebrow as I took another sip of wine. "I certainly am."

I longed to ask him of his life, where he had been and what he had been doing in the years since I'd last seen him. Had he ever left Venice, or had he been here the whole time?

But Bastiano spoke before I could ask. "As touching as this reunion is, time is a luxury of which we are very short at the moment. Fernando, perhaps we might explain why we've come—"

"I know well enough why you've come," Cortes interrupted. "The letters."

"Yes. I need them. Now."

"I've bad news on that front," Cortes said. "Zanetto is dead."

Bastiano shot to his feet. "Dead?"

Cortes nodded. "I went to the room he rents this evening, to see if I could convince him to talk to me in case you didn't make it back. I found him with his throat cut ear to ear. And anything he had of value is gone. Believe me, I looked."

"By the Virgin's tits," Bastiano swore. He dropped heavily back into his chair. "We are sunk, then." To me, he said, "Zanetto is the man I came back to Venice to meet with. The one who would only meet with me."

"Perhaps not," Cortes said. "There is one more man I can meet with, see if he might have anything. Some kind of clerk who's done work for Malatesta."

Bastiano swore. "We are out of time, Cortes."

"What letters?" I interrupted.

"Malatesta's letters," Bastiano said. "Signed by him. Promising bribes to certain senators and members of the Great Council in return for supporting his legislation. The legislation about the term limits for the Council of Ten."

"And this Zanetto," Cortes added, "also claimed to have a letter from Malatesta to an official at the Spanish court, promising all sorts of favors if the Spanish will give him the gold to pay the bribes. A copy, no doubt. He claims he was paid to carry the message—he's a sailor, so it's possible he took it right to Spain. Or was about to."

I felt the blood drain from my face. "Dear God," I breathed. "Once the Spanish get their fingers on any part of Venice, we'll never be rid of them." The Spanish and the Holy Roman Emperor—my old, most hated enemies.

Bastiano nodded. "Yes. Apparently Malatesta is willing to become a puppet doge for the Spanish rather than never be doge at all."

"The fool," I snarled. "He might well have become doge on his own someday."

"Men like him cannot wait and do things the right way," Bastiano said. "Once they get a taste of power, they must get their hands on the rest of it, no matter the cost."

I shook my head. "This is exactly what the Venetian government was built to prevent," I said.

"Yes. And still he decided to try it."

"Why are we out of time, Bragadin?" Cortes asked, bringing us back to the matter at hand.

"Malatesta knows I am working against him—have been working against him for a while. Thus he has given my beautiful lover"—he gave a nod to me—"until tomorrow to kill me."

Cortes's eyes widened in surprise at this. "He thought you would . . ."

"He threatened our daughter. But that is a story we haven't time for just now."

Cortes shook his head. "I don't have the letters," he said. "As I said, there is one more man who might have something. I'll go see him directly."

"Are we certain these letters ever existed at all?" I asked. "Malatesta is far too careful to ever put anything incriminating into writing, or so I would have thought."

"There are multiple people who claim to have seen them, and he would have had to send some kind of signed communication to the Spanish crown for them to consider his plot, I'd wager," Bastiano said. "Either no one has them in their possession anymore, or they are too afraid to cross Malatesta. I can't say I blame them, after Secco."

"You . . . you didn't let me kill Secco when you knew better, did you?" I whispered.

Bastiano reached out and took my hands in his. "No," he said, his eyes seeking and holding mine in the dim light. "I didn't know then. I would never have let you go through with it if I'd known differently."

From the corner of my eye, I saw Cortes looking between Bastiano and me, listening and piecing together my role in all of this.

"I suspected," Bastiano went on. "I suspected that Malatesta wanted Secco dead for not cooperating, for promising to thwart Malatesta's plans. But I wasn't sure. I couldn't be sure until after Secco was already dead."

"Until after I'd already killed him," I whispered. "I eliminated one of his rivals and implicated myself in his treason all at once. Then he had me trapped." I shook my head, pressing my hands against my face. "If only I'd seen how he was using me before it was too late. I could have—"

Bastiano gently pulled my hands away from my face, squeezed them in his. "You did what you had to do to survive," he said, his eyes never leaving mine. "Malatesta would likely have killed you if you'd defied him. He's . . . he's gone unhinged. Better Secco should die a thousand times than you."

He rose and turned to me. "We should go back home," he said. "I think you need to go to Ginevra. We must take the chance of trying to get to her before Malatesta can act. I will stay here and see if we can find the evidence we need to bring him up on charges before the rest of the Ten. I'll speak to my father, find out if he's come up with anything else. Cortes, send me word once you've spoken to this clerk."

Oh, how I had hoped this trip would give us everything we'd need, that we'd come sailing back across the Giudecca Canal with what amounted to a death warrant for Ambrogio Malatesta. But it was not to be.

Would that Tomasina had come through with something—if these letters the two men spoke of did indeed exist, they'd be in Malatesta's home somewhere, under lock and key. But had she turned up anything, I knew Bettina would have told me.

I took a deep breath and rose. But all was not lost. There was still work to do. I still had to save my daughter. I could speak to Bettina when I returned home, see if perhaps Tomasina could get me access to Malatesta's house so that I might search it myself, if nothing else.

"Andiamo," Bastiano said, interrupting my thoughts as he made for the front door.

"Wait," Cortes said, holding up a hand to stop me as I made to follow him. "A word?"

I threw a questioning glance at Bastiano. He huffed with impatience but said, "I will go hire us a gondola," and left.

I turned to face my old guardian in the dim light.

He regarded me silently for a moment, arms crossed over his chest. "I saw you once, you know," he said finally.

"You . . . what?"

"I saw you once, in Venice," he said, nodding in the direction of the city. "I saw you disembarking from a gondola at a fancy palazzo, dressed like a queen on the arm of some handsome patrician."

"Oh," I said. For once, I did not know what to say.

"I wasn't surprised you'd left the convent," he said. "But . . ." He shook his head. "I didn't want this life for you, Maria Angelina. To have to turn to whoring. That was why I took you to the convent in the first place."

"I couldn't stay there," I said. "I could not consign myself to that living death, not after how hard I'd fought to get here. To stay alive."

Cortes was silent at this.

"Do not pity me," I said, a bit angry now. "Or judge me. I *chose* this life, Fernando. I became a courtesan because I *wanted* to. Because I wanted to live my own life, by my own rules. And this is the only life I've ever seen that allows a woman to do that." I swallowed down a lump of emotion in my throat. "I survived because you taught me how. But surviving and living are two different things."

The only sound for a moment was the crackling of the fire. Then Cortes uncrossed his arms and nodded. "I understand that, I think. You should have the right to choose for yourself."

"And I did," I said softly.

He nodded again, and then he smiled that rare smile. "And you didn't forget the tricks with the dagger I taught you, I gather."

I smiled in return. "No. I . . . I've tried to use what you taught me for good."

"I've no doubt that you've done what you felt to be right."

His pride, his approval, ignited a warm glow in my belly, one to rival the embers in the hearth. "Would that you could use your skills on Malatesta," he said, his face darkening again.

"I long for the chance."

Cortes smiled again. "If you hunt him down, he'd meet his Maker before long."

"Or Lucifer, more like."

Cortes laughed gruffly. "Indeed. Well, you'd best get along. Get word to me once it's all over, if you can. That you're all safe."

"By the Shadow God, I hope we will be."

"The Shadow God?"

I paused. "I've . . . I've always thought that I serve a . . . a more sinister god, doing what I do. That a god who lurks in the shadows is the only one who can find favor with one such as me."

"Perhaps it is so," he said. "Though that's too much of philosophy for an old solider like me." He reached out and patted my shoulder. "Serve your Shadow God well, Maria Angelina—or Valentina, I think it is now. And if you can bring him Ambrogio Malatesta's head, then do it."

There was so much more I wanted to tell Cortes, so much more I wanted him to know, so much I wanted to say. Instead, impulsively I flung myself into his arms. And he returned the embrace awkwardly, just as he had once before.

Chapter 33

As Bastiano and I entered my palazzo in the growing light of dawn, speaking rapidly about our plans for me to collect Ginevra and for Bastiano to try to find more evidence, I did not even notice Lauretta until we nearly crashed into her at the top of the stairs. "Mi scusi, Madonna," she said, dropping a quick curtsey, more for Bastiano's benefit than my own, I was sure. "I was just looking for you; I did not realize you had left."

"Yes, yes," I said impatiently as Bastiano and I continued up to the third floor of the palazzo, Lauretta scurrying along behind us. "What is it?"

"I've a letter for you, Madonna," she said, handing it to me as we reached the third-floor landing. "Amalia Amante's maid just delivered it."

I stopped dead. "Amalia?" I asked, suddenly fearful of what might be on the bit of parchment I now held.

"Sí, Madonna."

"Thank you, Lauretta. You are dismissed."

"Shall I bring you and Signor Bragadin something to—"

"Not just now, thank you. You are dismissed."

Seeming startled by my abruptness, Lauretta nonetheless turned quickly and descended the stairs again, moving out of sight. I felt vaguely guilty for being so short with her, but there was no time for pleasantries just now. I would apologize to her later, once this was all over. However it ended.

Bastiano had resumed talking, but I scarcely heard him as we stepped into my bedchamber. My hands were shaking slightly as I turned the folded parchment over in my hands. What could Amalia possibly have to say after what had happened just a few short hours ago? And why would she choose a letter in which to say it? We never wrote to each other, save a brief note here and there to invite the other on an outing or for a visit. It was easier to simply stop over and see each other than to take the time to write and get a servant to carry the message.

So what had she put in this letter that she couldn't—or didn't want to—say to me in person?

Only one way to find out.

Tuning out Bastiano, I slid my finger under the thin wax seal and opened it.

The letter contained just five simple sentences, each one more extraordinary than the last. There was no salutation and no signature, just an address at the end.

Once back inside my bedroom, the door to the corridor closed, Bastiano turned to me and slapped his hat against his thigh in frustration. "I'd so hoped Cortes would have those letters," he said. "How much easier that would have made it. I certainly imagined Zanetto would still be alive when I got back to Venice to meet with him."

"You might have told me you were working with him," I said, momentarily diverted from the contents of Amalia's letter. "With Cortes—that he was here in Venice. That he was well. Saints, I . . . I suppose I thought him long dead."

"I didn't know he was the man who rescued you all those years ago," Bastiano said. "You never told me his name."

"Didn't I? I suppose I must not have."

"No. I would have remembered." He ran his fingers through his hair. "Why are we talking about this, of all things, now? By the Virgin's tits, Valentina. This is dire, this situation we find ourselves in. Those letters—" He broke off. "They are our last hope."

"We tried," I offered. "It was worth a try."

At my offhanded tone, Bastiano looked at me suspiciously. "You seem awfully unconcerned by this turn of events," he said. "These letters are our last chance, and we both know it. If Cortes cannot get them, I must . . . to save Ginevra, I . . ." His voice broke.

"No, you don't. And you won't."

He looked up at me, disbelief and hope on his face. "You . . . you've thought of something?"

"After a fashion," I said, letting the letter fall to the bed. "Let's just say an opportunity has presented itself to me."

He was on his feet at once. "An opportunity? What does that mean? What has happened?" he demanded.

"Follow me, and I will explain," I said, leading him out of the bedroom and into my dressing room. I went to a wardrobe and opened it, pulling out a cloak as well as a belt and some other clothing, bundling it all in my arms. "This letter I received," I said, "was a tip, I suppose you could call it. I know where Malatesta is going to be tonight. And he'll be alone."

"A tip from whom? From Amalia?" he demanded.

"Yes." With my back to him, I took the key to the dressing room off my dressing table and slipped it into my pocket.

"And you're sure this tip is . . . reliable? Sure enough to risk your life, and mine—and Ginevra's?"

I met his eyes coolly. "Yes. Wait here just a moment, and I'll show you the letter."

I went back into my bedroom and closed the door to the dressing room behind me. Before Bastiano knew what was happening, I used the key to the lock the door from the outside.

There was a moment of silence, in which he surely heard the lock clunking into place. Then, in an instant, he was at the door, pounding his fists against it on the other side. "Valentina, what are you doing? Let me out!"

"I'm sorry, Bastiano," I called to him. "I am. But I have to do this alone."

"Do what alone? Meet Malatesta? No! I need to come with you! Don't be a fool!"

"I need to do this alone," I repeated, "and I need you to wait here while I do it. I need to make sure you won't do anything heroic and stupid in the meantime."

"Valentina!" he cried, his outrage audible even through the heavy wood of the door. "You cannot be serious! This is utter shit!"

"It's not," I said serenely, with the same deadly calm that had overtaken me since reading Amalia's letter.

There was a pause, and I heard his footsteps move away, perhaps as he glanced around futilely to see if there was another possible exit. But there wasn't—the dressing room had no windows and was accessible only by the door to my bedroom.

"Just wait here, Bastiano," I called to him, beginning to dress in the clothes I'd pulled from the wardrobe. "When I come back, this will all be over. We'll all be safe. I promise."

"Valentina! Tu sei pazza! You must let me come with you!"

But I did not respond. I pulled on the pair of breeches I kept for those occasions, like this one, when I wanted to be in no way encumbered by skirts. I also donned a man's shirt and vest, and braided my hair back in one long, tight braid. With it tucked under my cloak, no one would glance twice at a slender young man making his way across Venice.

Ignoring Bastiano's continued shouting, I settled the belt about my hips. It had a dagger sheathed at either hip, and there was a dagger hidden in each of the boots I pulled on next.

I donned the cloak over everything, pulling the hood up over my face. I took the letter I'd received from the bed and slid it under the door to Bastiano.

"This is the letter I received from Amalia," I said, and he finally went quiet as he stooped to pick it up. "I must go. And when I return, this will all be over."

The silence continued as Bastiano no doubt read the same five lines that had so astounded me that I'd needed to read them several times to be sure they really said what I thought they said. What I needed them to say:

I have written to Ambrogio Malatesta and asked him to meet me at an empty house in Dorsoduro tonight at five o' clock. He and I have met there before, so he is sure to come. I have told him that I have information about you that will be of interest to him.

The house will be unlocked. Do what you must.

Below that was the address of the house in question, all in Amalia's hand.

Bastiano would, one day, forgive me for doing to him what Massimo had done to me all those years ago: locking me in to keep me safe. For I had vowed long since that I would never be the one locked up for her own safety again.

On my way out, I instructed my servants in no uncertain terms that they were *not* to release Bastiano from my dressing room, no matter what he may say or threaten. Then I was gone, down the stairs and out the door. I headed for the Rialto Bridge, where I would cross the Grand Canal and make my way into Dorsoduro. I was hours early, of course, but I did not mind. I would take no chance of missing him. I would lay my trap and lie in wait for him. And this time, he would not escape me.

I would make one last offering to the Shadow God.

Chapter 34

The house in Dorsoduro was neither large nor richly furnished. From the outside it was altogether forgettable, which likely was the point. I didn't know who owned it; perhaps Malatesta himself, to serve as a secret safe house, a place for the trading of information or goods or the stowing of secrets. It didn't matter. All that mattered was that I was there and that soon Malatesta would be as well, and then all of this would end.

Had the chance for me to kill Malatesta come about in any other way, I would still, incredibly, have felt a little remorse in doing it. Not because I thought the man deserved to live, and certainly not because I had any qualms about doing what must be done to defend my lover and my child. I had killed for far less, to be sure. No, the guilt I would have felt would have been entirely on Amalia's behalf. Yet she had absolved me of that guilt in putting pen to paper, in sending me that letter. In arranging this, my salvation. I could not know what it had cost her to do it, and I knew I could never adequately repay her. I was perfectly content to spend the rest of my life trying, though.

And I was not only saving Bastiano, Ginevra, and myself. This time, I was well and truly saving Venice, the city I loved, from the grasp of a would-be tyrant. One who would betray her, who would sell her to Spain and whoever else would bid just so that he might work his own will. I had been at the mercy once of men who wanted to inflict their own will on the world, and who had had the power to do it. Because of them, I had lost my home, and everyone I'd loved had been killed. I would never allow that to happen again. Not to me and not to everyone else in Venice—at Malatesta's whim just because he could not be sated by the power he already had.

And I would show Malatesta that I was not just a tool to be used by him, that I and the rest of the courtesans and women in this city were not simply objects for a man's pleasure or benefit. It was the women of Venice who would destroy Malatesta, the women of Venice who would defend our home and ourselves when needed. Not just me, but Amalia, Felicita, and Margarita, and even Tomasina and Bettina, all wanting revenge on a man who had done them wrong.

Men like Malatesta thought women were easily discarded. But we were not. We were resilient and unforgiving, and if we were to be confined to the shadows, then from the shadows we would strike.

Just as Amalia's letter had promised, the front door of the house was unlocked. I walked all about the place once, twice, three times, until I knew the basic layout well enough, knew where each hallway led, and where and how large each room was. There was the front door, which I had come in and which faced the street. There was also a back door, through the kitchen, which let out onto a small alleyway. There were no other entrances.

I guessed that Malatesta would come in the front door, but I could not be certain of that, and it would do me no good to be caught unawares. So I choose a small parlor in which to make my stand. It was nearer the front door than the back, but was preferable to the little dining room, which had two doors. The parlor only had one, so once Malatesta was inside, I could close the single door and ensure he could not escape. I removed all the blades from the house, from kitchen knives to a letter opener, and dumped them all in the Giudecca Canal. He would likely have at least a dagger on his person, but I wouldn't make it any easier for him than that.

Then, after walking through the house once more, I settled in to wait.

I paced about the room and shook my arms, wanting to keep the blood flowing to my limbs so that I was loose and ready when the time came. The hours marched by slowly, marked only by the changing of the light coming through the narrow windows in the parlor, by the early nightfall of these latter days of the year. I used a flint I'd found in the kitchen to light a single branch of candles in the parlor. Darkness would aid me, certainly, but I also needed to be able to see what I was doing, at least a little. I would only get one chance.

Then, at what must have been five o' clock or thereabouts, I heard the front door open.

"Amalia?" Malatesta's familiar voice called. I heard the door shut behind him. "Are you here?"

"In here," I called, in a fair approximation of Amalia's voice. I moved swiftly and silently to the door and pressed my back along the wall beside it.

A moment later he came through the door and into the room, looking around the dimly lit space. "Amalia? Where—"

I slammed the door shut and stepped in front of it.

I could see, even in the dim light, the rigid tension in his spine at the sound, even before he turned. He knew. He knew he was caught. That he was trapped.

But he turned to face me anyway—I'll credit him that much. And for just an instant, just a moment before he cloaked himself in his arrogant, confident facade once more, I saw the fear in the shadowed darkness of his eyes. And the sight was sweeter and more intoxicating than the finest wine I'd ever tasted. And I had tasted many a fine wine in my day.

"Valentina," he said, his smooth, aristocratic speech not managing to completely hide the dread in his voice. "I confess I am surprised to see you here. I should not be, and yet I am." He cursed under his breath. "Damn that lying whore, Amalia. Damn her!"

As if everything else were not enough, that last insult to my friend, the person closest to a sister I had ever had or ever would, cracked what shred of control I still possessed. I was on him in an instant, and as he was not expecting me to move so swiftly, was not anticipating the strength of my slender frame, he was taken off guard. I slammed him up against the front wall of the room, between the curtained windows that looked out onto the Giudecca Canal beyond, a blade at his throat. "You dare insult her with some of your last words?" I snarled, my teeth bared like a hunting lioness. "She is worth a hundred of you. She loved you, for some reason, a fiend who is not worthy of her attention or her love. You do not know the meaning of the word *love*."

He managed to chuckle, injecting a note of derision into the sound. "I loved her enough to trust her," he said. "That is my mistake. My fatal mistake perhaps."

I pressed the edge of the blade farther into his throat, drawing a trickle of blood. "Your mistakes are too numerous to list," I hissed. "But without doubt your biggest one was threatening my daughter and trying to force me to kill the man I love." Another bead of blood ran down his pale throat.

"And attempting to overthrow the Venetian state? Or perhaps not overthrow, but at least bend it to my will. Was that not one of my critical mistakes?"

I blinked, stunned even then that he would admit it so baldly, and he took that moment to shove me back. I stumbled once, and he made a dash for the door, knocking the dagger from my hand as he went. I sprang forward, cursing myself for a fool, and seized his arm, wrenching it back and out of its socket. He cried out in pain and tried to spin toward me. Remembering Fernando Cortes's advice all those years ago—*"Use your attacker's strength against him"*—I stepped toward him when he expected me to draw back, and he ran right into the knee I'd lifted to groin level. He let out another scream of pain, and while he was disoriented, I pushed him backward against one of the walls again, drawing the other blade from my hip and putting it back at his throat.

"A fine effort," I drawled, his face still contorted in agony. "It nearly worked."

He did not reply, still too winded from the pain.

"Certainly your plot to overthrow the Venetian state would have been your downfall sooner or later," I continued. "Someone would have caught wind—someone did, in fact. Several someones: Bastiano Bragadin. His father. A very fine man named Fernando Cortes. And Dioniso Secco as well. That's why you needed me to kill some of those men. And sooner or later they would have been able to prove it, and your colleagues on the Council of Ten would have taken your head." I clucked in disapproval. "Did you learn nothing from Marino Falier?"

"I would have succeeded where Falier failed," he snarled. "No one suspected me. No one who mattered. Many of them even agreed with me!"

"Maybe," I said, positioning the tip of the dagger just below his eye, so that if he so much as sneezed, he'd put out his own eye. He froze, even seemed to cease breathing. "But that is not why I'm going to kill you, Malatesta, though it does give me a bit of patriotic pride in doing so."

"Oh no?" he asked softly, still very aware of the tip of my dagger. "And was it patriotic pride that made you kill without a second thought all those men I told you to kill?"

"I'm going to kill you," I went on, "because you're a monster who tried to destroy everyone I love." I shifted the blade so that it was at his throat once more.

"Rather hypocritical of you to be calling anyone else a monster just now, is it not, Valentina?" His voice squeaked slightly with fear; he could not hide it anymore.

"I am the monster you made me," I said.

Three things happened at once. I tightened my grip on the dagger, ready to make the killing cut. I heard the door of the parlor, at my back, open. And Malatesta's eyes, turning wild with hope, looked beyond my shoulder, to the person who had come in.

"Help! Help me!" he cried. He began to struggle against me, to try to get to whoever the person was.

I could not pause, could not take the time to turn and see who had come in, if they were friend or foe, if they were a danger to me or not. Without further hesitation, I shoved Malatesta back against the wall, hard, and dug my dagger in deep, cutting his throat from ear to ear.

He made that horrible gurgling sound men make when they choke on their own blood. Crimson streamed over my hands, and I let him drop to the floor as he clutched at the wound. Only then did I turn to see who had entered the room.

I flinched with surprise and horror at the sight of Amalia Amante standing there, dressed in a dark gown and dark cloak, impassively watching her lover drown in blood.

He looked up at her, tried to speak, but of course he could not. Then his gaze moved to me, and with one last horrible rattle he went still, his head falling back to the floor and exposing the hideous gash at his throat.

I longed to go to Amalia, to embrace her, to turn her away from the sight before her eyes—the deed she had been instrumental in bringing about. But as my hands were coated with her lover's blood, I did not try to touch her. "Amalia," I asked, weariness and confusion mingled in my voice, "why did you come? You should have spared yourself this sight."

She walked over to stand near me, looking down at Malatesta's body. "No," she said quietly. "It was right that I was here. To see what I had wrought. I owed him that much, I think."

"You owed him nothing," I said savagely. "How many times must I tell you he was not worthy of you?"

"And you are right," she agreed. "I always knew that was true, you know, when he wished to keep me a secret, when he would not visit me openly. But . . ." She drew in an unsteady breath. "I loved him. I let that blind me to a lot of things—or if not blind me, then at least make me not care about them. I should have known better."

"We have all been fools in love at one time or another," I offered. I wiped the blade of my dagger clean on Malatesta's cloak and slid it back into its sheath at my hip.

She smiled halfheartedly. "Perhaps. You chose far better than I did, though. Bastiano is a good man. He truly loves you, without reservation, far beyond what you can do for him. And he loves your daughter." Her face sobered as she looked back down at Malatesta, lying in his pool of blood. "That was why I had to save him. Save you all."

"You did not have to do this," I said in a low voice.

She looked up at me, her eyes shining with tears in the dim candlelight. "But I did," she said, her voice raw with anguish. "I did. I could not let Ambrogio hurt you. And until you came to my house this morning . . . you should have seen your face, Valentina. White as a ghost's, but determined. You knew there was a very good chance you might die—I could see it. Even before you asked me to care for Ginevra. And for you to trust me so, even when your greatest enemy was my lover . . ." She shook her head. "I couldn't let him do it, couldn't let him work his evil against you."

"But you loved him," I whispered.

She nodded, and at last the tears fell. "I did, I did. I wondered why you were asking me about him a couple weeks ago. And then the night when you told me someone on the Ten had told you to kill Bastiano, I . . . I am ashamed to say it, but I refused to believe it was Ambrogio. He would not do that, I told myself. He would never. He could not be so cruel, so manipulative. But I knew he could be. He tried very hard not to show that side of himself to me, but I saw glimpses of it from time to time. Still, I told myself it could not be him, that there were other members of the Ten that could have given you your orders. What were the chances? But then that day that you came to my palazzo, when you saw him and he saw you . . ."

She trailed off and wiped her eyes, and I saw her expression harden, harden into the resolve that had no doubt propelled her to write me that letter and send Ambrogio Malatesta into the lioness's mouth. "I could no longer lie to myself. And because of all the hurt he had caused me over the years, and what he was doing to you, and what he was threatening to do to Ginevra—and I know he was capable of having a child killed, God help me; I knew there was darkness enough in his soul even for that—I could not let him. I could not let him do it, not when I had the power to stop it. I could never have looked you in the face again had I not done it, and this morning I realized that losing *you* was what was truly unthinkable." She looked up at me. "In the end I loved you more than him. It was that simple, I think."

Had I not been covered in blood, I would have thrown my arms around her right then.

Chapter 35

I collapsed in a chair in my private sitting room, relieved at what was written in the letter in my hand. "He has her," I said to Amalia, who had been visiting when the letter was delivered. "Bastiano found Ginevra alive and perfectly well, and he has her in his care. They are on their way back to Venice now."

Amalia closed her eyes, her lips moving in what seemed to be a silent prayer of gratitude. "Thanks be to the Blessed Mother," she said. "What will you do now?"

"We will decide that when he gets here," I said, passing her the letter so she could see for herself what Bastiano had written, so she could see the happy outcome that her actions, her sacrifice, had wrought. Once Amalia left, I would write a letter to Fernando Cortes on Giudecca, informing him my daughter was safe. A much cheerier letter to follow the one I had sent immediately after killing Malatesta, which simply read: *It is done. We are safe.*

"Bastiano is bringing Ginevra back to Venice for now. She can stay here for a time. I can put off my clients for a few days at least. I don't really want them visiting when she is here." I sighed. "She cannot go back to Vito and Sonia Abate, that much is plain. Perhaps Malatesta never shared her location with the rest of the Ten, but I cannot risk it. And I do not want to put the Abate family in any further danger." I sighed again, mournfully. "It pains me to take Ginevra away from the only home she's ever known, but I don't know that I have a choice."

"No, I do not think you do," Amalia agreed. "And so? Where will you send her to keep her safe?"

"I don't know," I admitted. "Bastiano and I will need to discuss it, will need to put some thought into it. I am not concerning myself with that just yet, though. All I want right now is to see my daughter and hold her in my arms." Tears stung my eyes as I looked up at Amalia. "Thanks to you, I can do that."

She reached out and squeezed my hand, tears in her own eyes.

Two nights ago, the night I'd killed Ambrogio Malatesta, Amalia and I had waited until the small hours of the morning, then dragged his body from the house and dumped him into the nearby Giudecca Canal. He had yet to be found; it would be the talk of the city once he was.

Then I had gone home to free Bastiano from his prison. I had tried to insist Amalia come with me so that she need not be alone that night, but she had firmly declined, saying that being alone was just what she needed right then. I had acquiesced, albeit reluctantly, and later realized it was likely for the best, what with all the arguing and joyous shouting Bastiano and I did.

He'd fallen to his knees in relief when I told him that Malatesta was dead, that I had killed him myself, and that he and Ginevra were safe. He then began to let me know, loudly and with many choice words, what he thought of my locking him up and taking care of Malatesta myself. I endured his angry words mostly silently, knowing that I would have been incandescent with rage had he done the same to me.

When he had finished expressing his anger, I simply shrugged and said, "I couldn't risk you running off and doing something tragic and heroic before I put an end to the whole matter."

"Oh, is that how you see me, then?" he'd demanded. "Some sort of foolish, arrogant, tragic hero?"

"Yes."

"Good Christ, Valentina—"

"If you are quite done," I said, cutting him off, "we need to get to Ginevra immediately. We must make sure she is safe and that there is no one lying in wait, ready to do her harm."

"By the Virgin's tits," Bastiano swore. "You let me rant and rave all this time before reminding me of that?" He went about hunting for his cloak and hat. "I must go at once."

"Not alone, you won't," I said. "Let me wash and change into something without blood on it, and—"

"No," he said vehemently. "I don't think so. You'll stay here."

"If this is your juvenile idea of retribution . . ." I flared, my nerves stretched to the breaking point, not willing to put up with any more of his nonsense.

He glared at me. "Think about it for just a moment, Valentina," he said. "Malatesta has, as far as anyone knows right now, disappeared. How will it look if both of us are seen to be leaving Venice the same night?"

"Does anyone even know you're in Venice? And no one will be missing him yet."

"No, not yet, but in a day or so someone will, and they will begin tracing back when he was last seen, and by whom, and people—most likely the other members of the Council of Ten—will begin asking questions. And while there are some who never knew I left in the first place, they might hear about my leaving now if they are asking questions. If we both left Venice the same night Ambrogio Malatesta was last seen alive, what then?"

"Hell and fury," I grumbled. "Yes, I suppose you're right."

"I am right. So I will go alone and bring Ginevra to you. Then we'll decide what to do next."

"Very well," I agreed, albeit grudgingly. "Then go quickly. Go now, and do not stop until you have her safely with you."

Bastiano had done just that, and I had spent two days in an agony of suspense until his letter reached me.

It had turned out to be a boon for another reason entirely that I had stayed behind.

Not long after Bastiano had departed, as I paced my bedroom, exhausted but too exhilarated to sleep, Bettina appeared at my door. At her side was a girl of perhaps twenty, whom I had never seen before. And yet the resemblance between them was plain enough.

"Bettina," I said, stopping my pacing. "And this must be Tomasina."

Bettina nodded. "It is, Madonna." She gave her daughter a slight shove. "She has something for you."

Tomasina crossed the room to me, chin held high, and handed me a few sheets of paper. "This was in Malatesta's study," she said.

I looked over the pages, my eyes widening as I began to comprehend what I held in my hand. "He just . . . left this out?" I asked.

"Well, not exactly," Tomasina said. "I was poking about his desk—I could always make the excuse that I was cleaning it—and I found a false bottom in one of his drawers. And these were inside."

I began to laugh. "Oh, Tomasina!" I said. "You marvelous, marvelous creature."

She smiled and it lit up her pretty face. "I thought it would be important," she said. "I thought it would hurt him if anyone knew. And I want him hurt."

Again, Malatesta had underestimated the women around him, those he thought existed just to do his bidding. He'd thought that how he treated us did not matter. So many patrician men thought the same. Yet we, together, had the power to bring them down.

If only more of them were aware of that fact. Still . . . perhaps it was for the best that they weren't. Perhaps it was better, for now, that we women continued to wield our power from the shadows, and when they least expected it.

"He is . . . hurt quite badly already," I informed her, and saw her face fall slightly. I held up the papers. "But this will ruin his name. The Council of Ten will want to see this, to ensure that nothing like this can happen ever again."

Her expression brightened once more. "Good," she said. "Good! I wouldn't want such a thing to happen. And by the Blessed Mother, I want his name ruined." She cleared her throat and glanced at Bettina. "My mother said that . . . that you might have a position for me?"

I smiled. "I do. Tell me, Tomasina, do you like children?"

"Oh, very much!" she exclaimed.

And so it was that Ginevra had a new nursemaid ready and waiting for her at my palazzo.

And I had, locked in a secret drawer of my own, a written reply from the Spanish king, promising gold and troops if needed to back Malatesta's play for ultimate power in Venice. I planned to have Bastiano take it to his father, who could make it public in whatever manner he saw fit. Everyone would know what Malatesta had done, and if it ever came out, somehow, that I had killed him once the deed was discovered, I would be hailed as a hero.

Though I very much hoped that fact never came out. It would wreak havoc on my client list.

Now I watched Amalia carefully as she put Bastiano's letter aside. "Are you quite well, Amalia?" I asked her quietly. "Truly?"

She smiled, and though it was a thin, watery smile, I could see a trace of her usual smile beneath it all the same, and that heartened me. "As well as I can be," she said. "I am grieving. Perhaps I always will be, in some way."

"Do you regret it?" I asked, the question I had been wanting to ask, although I dreaded her answer. "Do you regret giving him up?"

"No," she said. "I don't. And even if I did, I would blame only myself, Valentina, not you. Never you."

"But you truly do not regret it?" I pushed. "Truly?"

"Truly, I do not regret it," she said, her voice quiet yet strong. "I do not grieve Ambrogio quite so much as I grieve the man I thought he was, for so long. The man I wish he had been. The man he might have been, had he not allowed power and the lust for power to warp him and turn him into something malicious and deceitful and twisted."

"I understand, I think," I said gently.

She smiled sadly. "And of course I grieve the love I had, that heady, breathless feeling when all the world seems brighter. I grieve that I did not spend that love on someone more deserving of it."

"We cannot help loving those we do," I said, thinking of me and Massimo, and then me and Bastiano, of all the men over the years who had professed to love me, in whatever way they meant that word. Niccolo Contarini. Francesco Valier. And I thought of how much Amalia must love me, to betray her lover for me and mine. "And you will fall in love again, Amalia. You will feel that way again—I know it. Venice, the world . . . they're full of men ready to love you. Men who are worthy of your love."

She smiled. "I hope you are right, Valentina. I do. I hope I am still worthy after what I did."

"You are," I said fiercely. "Never think otherwise. If God is just, then He will see that you did the right thing. That you did more good than harm, when your deed is placed on the scales. And the Shadow God applauds you, I think."

She frowned. "The Shadow God?" she asked, just as Fernando Cortes had done. "I have heard you use that phrase before, but I never asked what it meant." She chuckled. "I think I did not want to ask."

I laughed. "That is how I thought of the god I served, if a god he can be called," I said. "But I do not serve him anymore."

Amalia, bless her, seemed to understand. "And so what will you do next? You and Bastiano?"

"I am done with the Council of Ten—that much is certain," I said, and shuddered. "I know Bastiano is as well. We can only hope the Ten is done with us as well."

Chapter 36

The Council of Ten, as it turned out, was not entirely done with us.

Bastiano had been back in Venice with Ginevra for two days when the body of Ambrogio Malatesta was brought up in a fisherman's net. There had been whispers of gossip before then, as it had been some time since anyone had seen him, and so his servants and associates had begun to ask questions. But those whispers exploded into a maelstrom once his body was found, his throat clearly cut. He was partially decayed from his time in the water, but not so much so that he could not be identified.

Speculation was furious, and while I heard the usual salacious rumors—a jealous husband, a jealous lover, gambling debts, even some sort of involvement with the dark arts—it soon came to be generally agreed upon that his work with the notoriously secretive and ruthless Council of Ten had somehow played a part in his demise. A wrongfully accused prisoner, perhaps, or an assassination by some foreign nation in retaliation for the execution of one of its spies.

Bastiano gave the letter from the Spanish crown to his father, who took it to the Ten. After that, the whispers about

Malatesta began to change. He had been plotting against his own country. The Ten had executed the traitor in their midst. All unsubstantiated rumor, of course. Yet even so, before too long, his name would be ruined, just as I had promised Tomasina.

I had also received a letter that read: *I thought you might wish to know that Senator Gritti owes a favor to whoever rid the Republic of Ambrogio Malatesta, or so he was overheard to have said.*

It was signed simply, *F.*

I could not know how much Felicita knew about my involvement in Malatesta's death, and even if she guessed at the whole of it she would never be able to prove anything. But for whatever reason, I trusted that she would never speak of it to anyone, in any case—in a way that was quite unlike me. And yet I trusted Felicita all the same.

⋆ ⋆ ⋆

One night, about two weeks after the body was pulled from the lagoon, I was home with Bastiano, enjoying a late meal, when Lauretta came, breathless, into the dining room. "Mi scusi, Madonna," she said, throwing an admiring gaze Bastiano's way. Some things never did change, I thought, rolling my eyes. "But there is a man here to see you. A patrician, a man from the government, he says."

"Who?" I demanded. "I am not expecting anyone tonight." Not with my lover there and with Ginevra in the house. She was asleep in the spare bedroom on the top floor of the palazzo, with her new nursemaid nearby. We had not been able to bear parting with her, and so Bastiano had installed her at his home, the Bragadin palazzo, with Tomasina accompanying her there. His parents had not been thrilled at his bringing his bastard daughter under their roof, but they tolerated her, which was all we could hope for just now. It was truly the least Bastiano's father could do, after his political intrigues had almost gotten his son killed and after we had obtained the letter that had forever destroyed Malatesta's reputation and burnished Senator Bragadin's in the process.

"A Signor Loredan, Madonna," Lauretta said.

I froze in my chair, looking over at Bastiano. He wore a shocked, stricken look that I was sure was a mirror of my own. Bartolomeo Loredan was from an old and powerful Venetian family and was said to be the doge's most trusted advisor. He also sat on the Council of Ten, and just at the beginning of that month had been chosen as one of the Tre Capi, or so gossip relayed.

The Tre Capi were forbidden from leaving the Doge's Palace during their monthlong tenure leading the Council of Ten. His coming here was extraordinary, and I was quite certain it wasn't for a happy purpose.

"He did say you were not expecting him," Lauretta went on, "but he is insisting on seeing you, Madonna. And Signor Bragadin."

"And . . ." I cleared my throat. "He . . . he knows Signor Bragadin is here?"

"Sí, Madonna," Lauretta said uneasily.

I looked across the table at Bastiano, who had gone still as a marble statue. "I suppose we had better see what he wants, then," I said.

Bastiano blinked and rose. "I suppose we must," he said.

"Show him up to the parlor, Lauretta," I said.

She nodded and left to do my bidding.

"By the Virgin," Bastiano swore once she'd left. "What's this about?"

I nervously twisted my napkin in my lap. "Nothing good, I'm sure." Mentally I began recalling where all the weapons in my public parlor were hidden, then shook off such thoughts. I could not kill the head of one of the most illustrious families in Venice. That would be suicide, even for me.

"If he were going to arrest us," Bastiano pointed out, "or torture us for information, or some such, he would not have come to your palazzo. He would have had us both hauled into the doge's prison. And we are the heroes of this tale, ultimately."

"That is true," I said, feeling a bit more optimistic at his words. "Still, I do not like it."

"Nor I."

We both rose and went into the parlor where Bartolomeo Loredan was waiting.

"Signore," I said, crossing the room and offering my hand, which he kissed courteously. "You are most welcome in my home. And you know Bastiano Bragadin, I'm sure."

"I do," Loredan said, inclining his head to Bastiano, who returned the gesture.

"Please, sit," I invited, and we all took a seat. "I wish that you had given us some warning of your visit, signore. We could have received you properly and had refreshments ready."

"Think nothing of it," Loredan said. "This is not a social call, and I shall not be staying long."

"No? Then in that case," I said, my voice hardening slightly, "perhaps you might enlighten us as to the purpose of your visit."

"I certainly shall," he said. "I understand that you were both familiar with my former colleague, the late Ambrogio Malatesta."

My breath caught in my throat, though I had certainly guessed this was coming. "Yes," I said. "I had a . . . professional association with him."

"As did I, from time to time," Bastiano said.

"I am well aware of that," he said, "just as I am well aware of the specific details of the . . . assignments with which Ambrogio entrusted you particularly, Signora Riccardi."

"As I would expect you to be," I said smoothly, "given that those assignments were given on behalf of the Council of Ten, were they not?"

"They were," he said, looking from me to Bastiano, "in most cases."

I had not expected an admission such as that.

"I have recently become aware that there were instances in which Signor Malatesta gave you, Valentina Riccardi, certain assignments that had not been cleared nor even discussed with the rest of the Council of Ten." His gaze went to Bastiano. "And that you, Signor Bragadin, became aware of the senator's . . . extracurricular activities, shall we say."

"I was," Bastiano said uncomfortably.

"And why, may I ask, did you not bring these activities to the attention of the Ten?" Loredan asked.

"I did not wish to alert Malatesta himself to what I knew, of course," Bastiano answered at once. "Though it seems he found out anyway. I feared bringing the matter to the Ten might so alert him. And I wanted to wait until I had more solid proof."

"Sound reasoning indeed," Loredan said. "I can assure you, however, that there were those within the Ten who had their suspicions of Ambrogio Malatesta and that your information, however incomplete, would have been most welcome." He waved a pale, aristocratic hand. "But that is neither here nor there at this point, of course."

I did my best to steady my breathing. Where was he leading us with all this?

"We are all—His Serenity, the Doge, included—now certain that Ambrogio Malatesta was a traitor to the Venetian Republic," Loredan went on, "thanks to a letter from the Spanish crown obtained by your father, Signor Bragadin." His gaze then slid over to me. "However he came into possession of it, we are grateful that it came to light."

That was all the thanks we were likely to get, I knew. "As am I," I said carefully, "but if I may ask, signore, why are you telling us all this?"

"Ah," he said, leaning forward slightly in his chair. "A fair question. Normally a traitor such as Ambrogio Malatesta would be questioned and eventually executed. But as he is, of course, already dead, this will not be possible. As such, His Serenity, the Doge, as well as the Council of Ten, wish for Signor Malatesta's true nature to remain unknown to the general public." He shook his head, a faint expression of disgust twisting his lips into a sneer. "As unknown as anything salacious can be in this city, of course."

"Perfectly understandable," I said, "and yet that still does not explain why you have come here."

"Far be it from me to condone murder, of course," Loredan went on, as though he and the rest of the Ten did not condone murder on a regular basis. "But I will say that whoever rid Venice of Ambrogio Malatesta did the Republic a great service."

My entire body relaxed at that, though I did what I could to prevent Loredan from seeing it. "Ah" was all I said.

"Indeed. It would be rather unfortunate, wouldn't you agree, for the Venetian people to learn that a one-time member of their most illustrious Senate, as well as a member of the very body charged with keeping them safe, had sought to betray that most honored office and the sacred trust that accompanies it?"

"Indeed it would be," I said. "Most unfortunate." Bastiano, too, murmured his agreement.

Loredan smiled a rather cold smile. "I am glad we are in agreement. And so I can trust that this conversation, and everything that preceded it, will remain in confidence?"

"Of course," I said.

"Of course," Bastiano echoed.

"I am delighted to hear it. I thank you both for your time this night, and for the hospitality." He rose and donned his hat. "Oh," he added offhandedly, "I would advise that both of you stay well clear of affairs of state from now on. Is that understood?"

My blood went cold at the barely disguised warning in his voice, but I lifted my chin defiantly. "I would like nothing more, signore," I said. "My question for you is whether the affairs of state will stay clear of me. Of us."

Bartolomeo Loredan gave me a hard, assessing look, as though, upon entering the room, he had made a certain calculation as to who I was, and was now forced to rework that calculation. Then he chuckled. "You are an interesting woman, Valentina Riccardi. Most of what is said about you does not do you justice."

I kept my gaze on his, never wavering.

"Very well. I shall be as frank with you as you were with me. The Council of Ten shall no longer seek your services, either of you, for any reason," Loredan said. "You may rest easy in knowing that you have done great service to the Republic." He smiled sardonically. "My personal view, however, is that you are both more trouble than you are worth." With that, he nodded to each of us, then took his leave.

Once he was out of sight, I slumped back in my chair, going weak with relief. Bastiano shook his head, baffled, running his fingers through his hair.

"More trouble than we're worth," I muttered under my breath. "The Council of Ten can go fuck itself."

Bastiano let out a bark of laughter, and soon he was laughing so hard that his shoulders shook and tears ran down his face.

"What is so funny?" I demanded. Maybe it was naught but the giddy relief of knowing we were safe, that we were finally free, but soon I was laughing as well. We both sat there and laughed uncontrollably for I knew not how long, until we could scarcely breathe with the heady pleasure of it.

Author's Note

So now you're probably wondering, as many readers do upon reaching the end of a work of historical fiction: How much of this story was real, and how much was invented? The short answer is that *The Assassin of Venice* is one of my more fictional works of historical fiction, but there is a great deal of real history underpinning it all the same.

All of the characters in the novel were invented by me, though for authenticity I borrowed the surnames of many real patrician families of the Venetian Republic (such as Bragadin, Contarini, Gritti, and Loredan, among others). The one exception is Pietro Aretino, who was a real historical figure, with a notoriously wicked pen, who did often satirize courtesans and their profession, among many other topics.

The Council of Ten was very real and was as I've described them here: a subset of the Venetian senate that dealt with espionage, intelligence, and the general protection of the state. And yes, they did order the occasional assassination. I am particularly grateful to Dr. Ioanna Iordanou's book *Venice's Secret Service: Organizing Intelligence in the Renaissance*, which provided a wealth of information about this particularly secretive organ of the Venetian state.

The Venetian Republic—though in reality more of an aristocracy—was indeed built to prevent corruption and cults of personality in their politics, as Valentina put it. The idea of any one man having too much power was abhorrent to Venetians throughout the duration of their Republic, which remains one of the longest lasting governments in human history. (And it was true that they loved term limits!) Beginning in the late thirteenth century, a patrician class was firmly established, with all the male members of each patrician family over the age of twenty-five eligible to serve in the Great Council and vote in its weekly meetings and make or approve political appointments throughout the Republic. The Great Council also elected the doge through an extremely complicated and Byzantine (literally) process designed to make rigging the election impossible. Though the doge was ostensibly the head of the government, he was truly more of a figurehead than anything else, as his actual powers were quite limited.

The members of the Senate were elected from the Great Council, and the Senate was where most of the serious legislative business of the government was conducted—it was much easier getting things done in a Senate of three hundred as opposed to the Great Council, which had membership of over a thousand.

There is much more to the architecture of the Venetian government; the above is a very basic overview. For further information about the Venetian government as well as an excellent general history of the La Serenissima, I recommend Thomas F. Madden's highly accessible *Venice: A New History.*

Venice was certainly famous for her courtesans, who were as I've described them here: cultured, beautiful, talented, and highly educated. As described in the novel, Venetian patrician women unfortunately were barely educated, as intellectual pursuits were not considered appropriate for "good women." As such, their highly educated husbands had to seek intellectual companionship elsewhere. This is where the cortigiane oneste, or "honest courtesans," came in, providing conversation and entertainment as well as sex. They were also, essentially, a tourist attraction, as visitors to Venice would often engage their services. For more about the lives and world of Venetian courtesans, I recommend Margaret F. Rosenthal's *The Honest Courtesan: Veronica Franco, Citizen and Writer in Sixteenth-Century Venice*, about the most famous Venetian courtesan.

But were there courtesans who were also assassins?

I couldn't find any evidence that there were, but nonetheless, if any courtesans had engaged in such clandestine extracurricular activities, we might not know about it, right? In all seriousness, though, sex workers throughout history have engaged in espionage and intelligence gathering, as they are certainly perfectly placed to covertly collect or coax information from their clients. I took this a step further and wondered: What if a courtesan, in the often paranoid political climate of Renaissance Venice, were asked to actually kill men deemed a danger to the state? She'd be perfectly placed for that too. Hence, this novel is a bit of a thought experiment on my part, built on the very real history of Venetian courtesans and intelligence services in the Venetian Republic.

Because again, this novel is a work of fiction. And if there's one thing we fiction writers love, it's the question: "What if?"

Acknowledgments

Books are written in isolation, and this one was written in the deepest isolation of all: the early days of the COVID-19 pandemic. These characters and their dramas and intrigues and banter kept me sane through that awful, uncertain time, and I've been so very grateful to get the chance to pull this story out of that isolation and work with some truly incredible people to bring it to the world.

First and foremost, my most heartfelt thanks are due to my absolute rock star of an agent, Sam Farkas. She signed me for another book entirely, then didn't bat an eye when I said "I've also got this book about a courtesan assassin, is this anything?" Turns out it was something! She believed in this book even when I was ready to give up on it. For that, Sam, you have my and Valentina's eternal gratitude.

Thanks as well to the excellent team at Jill Grinberg Literary Management for all their support.

I'm very grateful to Toni Kirkpatrick for giving this strange, dark, and sexy book a shot, and for seeing what was special about it. Toni, it's been so wonderful to work with you!

It has also been wonderful to work with the team at Crooked Lane Books. My sincerest thanks to Rebecca Nelson and Thai Fantauzzi Pérez for their helpful and timely communication and for keeping me and this book on track. Huge thanks as well to Westchester Publishing Services for all their insightful and thorough work on this book. And thank you so much to Lynn Andreozzi and the art team for an absolutely incredible cover that captures Valentina's vibe so perfectly.

Thank you to Brianne Johnson for her input on this manuscript.

Thank you to my friend and critique partner Diana Giovinazzo for reading some early pages of this one and rooting for Valentina right from the get-go.

Thanks to the Wonder Writers for all their conversation and commiseration about publishing, and for all their support.

Thank you to the wonderful community of supportive and talented historical fiction writers who celebrate each other's accomplishments and are always uplifting one another. I've been privileged to chat with, get to know, and also present at conferences with so many incredible fellow authors, too many to name here (since I might forget someone and then feel terrible), so please just know how fortunate I feel to count so many amazing writers as my colleagues.

My immense gratitude always to the wonderful booksellers at Talking Leaves Books in Buffalo for all their support of my work and of Buffalo's writing and reading community as a whole.

No acknowledgements in an Alyssa Palombo book are complete without a shout out to all the amazing musicians whose work so inspired me while writing this novel: Within Temptation, Nightwish, Evanescence, Charlotte Wessels, Lacuna Coil, Kamelot, Delain, Halestorm, In This Moment, and Katatonia, among others. Music is both the fuel and the fire that keeps me going.

My undying gratitude, always, to Lindsay Fowler, one of my best friends and also (whether she likes it or not) my writing therapist. Thank you for always being there and always being willing to talk it out.

Thank you so very much to all my incredible friends: Jen Hark-Hameister, Amanda Beck, Andrea Bieniek, Alex Dockstader Schwob, Katie Schrader, Jen Pecoraro, and Jenessa Irvine. I am so lucky to have all of you cheering me on every step of the way. I never take it for granted.

Thank you, always, to my wonderful family, who have never been anything but supportive of me and my writing career. Thanks especially to my parents, Debbie and Tony Palombo, for everything they have done and continue to do for me, for always being proud of me, and for sharing my love of Italian history, culture, and food (of course, the food!).

Thank you to my brother, Matt Palombo, the most excellent brother and travel companion. (Matt—I stand by what I said in the dedication, but it shall not be legally binding as I heretofore reserve the right to sit down and have a glass of wine and chill out when next we travel together).

Thanks also to the world's best writing assistant, Fenway the silky terrier, who is even more ferocious than Valentina.

And a huge thank you to YOU, dear reader! If you are holding this book in your hands (or on your e-reader, or what have you) please know that you have played a part in making a writer's dream come true.

Last but certainly not least: grazie mille alla bellissima città di Venezia, per tutta l'ispirazione. Ti vedrò presto.